MATA HARI'S LAST DANCE

a novel

❦

MICHELLE MORAN

ATRIA PAPERBACK

New York   London   Toronto   Sydney   New Delhi

ATRIA
PAPERBACK

An Imprint of Simon & Schuster, Inc.
1230 Avenue of the Americas
New York, NY 10020

First Atria Paperback edition July 2016

ATRIA PAPERBACK and colophon are registered trademarks of Simon & Schuster, Inc.

For information about special discounts for bulk purchases, please contact Simon & Schuster Special Sales at 1-866-506-1949 or business@simonandschuster.com.

The Simon & Schuster Speakers Bureau can bring authors to your live event. For more information or to book an event, contact the Simon & Schuster Speakers Bureau at 1-866-248-3049 or visit our website at www.simonspeakers.com.

Interior design by Jill Putorti

Manufactured in the United States of America

7   9   10   8   6

The Library of Congress has cataloged the Touchstone edition as follows:

Names: Moran, Michelle, author.
Title: Mata Hari's last dance : a novel / Michelle Moran.
Description: First Touchstone hardcover edition. | New York: Touchstone, 2016.
Identifiers: LCCN 2015051095
Subjects: LCSH: Mata Hari, 1876–1917—Fiction. | World War, 1914–1918—Fiction. | Women spies—Fiction. | Stripteasers—Fiction. | BISAC: FICTION / Historical. | FICTION / Romance / Historical. | FICTION / Biographical. | GSAFD: Biographical fiction. | Historical fiction.
Classification: LCC PS3613.O682 M38 2016 | DDC 813/.6—dc23
LC record available at http://lccn.loc.gov/2015051095

ISBN 978-1-4767-1638-1 (pbk)
ISBN 978-1-4767-1639-8 (hc)
ISBN 978-1-4767-1640-4 (ebook)

MATA HARI'S
LAST DANCE

ALSO BY MICHELLE MORAN

Rebel Queen

The Second Empress

Madame Tussaud

Cleopatra's Daughter

The Heretic Queen

Nefertiti

A very heartfelt thank-you to everyone
who worked with me on this book. Sally Kim,
Etinosa Agbonlahor, Dan Lazar, Susan Moldow,
Brian Belfiglio, David Falk, Laura Flavin, Maria Whelan,
and, most of all, Allison McCabe.

The divine attributes of Brahma,
Vishnu, and Shiva—creation, fecundity, destruction.
This is the dance I dance tonight.
The dance of destruction as it leads to creation.

MATA HARI

MATA HARI, BEAUTIFUL DANCER, IS SHOT BY
FRENCH AS SPY; WAS KAISER'S CLEVER AGENT

PARIS, FRANCE, OCT. 15—Mata Hari, the Dutch dancer, who two months ago was found guilty by a court martial on the charge of espionage, was shot at dawn this morning.

Mme. Mata Hari, long known in Europe as a woman of great attractiveness and with a romantic history, was, according to unofficial press dispatches, accused of conveying to the Germans the secret of the construction of the entente "tanks," this resulting in the enemy rushing work on a special gas to combat their operations.

Posed as a Japanese Dancer.

Mata Hari, who got her name through posing for some years as a Japanese dancer, was famed in the music halls of Europe for her great beauty. One of her specialties was, after singing, to mingle with diners on the floor, pick out some attractive officer and engage him in conversation. These informal meetings frequently developed into acquaintances which were profitable to Mata Hari in the way of gaining military information which, it was afterward found, she sent to Germany.

Intimate with Many Officers.

Mme. Mata Hari was found to have been on intimate terms with many French and British officers who did not dream of the real nature of her work. She was said to have worn a gold dragon, the insignia of the British tank service, indicating that it had been given her by a tank officer from whom she may have learned the secret of the tanks which she communicated, far in advance of the appearance of the tanks in battle, to Germany.

Suspicion Fastened on Dancer.

It was apparent, as soon as the tanks were brought into use, that Germany had had advance knowledge concerning them. Suspicion was soon fastened on Mata Hari and she was closely questioned by French officials. Her explanations proving apparently satisfactory, she was allowed to remain at liberty and at once moved to England. As soon as she landed, however, she was placed under arrest and a formal charge of Espionage placed against her.

Maintains Complete Composure.

The beautiful dancer manifested complete composure throughout her investigation and subsequent trial, even after documents of the most damaging nature had been produced against her.

It was found that she had communicated to Germany many secrets other than that of the tanks and had been, in fact, one of the most dangerous of the Kaiser's agents in France and England.

Part 1

CREATION

Chapter 1

TELL ME WHERE YOU
LEARNED TO DANCE

1904

*W*e don't take a horse-drawn cab to his office. Edouard Clunet is a lawyer—he owns a car. He opens the door for me and I find a wilted rose on the black leather seat. I hold it up. "Recent lover?"

He takes the rose and tosses it out the window. I can imagine him acting as casual with the women he makes love to. "You're young. Nineteen? Twenty?"

"Twenty-five."

If he's surprised by this he doesn't show it. "Still, you haven't seen much of the world." He starts the car and we drive down the Boulevard de Clichy, past empty shops and seedy bars. Men stand in tight clusters along the sidewalks, smoking, talking, whistling at women.

"I was born in India," I say. I'm about to elaborate when we jerk to a halt, narrowly avoiding an outraged pedestrian.

"Listen," he says when we are driving again. "I don't care how many men you sleep with or who you charm by describing fanciful holidays in Egypt, sipping champagne on a felucca in the Nile. If you can mesmerize a man by claiming you took high tea with Edward VII during the durbar to celebrate his succession to Emperor of

India, fantastic. The bigger and more believable your lies, the better. That being said—with me, cut the act."

We are driving downhill toward the nicer part of town, an area much more respectable than where he found me. He stops the car for another pedestrian and I look out the window, imagining myself in one of the boutiques. I'd wear black silk gloves and pearls around my neck at least three strands deep. I'd wear a hat with feathers.

"When I introduce you to my client, I'm responsible for how you behave. Understand?"

"No."

"Let me explain it clearly. I am going to present you to my client, M'greet."

The car rolls past La Madeline. A month earlier I auditioned for them. I wore a wine-colored sarong while all the other hopefuls dressed in moth-eaten furs. I told the men who owned the theater that I had traveled from India to share the dance of my people with the citizens of Paris. I danced without music, imagining the sounds of a gamelan, the strum of a sitar and surmandal. I was exotic. Too exotic.

"Thank you. We'll be in touch," they said and rejected me.

"He is a very rich client and a very respected man. I will tell him that you are Indian, that you were born in India, and you are going to behave as if everything I say is true. I can make you famous. But you must follow my advice and never lie to me. Ever."

After La Madeline's rejection I went to L'Ete. A shack where the poor entertain the poor, everyone's last stop before trying something desperate. At L'Ete the girls stank of alcohol and poverty. It was my last audition, and where I met Clunet. He watched me perform with his fingertips pressed over his lips. As I danced, I thought he looked out of place in such a rundown playhouse. His suit was immaculate. I tried to guess his age. Thirty-three, thirty-five? I focused on him rather than on the men who were judging me from behind a wooden table as I spread my arms like the mother goddess and moved my hips to the silent gamelan. But I was "too dark and too slow" for L'Ete. "Too," one of the men at the table said, waving his hand to search for the right word, picking fruit from trees, "Eastern." They wanted blonde girls; they didn't want me.

Clunet sought me out immediately afterward.

The sun had begun to dip behind the Sacré-Coeur and I had braced myself against the side of the theater. If I couldn't dance, I told myself, I could sing or play piano.

Clunet interrupted my thoughts, introduced himself, and said he had a client, a man who had built an expensive library dedicated to Asian art, and that this individual desired something spectacular for its opening.

"Why should he think that I'm spectacular? No one else does," I said, stinging with the humiliation of failure.

"Because this is a man with class and taste. Someone who will appreciate your art."

I catch my reflection in the car window now and smile. My *art*.

"What other languages do you speak?" Clunet asks.

"French, English, Dutch, Malay. I learned some Hindi," I say, "but not enough to call myself fluent. I was taught German in school."

"Well, mademoiselle—or are you madame?"

"Mademoiselle."

"Tell me where you learned to dance."

"Java." I paint the picture for him. Gamelan orchestras playing in the night. White orchids floating in private pools. Parties so lavish the queen of Holland might have attended. "There was a woman who danced at these affairs. Mahadevi." I describe how she taught me to dance and I can see him struggling to decide whether or not I'm telling the truth. But he doesn't say anything. He must believe me.

"Here we are." He parks in a suburb I've never visited before, in front of a magnificent villa that soars five windows high. The magnolias lining the street are in bloom. We walk to the front steps and immediately a bellman opens the door, expecting us. The man ushers us inside, into a hall lined with paintings of stern-looking men. At the end, in a small circular room, a woman smiles at us.

"Mathilda." Clunet tips his hat to her.

She blushes a little and fumbles with her papers. "Monsieur Clunet." She looks in my direction, but Clunet doesn't introduce me.

We climb the stairs toward Clunet's office: two desks and half a dozen glass and mahogany bookcases. I know that he is watching me, waiting to see if I am impressed. I take a seat and keep my expression neutral.

"There are things I must tell you, M'greet, about my client, Monsieur Guimet. About this engagement and what it will mean for you—and me—if you succeed." He sits behind his desk and folds his hands. They are perfectly manicured, like the rest of him. "I'm not an agent," he says. "My field is international law. But my client has a very special request and it occurs to me that he might not be the only one interested in the Far East."

"Are you changing professions, then?"

He laughs, and I feel foolish. Of course he isn't—look at his office. The leather chairs, the Persian carpets.

"No. I'm pursuing something that may be interesting for a time. There's a great deal of money to be had in this, M'greet. But first, Monsieur Guimet has to believe that you are truly exotic, the daughter of a temple dancer in India. So when my client asks what your name is, you are going to say—"

"Mata Hari." I embellish, "My mother *died* giving birth to me in a temple."

He nods, impressed. "Good. And your age?" He reaches behind his desk and takes out a box.

"Twenty-two?"

He opens the velvet top. "Eighteen." Inside is an emerald in gold filigree. "One of many, acquired on trips to India," he says. "There are pieces in my client's home that he knows to be fakes; he keeps the originals here, with me." He holds out the jewel and I touch the Far East, running my fingers over the lives of princesses forced into marriage, mothers who lost children, lovers who cried on their wedding day. History wrought in emerald and gold.

"Monsieur Guimet isn't one of your Montmartre customers." He closes the box and puts it back, turning the key in the cabinet door. "He is an industrialist, an intrepid traveler, and one of the richest men in Europe. When we meet him tonight, I want you dressed as you were at L'Ete. Wear your most elaborate sarong. Wear all of your jewels."

"I don't have any," I tell him. Rudolph, my husband, was the last person to buy me anything expensive—and everything I owned that had value I sold in order to eat.

"No matter. I'll loan you jewels to wear," he says. There is a piece of paper on his desk. He pushes it toward me.

"What is this?"

"Our agreement."

I consider it carefully. "This is a partnership?"

"Yes. I found you, M'greet."

"Then you're my lawyer?"

"And your agent. As soon as you sign."

That evening, in my apartment in Montmartre, I lay my best sarong on the cheap brown comforter that covers my bed. Red silk trimmed with embroidered leaves of gold. I trace a finger across the cloth and in the ripples of the fabric I can see my father sitting like a bronzed sentinel by the fire, his black hair tinged gold by the orange flames. I climb into his lap and rest my head against his shoulder. He's staring out our parlor window at the canals. It's snowing and the houses along the water have disappeared like painted women beneath white veils. "I hate snow," I whisper into his beard. He smells of fresh wood and rain.

"Why? It wipes everything clean. Makes it fresh, new."

We both look outside at the color of nothingness. "But white is plain," I tell him.

"Plain can be nice. But you're right. White is not your color, M'greet."

I like it when my father reveals things about me. I bury my head in his neck. "What is my color?" I don't have white-gold hair like my mother or Dutch-blue eyes like my brothers.

"Red." My father pauses. "Because red is passion. It's life."

Passion, I think as I dress. I stand in front of the mirror in the color my father envisioned for me and I know my papa was right. I am striking; unusually tall for a woman and in the sun my skin bronzes to cinnamon. When I was a girl, my dark eyes and hair made people whisper that my mother had taken a Jewish lover. "An orchid among buttercups," my father called me. Tonight, my dark hair is pulled back from my face. The deep red of my lips matches my sarong. I move my arms and my hips into different poses and the silk reflects the room's light like water.

There's a knock at the door and I am startled. I had planned to meet him outside my building. Yet here he is, early. I open the door and before I invite him inside, Edouard Clunet welcomes himself into my apartment. If he's shocked by the silk scarves I've hung to cover the shabbiness of the walls or the aroma of the urine-scented halls that my incense can't hide, his expression doesn't betray him.

"Your costume is excellent," he says. He produces a box and opens the lid. "I want you to wear these," he says. I count six bangles—all gold—and a heavy necklace encrusted with rubies.

I catch his eye. "Are these—"

"Most certainly real. He's the greatest collector of Asian art in the world. I can't have you meet him wearing inauthentic jewels."

I tease the bangles over my wrists and he clasps the rubies around my neck. We both look at me in the mirror; my image is regal.

"If you can charm him this evening, M'greet, your entire life will change."

I imagined Guimet as old, thin, eccentric. But the man who stands in the finest parlor I've ever had the pleasure to be invited to is taller than Clunet, bearded, distinguished looking. In the light of the crystal chandeliers his hair is silvered, but beneath his tailored suit, his shoulders appear to be broad and strong.

"Émile Guimet, it is my privilege to acquaint you with Paris's next sensation." Clunet makes a sweeping gesture toward me. "May I introduce Mata Hari, the Star of the East."

Guimet inspects me from head to toe, then we meet each other's eyes. I know he is calculating the worth of my jewels, the quality of my sarong. "Please, have a seat." He gestures to some silk-covered chairs. I sit slowly, crossing my legs so that the sarong rises along my thigh.

He nods for Clunet to take a seat, and then sits himself. "Edouard tells me you were born on the altar of Kanda Swany," he says.

"It's true," I say softly, lilting my vowels. "My mother gave her life to the temple. She died on the very day I was born. The priests of Kanda Swany adopted me. My name means 'Eye of the Dawn' and from the earliest days of my life I was raised in the hall of the pagoda of Shiva, trained to follow in my mother's footsteps through the holy rites of the dance."

"Yet your accent—I do not recognize it. You do not sound like someone from India."

I touch his arm. "I have lived all over the world and speak many languages," I say, as if confiding a great secret. "My favorite tongue is French. *Vous avez une belle maison,*" I compliment him, then steer us on to another topic. "I have been told you are curious about the sacred arts of my people. The secrets of Borobudur, Kelir, Brahma." I drop the names like small pearls for his delight.

"Tell me about Borobudur," he says.

"What would you like to know?"

"The temple. Is it Buddhist or Hindu?"

He is hoping to trick me. "No one knows. The men who built the temple were followers of Buddha. If you journey clockwise through the five levels of the pyramid, you will witness the life story of Buddha unfold." I hold my hands before me, as if weighing the weight of a pear against an apple. "Yet the inscriptions on the temple walls suggest Hinduism. There is mystery in the temple." He looks at my hands. Perhaps they don't look like the hands of a temple dancer. I quickly drop them to my lap.

"Tell me about the stupas," he says.

"The bell-shaped stones in which meditating Buddhas sit in quiet bliss contemplating the world? They are part of the temple."

"You've seen them?"

"Many times." They are a piece of paradise overlooking Yogyakarta.

"How many are there?"

"Seventy-two, if you do not include the largest one in the middle."

He rises abruptly and I look at Clunet. Have I said something wrong?

"Come," Guimet says.

I exhale and Clunet and I share an uneasy glance. We follow him into an antechamber. The dark velvet curtains are drawn and the air is cool. In large glass cases illuminated books are displayed. He walks to one work in particular and stops. I recognize it immediately.

"*The Kamasutra*," I say. A book of sex, and this particular volume contains explicit pictures. I move closer to Guimet and begin to read in Malay, the language my barbarian husband hated with such ignorant passion. I make certain to catch his eye each time I pronounce an evocative word.

After I fall silent, Guimet immediately asks, "Is this book truly held sacred in India?"

"In certain places, yes." I gaze deeply into his eyes. "Very much so."

He nods and I know he is imagining himself in such places, with lovers capable of gravity-defying sexual positions. Although, in fact, the book is largely about virtuous living.

"When you danced in the temple, what did you wear?"

I look briefly at Clunet. We did not discuss this earlier. "When one dances for Shiva, it is done in the nude. Of course, jewels are like offerings to the gods. They never interfere with the sacredness of the dance. Unlike clothing."

I enjoy Guimet's shock. And from behind me, I can feel Clunet's approval like warm light. Guimet sweeps back a velvet drape to reveal an astounding collection of jewels: stunning necklaces, bracelets, and a ruby-studded brassiere.

"This piece is from my last trip to India." He hands me the silver brassiere. I touch it reverently, holding it up to my chest, pinning his eyes to me.

Clunet breaks my spell in a clumsy instant. "Is that insured?"

Guimet pulls his gaze away from my chest and claps Clunet on the back with a sigh. "Everything's in order." He turns to me, his new confidante. "He's a good lawyer, Mata Hari. Always concerned. But does he have an eye for beautiful things? Does he appreciate art and the East like we do? Why don't you select your favorite pieces to wear for your performance at the launch of my library?"

I pretend to hesitate.

"Please," he says. "I insist."

I caress necklaces of gold encrusted with gems. Run my fingertips along silver so pure it's white. I hold twisted pieces of bronze in my hand, weighing the history in them. In the end, I choose Guimet's favorites: the brassiere, two snake bangles, a diadem that has pride of place in its own case, and a necklace that—as Guimet observes—will hang at "a lovely length" between my breasts. I pass my selections to Clunet and he locks the jewels in a long metal case.

"My new library is across the street," Guimet says. "It is both a house and a museum; I've recently added a second floor. It's home to my greatest collections, gathered from all over the world. I'd like to show it to you, Mata Hari."

"Of course," Clunet says. "We can go now if you'd like. I've been curious to see what you've accomplished."

Guimet looks at him and I wonder if Clunet realizes he hasn't been invited.

The three of us walk across the Place d'Iena and Guimet produces a key from his suit pocket. Before us is a two-storied building that stands opposite a life-size statue of George Washington on his horse.

"They installed that five years ago," Guimet says with distaste.

I read the statue's inscription. "A GIFT OF THE WOMEN OF THE UNITED STATES OF AMERICA IN MEMORY OF THE BROTHERLY HELP GIVEN BY FRANCE TO THEIR FATHERS IN THE FIGHT FOR INDEPEN-DENCE."

"Have you visited America?" I look at Washington's raised sword. He never visited Paris in his lifetime.

"New York." He smiles at a pleasurable memory. "There's no finer city in the world."

I'm surprised by his answer. "You found New York more appealing than Paris?" I can still remember my first glimpse of Paris, her wide boulevards, her sparkling lights. Everywhere I went there was something new to see. And the women . . . they were all dressed like starlets in lacy Callot Soeurs gowns and Paul Poiret dresses.

"Absolutely," Guimet says. "There are buildings so tall in New York that some people are afraid to ride the elevators to the top. The entire city is magic."

Perhaps someday I will visit New York. A city of magic.

He pushes open a pair of double doors and we step into a round library so beautifully designed that I hold my breath just entering. It's a domed cathedral of light and space. The patterned wooden floors are polished to a sheen, and eight graceful columns rise toward the second floor. Everywhere you turn there are books, leather-bound and encased in glass.

"My God, this must have cost a fortune," Clunet says, stepping into the center of the room, marveling at the spectacular glass skylight in the ceiling.

"A small one," Guimet concedes.

"*Indah*," I say for Guimet's benefit. In Malay it means, "beautiful."

Guimet leads us to the stairs and motions for us to follow behind him. Viewed from the second story, the entryway floor becomes a starburst of mahogany and pearl. I look at the priceless works of art assembled in this building and I imagine all the countries Guimet must have visited to create such a dreamlike, enchanting space— India, Java, China, Japan. His library is breathtaking. I study him in the soft light with new appreciation. A man capable of executing so many fine details to fulfill his own desire to create a cathedral to Asian art must be a gentle, tasteful lover. Clunet said Guimet was married once. I wonder what became of his wife, whether she died or ran away like I did.

We stand at the wooden balustrade and Guimet clears his throat. "Edouard, do you still have my lapis necklace in your office?"

"Of course."

"Will you retrieve it for me?"

"Certainly. Tomorrow—"

"Actually, I would like to have it now."

Clunet frowns. "Very well. Mata Hari, shall we—"

"I believe that Mata Hari is quite comfortable here. No need for her to join you."

Both men look in my direction and I weigh the choice in front of me. Clunet holds my gaze for several moments and I wonder if he's instructing me to say no. Or is he willing me to stay?

"I'm sure there are many treasures in this enchanting library that Monsieur Guimet would like to share with me," I tell him. "I see many intriguing books that I would like to know more about. You take care of business, Monsieur Clunet. I'll find my way home."

I look at Guimet and he smiles.

When we're finished, Guimet reclines on his bed and stares at the ceiling, breathing deeply. "I had no idea," he keeps saying. "*No idea . . .*"

I run my hands over cotton sheets so fine they feel like silk. This is where I belong.

As I dress the following morning in the cavernous luxury of Guimet's bedroom, he asks what I will require to enhance my performance when I dance at the unveiling of his museum. "Anything," he stresses, as he tightens the blue sash of his silk robe. "Tell me what you need and I will give you absolutely anything."

Countless things I need leap to mind. But I limit my request to statues I've seen in Hindu temples and heavy bronze incense holders that are common in Java. "Also," I say, "I will need a set of Javanese gamelan. Eight instruments. And a flute and zither as well." It's a tall order. But Guimet appears unfazed.

"Consider it done."

Chapter 2

MY DANCE IS A SACRED POEM

This time I am the one who is early. I wait for Clunet in the foyer of my run-down building. I rent my tiny room from a man who beats his wife. The carpets stink of urine and mold. I force myself to take a deep breath. After tonight, when Guimet and his guests meet the "Star of the East," perhaps I'll never have to live with the scents of poverty again.

"What are you doing?" Rudolph snapped the first time I allowed myself to inhale the fragrances of Java. The air was heavy with the scent of the yellow and white blossoms of frangipani trees.

"Smelling the air," I said, already regretting my marriage to him.

"You enjoy the scent of cow shit?"

I ignored his comment and pointed to where terraced gardens were being cultivated in shades of emerald and jade. "What's being grown over there?"

He licked a stray morsel of food from his mustache. "Those are rice paddies and coconut palms. The natives call the paddies *sawah*s," he said with a dismissive grunt.

*Sawah*s. I committed the word to memory. "And that grass, what's it called?"

"*Alang-alang*. A bloody uncivilized language if you ask me. Too much damn singsong. It's no small wonder these people never contribute anything to society. They're all too lazy and too busy singing." He checked his pocket watch. If the driver went any faster our luggage would topple over and litter the streets. "It's shameful. We colonized this land fifty years ago. But with darkies, what can you do?"

We were on our way to Yogyakarta, to the house that would have cost a prince's fortune if it were built in Amsterdam. It was only a few days after my eighteenth birthday, and when we arrived, I ran inside and danced through its whitewashed rooms, admiring my burnished teak furniture and bamboo tables. "I can't believe it," I kept saying. I touched everything. The oyster-white countertops, the cinnamon and beige curtains, the flowers in terra-cotta pots. I took off my shoes so I could feel the polished floor, cool as silk, against my feet. "There are servants," Rudolph said, impatient with my excitement. They appeared on cue behind him. Two women and a man. All three bowed. The women smiled and I recognized my amber tones in their skin, my long, dark hair in theirs. I felt I had come home and I thought that I would live there forever as Margaretha MacLeod. Lady MacLeod.

Now I know I should have married a man like Guimet. Intelligent, refined, a lover of art. A gentle man.

Three uncouth-looking men pass through the dingy lobby and try to engage me in conversation. I shiver inside my black cloak. I'm wearing almost nothing underneath it—only a few veils and a thin top. I turn my back on the men and wish Clunet would hurry. When he finally arrives, he parks across the street and I watch as he walks up the three steps into the lobby. As he enters, I'm certain he is appalled by the same things that dismayed me the day I made this building my home. The stains on the carpets, the old tarnished mirror decorating the wall—the odor. Still, this is preferable to having him inside my apartment again; I know how shabby it is. Rue Durantin is all I can afford.

"Ready?" he asks, and pretends not to notice my embarrassment. He offers me his arm as if we were in an elegant hotel, and he walks me to his car. I wait as he opens the door for me. He tucks in the edges of my long cloak as well.

"Thank you," I say. Rudolph never opened or closed my carriage door.

Clunet starts the car. As we drive toward the Place d'Iena I begin to feel nervous. I try not to imagine what will happen to me if my dance is rejected; life won't be worth living if this evening is a disaster. Then the dream of Paris will truly be gone. I glance at Clunet, his expensive blue suit and thick salt-and-pepper hair. If I fail to impress, he'll toss me away as easily as he tossed that rose from his car the day we signed our contract.

He must notice the way I am twisting the fabric of my cloak because he says, "Nothing to be frightened about, M'greet. I've seen you perform. You'll conquer them tonight."

But there is everything to be frightened about. "There will be so many guests—"

"Yes. Think of it as performing in a theater."

"An exclusive theater; every member of the audience is astoundingly wealthy."

He smiles. "That is the very best kind of playhouse."

I recognize the statue of George Washington. We have reached the Place d'Iena. There are still three hours before the two hundred guests are due to arrive, but I'll need the time to practice and dress. A butler answers the door and as soon as we're inside, Guimet pounces on us. He's all compliments and smiles with me, but with Clunet he's more formal. He offers his hand and says, "Looking forward to tonight." Then he turns back to me, as excited as a boy. "Wait until you see what I've done."

He escorts us across the street to the library and I'm truly amazed. He has transformed a cathedral of books and art into an Indian temple. Incense wafts, thick and heady, between the columns, while men dressed in gold silks and wearing jewel-encrusted turbans wave ostrich-feather fans. A three-foot statue of Shiva Nataraja, the destroyer of worlds, glitters from the center of the room. I close my eyes for a moment and breathe deeply. He has spared no expense and the authenticity is exquisite; it is as if Paris is thousands of miles away and I am standing in a temple in Java.

Exactly as I requested, a gamelan orchestra is poised, waiting for me. The musicians have set up in the back of the room. In the car I was nervous; the stakes are so high. If I succeed, I am guaranteed entry into high society; if I fail, it is back to Montmartre and misery. Yet standing in front of Shiva—who is trampling Illusion with his right foot—I feel powerful and strong. I take off my light cloak. I am wearing only the silver brassiere and a thin silver band on my thigh that is clearly visible through my diaphanous skirt. Guimet cannot take his eyes off me.

"I must rehearse," I say, dismissing the two men.

Guimet immediately kisses each of my cheeks. "*Bonne chance,*" he says on the first, and on the second kiss, "*Shubhkamnaye.*"

Good luck in both French and Hindi.

But it's clear that Clunet isn't going to leave. "Thank you, Edouard," I say, handing him my cloak. Then I focus all of my charm on the men in my orchestra. "And thank you for joining me for tonight's experience. This dance is unlike anything you've witnessed before. While we rehearse I ask but two things of you: If you are shocked, hide your emotions. If you are offended, leave."

The men exchange looks between themselves. A few of them have glanced at Clunet; none have met my eye.

"My hope, however, is that each of you will stay. That you will help me create one of the most memorable evenings in Paris, one that will make you famous throughout this city."

The men look intrigued; one or two has risked meeting my glance.

"We have less than three hours to come to know each other, to anticipate each other's needs. We will practice the entire dance together. We will rehearse until we know we are perfect. I will enter from beneath the stairs." I indicate the exact spot. "You will start to play moments before I come out, gently transporting our audience away from the present, away from their everyday lives. Then—at the instant I appear—the music must crescendo."

We run through the dance and my hips sway to their music, the movement and the percussion carrying us all to another world. I am certain some of these musicians have seen dancers partially disrobe; they have knowing looks in their eyes. But when I slip off the last of my layered skirts and kneel before Shiva, my back arched, everything I was born with displayed, I know their shock is genuine. I glance over in time to see Edouard Clunet with his eyes as wide as those of the men in my orchestra.

His expression tells me I'm in exactly the right position.

I hear the sounds of people moving into the library, members of French society talking and laughing and taking their places.

"This is quite a spectacular room."

"I hear the entertainer is Japanese."

Chairs scrape across the floor. Then the lamps dim and all conversation stops as Guimet begins his introduction.

"Our guest was born in the south of India at Jaffnapatam. She is the daughter of a great Brahmin family. Tonight we will witness one of the sacred dances of India."

The audience murmurs as the orchestra begins, filling the room with music few people in Paris have ever heard.

"She will honor us with the dance of the *devadasis*, a sacred art belonging to the Hindu god Shiva. In doing so, she will bless this library. I present to you the dancer, Mata Hari."

I enter the room and the music crescendos.

Two hundred pairs of eyes turn toward me.

"My dance is a sacred poem," I begin, as the orchestra plays a slow rhythm. I am offering them the precise speech Mahadevi fabricated in Java, a Dutch colony worlds away from this exclusive gathering. I have memorized it faithfully, to the letter. I spread my arms. "Each movement is a word and every word is underlined by music." I pause; *la gratin* listens, spellbound. "The temple in which I dance can be vague or faithfully reproduced as it is here tonight. For I am the temple. All true temple dancers are religious in nature and all explain, in gestures and poses, the rules of the sacred texts."

I begin to move my hips. "One translates the divine attributes of Brahma, Vishnu, and Shiva—creation, fecundity, destruction. This is the dance I dance tonight. The dance of destruction as it leads to creation."

The room is mesmerized as I translate the speech into English, Dutch, German, then Javanese. By the end, no one understands what I'm saying, but I see that they are enraptured with the foreignness of my words, hypnotized by my movements.

The music changes, becomes a slow sensuous beat. I close my eyes and free the knots that hold the veils of my skirt in place, letting them drift, like petals, to the ground.

The hypnotic sounds of the flutes rise and yet I hear the audience gasp as one.

I kneel before Shiva; all that clothes me now are the silver arcs on my breasts and the silver band across my thighs. The wives in the audience are wide-eyed. I imagine the husbands are wishing for looser trousers.

The music becomes deeper, more urgent. I crouch, exposing myself to the men in the front row. Quick as a flash I lift my arms and offer myself to the audience in seductive, orgasmic waves. The men sit forward. The women lean back.

I fall on my knees before the statue of Shiva and arch my back in ecstasy.

As the music climaxes, Guimet is the first to leap to his feet, applauding.

"Excuse me," Edouard interrupts my conversation, cupping my elbow and guiding me toward a secluded spot. The entire library is abuzz. I overhear the words "brilliant" and "incomparable." The line of people waiting to talk with Guimet will easily take several hours to get through. I look over my shoulder at the handsome young officer I've been pulled away from and wink at him, promising my return. Is anything more attractive than a man in uniform?

"Did you say a *woman* taught you to dance like that?" Edouard asks the moment we are alone. "Mona Devi?"

"Mahadevi," I say, irritated that he's mangled her name. "She danced at the elegant parties I attended in Java. She wore silver bangles and sheer yellow veils. She owned rubies and sapphires as big as my thumb." I leave out other details: that I was the hostess of those parties, not a guest. And that my husband forbade me to learn the magic of her dances. That she promised me "with every new sun comes new chances, a new day to reinvent yourself." That she was the first to call me Mata Hari, "Eye of the Dawn."

"Who is that man I was talking to?"

"In the uniform? No one."

"He has to be *someone*."

"An Italian officer, judging from his costume."

"Ah. A poor mortal like yourself."

Edouard looks genuinely astonished. "Are you quoting Petrarch's *Lives?*"

"My father read it to me. When I was a child, he'd quiz me on the names of the ancient Romans. Greeks as well. The gods they worshipped, the temples they built." Sometimes, instead of reading, he would tell stories from his childhood. How, when he was a boy, he was asked to pose as King William's horse guard in a portrait painted for the Royal Gallery.

Guimet laughs loudly at something one of his guests has said. Edouard's hand drops from my elbow. "He was impressed with you tonight." He pauses. "And I'm sure last night as well."

I don't deny it. We are both adults. He said he wants no secrets between us.

"I'm going to find you a better place to live. To maintain his belief in you, you'll need an apartment that he can visit."

I am a child in an instant. "Can I have a bathroom, and running water, and a balcony that looks out over the city?"

"All of that and more. But first, I believe I have secured another engagement for you. Have you heard of the Rothschilds?"

Have I heard of them? Of course I have. They're as rich as kings.

Chapter 3

EVERYTHING I HOPED FOR

*C*lose your eyes and I'll transport you to a temple called Borobudur," I whisper in Guimet's ear as we lounge in his bed and listen to the rain. I've convinced him that I conceived my sacred dances at this sanctuary and offered them to the faithful, but this isn't true. I did visit the holy place once, on a morning as warm and fragrant as this March morning is damp and chill. Sofie, my only friend and the wife of one of my husband's subordinates, arranged the outing. We made the trip without the men, accompanied by my servant, an Indian woman named Laksari.

Guimet closes his eyes and I paint him a picture with words. Gone is the mahogany four-poster bed. Now, we are traveling in a rickety andong. I am pressed between Laksari and Sofie. We pass by roadside stalls where the scents of fresh fruit and cardamom waft heavily in the air. Bananas hang in bunches from the tops of bamboo huts and signs promise *Freshly Picked* and *Ripe*—I know this because Laksari is translating as we pass them by. There is absolutely nothing of Leeuwarden here. In Yogyakarta one can see reflections of The Netherlands in the way the officers' wives dress, in the foods offered in the market—but this is a world of its own. We pass through a river valley with thatched-roofed houses on stilts. The houses climb up the tiered slopes and sweep down into rice paddies.

"They allow ducks to eat the rice?" I ask, watching the emerald-throated birds bob and nibble.

"The ducks do not eat the rice," Laksari corrects me. "They eat the insects that hurt the rice."

We wind along palm-fringed roads and listen to women singing in the fields while men at the warungs—tiny shops—call out to us to buy fresh coconuts. The andong takes us through a small grove of heavenly smelling pine to where bamboo houses nestle against the hills. They are covered by twisted magenta garlands. Laksari tells me the funnel-shaped flowers are called ipomoea.

When the andong driver announces, "Nearly there, my ladies," we are transported back in time. Before our eyes an ancient temple rises from the jungle floor, partially obscured by abundant flora and twisting vines. Dutch soldiers work in complete silence, laboring to clear off the lush vegetation; it appears as if the verdure wishes to reclaim the terraces that rise, one above another, as the temple ascends to the sky. I breathe deeply and believe I am inhaling the wisdom of a thousand years.

"I am sure you know Borobudur was built by the Shailendra dynasty. And that it took eighty years of labor to build," I say to Guimet, tracing my finger over his chest.

In my memory, Sofie, Laksari, and I walk to the base of the holy place and I touch the wall. It is made of basalt. On the first level, inside, are friezes illustrating the stages of life.

We go inside and the temperature drops. It is cool and the air smells of soil, of the earth itself. Sofie points to images depicting Greed, Ignorance, Envy. According to Buddhists, she says, you reach enlightenment by overcoming desire. If you are a slave to earthly desires, you will never achieve Nirvana, the ultimate enlightenment . . . heaven, I suppose.

Slowly, we make our way to the top of Borobudur, an ascent that elevates us, delivers us so close to the heavens that you can view volcanoes jutting through the forest canopy.

At the topmost level of the pyramid we discover the meditating stone Buddhas. They are sitting in quiet bliss, feet crossed one over the other, palms outward, contemplating the world from inside stone bells. At first glance they look identical; closer inspection reveals subtle differences in the placement of their hands. In the very center rests the largest bell pointing toward Nirvana.

"Ah. Nirvana," says Guimet, startling me back into the present. He cups my breast and jiggles it in his hand.

I search the papers later that morning and I find my review under the headline SACRED DANCES OF BRAHMANISM. I read it as quickly as I can, holding my breath.

"This is different from any dancing I have seen in Paris," said M. Mollier, who spoke to the director of the Guimet Museum, an establishment devoted to art pertaining to religions of the extreme East, and where lectures are given to students twice a week.

Different from anything he has seen.

The article continues:

"The dance begins in slow rhythms and gradually becomes highly impassioned. The costume is purely Indian, disclosing the skin, which is profusely ornamented with jewels and slender gold chains. The feet are bare, and in her improvisations derived from the 'Mantras,' or sacrificial incantations, she often works herself up to a pitch of excitement and frenzy that may be more readily imagined than described. The dance symbolic of worship to the three deities of Brahmanism, Brahma, Vishnu and Shiva, are intensely emotional . . ."

I skim to the end:

"The Brahman dances present the most original novelty of the Parisian season."

I feel pure exhilaration.

Edouard has taken me to a building on Rue du Faubourg Saint-Honoré, a fashionable street in the eighth arrondissement. We are standing on the threshold of my new apartment, yet he refuses to open the door. First he asks me if I know that Saint-Honoré is the patron saint of bakers. Now he delays further by asking me to imagine what's inside.

"A room," I say, too excited and impatient for games.

"Very clever. What manner of rooms?"

"I don't know—oh, Edouard, please, open the door!"

Inside is absolutely everything I've ever hoped for: parquet flooring, heavy cedar-wood beams, chandeliers with crystals, a bathroom with running water, and a balcony overlooking Paris. I hug him; he has given me everything I asked for. I run my hands over the satin chairs and breathe in the scent of the fresh-cut yellow roses in crystal vases. I have read that yellow roses are symbolic for "new beginnings." I hope this is true. I absorb my good fortune. It's obvious the furniture choices are his: heavy masculine pieces in mahogany and glass. Large gilt-framed paintings. Persian carpets.

"I love everything," I tell him, as I spy a telephone. My own telephone!

"It is a luxury you will need, I am sure. The two of you will have all the time in the world to become better acquainted later this evening. You may want to join the Telephone Subscribers' Association. But this afternoon we must go shopping." When he sees my expression of surprise, he searches for the right words before admitting, "You require a wardrobe. A proper wardrobe."

I am not insulted by the implications. I am thrilled to be considered a courtesan—I have read of mistresses to barons and princes who live in splendor like this.

"Money for emergencies," he says. He reaches into his jacket pocket and withdraws a purse. "Before we leave, let's find a safe place for it."

It holds one hundred francs. My God, it's enough to live for two months.

As we drive together down the Rue du Faubourg Saint-Honoré, he explains what I can expect from the Rothschild's event. They have planned a party for more than six hundred guests, and Madam Rothschild has requested that I perform something from the classics.

"*Tristan and Isolde*," he suggests.

"Lady Godiva," I counter. Her story was a favorite when I was a child. My father knew I loved the tale and only told it late at night when my brothers were in bed. "Tell her I absolutely must have a horse. That is a requirement. A white horse," I add.

"Do you ride?"

"Of course. Would I ask for a horse if I couldn't ride? My father taught me." Before he disappeared, leaving bills and empty cupboards to remember him by.

Edouard is nodding. "A white horse, nonnegotiable."

I glance out the window and watch the women walking along the Champs-Élysées. They are breathtaking, wearing dresses of such rich fabrics that Marie Antoinette would be envious. I imagine myself in a metallic brocade with lace. I add delicate sleeves and a high black belt to accentuate my waist, and improve the whole ensemble by including pearls around my neck.

"Everyone who sees you must remember you," says Edouard.

"That is our goal. This requires strategy; none of your dresses are to be repeated. The same rule applies to your performances."

Edouard stops the car in front of an exclusive-looking women's boutique. I've never been inside such an expensive shop. The moment we step out of the car a man in a black suit takes Edouard's keys.

"You're giving your car to a stranger?" I ask, astonished at his lack of concern.

"The man's a valet, M'greet. It's his job to watch cars."

I blush and say, "Of course." But as we walk away I keep turning around.

Inside Le Bon Marché the air is lightly perfumed—lavender and vanilla, I think. And suddenly it's my thirteenth birthday again and my father has taken me to the finest dress shop in Leeuwarden. *Find her a dress that's fit for the queen*, he says, and the shop girl is more than happy to oblige. But here, in this shop, there are so many exquisite items to look at that I feel slightly overwhelmed. I linger by the front window, where there are rows of shawls. Each looks as soft and rich as butter. I delicately brush them with my fingertips, and feel intoxicated.

"Choose," Edouard tells me, gesturing expansively. "You need four or five ensembles for this engagement, minimum." Then he sighs, and says almost to himself, "A Rothschild event waxes on for days."

I try on a dozen different dresses, hats, cashmere shawls. I am one of the women on the Champs-Élysées. I hold up a gleaming string of pearls. "These?" I ask, although he has said nothing about my lack of jewels. "Every woman needs pearls."

Edouard nods his approval and the shopkeeper asks, "Would madam like to try this matching bracelet?"

*   *   *

That evening I don't go back to Montmartre. I return directly to my elegant apartment on Rue du Faubourg Saint-Honoré. I unlock my new life and stand on my private balcony to gaze out over Paris while I wait for Guimet to arrive. The air is chilly and the sun is setting but I have wrapped myself in cashmere and I feel deliciously warm and safe. I will leave my old possessions in that miserable rented room. They belong to the past. I have no desire to claim them.

Chapter 4

LOOKING FOR FAME

$\mathscr{I}$ have lived in Paris for more than a year, yet in all that time I never realized that a few minutes of travel could take me from Notre Dame to Baron Henri de Rothschild's château. It's the most beautiful building I've ever seen, hidden from the road by a thick bed of trees and protected from outsiders by a great stone wall. Edouard's car pulls into the circular drive and I see reporters crowding the columned steps of the estate.

"Are they here for *me*?"

"They're certainly not waiting to hear my opinion on international law," Edouard says drily.

I bite my lower lip.

He places his palm on my knee. "You'll be fine." He steps out and opens my door; then the barrage of questions begins.

"Is it true that you were born on the Malabar Coast?"

"Yes," I say, before I'm even out of the car. "In the city of Jaffnapatam."

"Is this how you spell it?" A reporter thrusts a notebook under my nose. He's wearing a card that says *Press* in the hatband of his fedora.

"Exactly."

I get out and a second reporter maneuvers through the crowd. He is wearing a bright yellow bow tie. "So tell me, Mata Hari, what is required of a temple dancer?"

"The most sacred festivals require the ability to charm snakes," I say. "It is dangerous work. My mother—"

"What makes you different from Isadora Duncan?" someone else shouts.

Edouard pushes several reporters out of the way and we climb the steps of the château. At the front door he turns to the crowd: "As she's said, her mother danced at Kanda Swany, and yes, she died giving birth in a temple. Now if you'll excuse us, she has a dance to perform."

"Tell me about India," Bowtie persists, and the crowd of men surge, pushing us against the door. "When will you be returning?"

"Never," I say. "France is my home now."

A dozen pens begin to write.

"Now if you'll excuse us."

A butler opens the heavy oak doors as if on cue and Edouard ushers me inside.

"Can you believe that mob?" I whisper. "Those reporters would have followed us inside if you hadn't blocked them."

"Yes, they're a real pain in the ass. Isadora Duncan?" he asks, in a tone of disgust. "That woman clomps about wrapped in blankets. She's as seductive as a nun. There's no comparison between the two of you."

As the butler ushers us down the hall I keep looking out the windows to see if they're waiting for me.

"Stop that," Edouard says. "You'll only encourage them."

"Isn't that what we want?" They've all gone away. All except Bowtie, who's trying to push through the hedges so that he can see through the glass. I walk closer to the windows, hoping he'll catch a glimpse of me.

"Yes." Edouard guides me away with his arm. "But not here. The Rothschilds are private people," he whispers.

What kind of private people, I wonder, *host an event for six hundred guests?*

I don't have to wonder for long. We meet them in the salon, decorated in loud pink brocade chairs and heavy silver mirrors. Baron Henri de Rothschild is short and fat: He makes me think of a little toad. I have heard that he is a playwright, that he uses a pen name. I tower over him as I execute a well-practiced curtsy, allowing him a quick glimpse of breasts. His bejeweled wife, Mathilde, frowns.

"So. We have heard that you were born on the Malabar Coast," Rothschild says, offering me a seat.

"Yes. My mother danced at Kanda Swany. And now I am honored to dance for you."

"I understand you will deliver something different from your performance at the library?" He sounds disappointed, but his wife looks relieved.

Edouard catches my eye; he told me that the baron begged for a repeat of the temple dance. But his look says, we *never* repeat performances.

"Tonight," I tell him, "I will give you Lady Godiva. A noblewoman who defied her husband while clothed by her long, lovely hair." When the baron's wife gasps, I add, "She was bold, acting for the welfare of the poor."

"I believe those who did not merit an invitation to tonight's event will deeply regret their absence," Edouard says quickly. "This evening we will bear witness to a once-in-a-lifetime performance."

"Indeed!" The baron's pleasure is evident. He summons a servant and tells him to show us to our rooms. "Mata Hari must rest and prepare."

The room is spectacular and the view of the lake calms my nerves.

I sink into the cloud of expensive linens on the bed. I wonder what Bowtie is writing about me. I close my eyes for only a moment before a sharp knock on the door disturbs my peace.

Outside, the baron is smiling. He is so fat that the exertion of climbing his own stairs has left sweat on his brow. But his eyes are beautiful and his taste—the cut of his suit, the soft leather of his shoes—is impeccable. I invite him inside and he notes that I've unpacked.

"I hope the accommodations are to your liking?"

"This room is wonderful," I say.

"Occasionally my foreign guests find these suites too large. Too lonely."

"It's very big," I say, understanding him perfectly. "Yet how can I be lonely now that you are with me?"

Under the full moon I arrive in the jasmine-scented garden on a white horse, covered only by my hair and a translucent veil.

"Is she wearing anything?" a woman whispers. "Anything at all?"

"I think she's naked!"

I slip off the horse without a word. Six hundred people who have never known hunger stand still, breathless in the face of my nakedness. The music begins and I bend over backward, a silver-skinned diva in the jasmine night.

At the threshold of my room, Edouard appears absolutely delighted. He holds out his hand and I slip a gloved arm through his. "Ready?" he asks.

"I should think that my performance merits at least one compliment," I say, as we journey down the thickly carpeted hallway. "Did you admire my horsemanship?"

"I admired more than that; you were stunning. Breathtaking. More regal than Godiva herself."

"And this dress?" I prod.

"I am the person who bought it for you," he reminds me. And then adds, "No woman in Paris—on earth—could hope to look more lovely in lavender. And those pearls . . ." He puts his hand over his heart.

"You are looking handsome yourself." And it is true. In his formal-wear his appearance is dashing.

"I know."

"Rascal."

We descend the stairs to join the Rothschilds' party and he leans in to whisper instructions to me. "Everyone who matters is here. Don't speak at length with anyone who appears drunk, in particular the German ambassador, an unpleasant man called von Schoen."

At the bottom of the stairs a butler escorts us into a mirror-lined ballroom illuminated by dozens of chandeliers. And beneath them, on the polished wooden dance floor, hundreds of people are laughing and chatting.

"And be careful of Lady Brochard. That's her, near the window." He inclines his head slightly to indicate a plump woman in a bur-gundy dress. "She's known for her sweetness and for passing on mali-cious gossip. But Lady Saint-Amour is a gem." I follow his gaze to a slender woman with auburn hair. "And all of the Barton sisters are delightful. Although I haven't spotted them yet."

"Is there anyone you don't know?"

"In Paris? Not really."

Over the sounds of tinkling glasses and conversation are the high, sweet notes of a string quartet. We move through the room and I catch snippets as we walk. Women talking of horses and furs. Men concerned that the price of food is rising. Is this a good time to invest in wheat? What about corn? A dark-haired man meets my gaze and we both smile. Who could possibly care about wheat on a night as elegant and promising as this?

The string quartet is playing something slow. Edouard disappears and the dark-haired man asks me to dance. Henri de Marguerie. His suit is immaculate and the band on his wrist reads Rolex. It looks to be a tiny clock of some sort. "It's a wristwatch," he says when he catches me staring.

"I've never seen one," I confess.

"Soldiers use them. In a few years, everyone will have one."

"You're military?" I imagine his uniform: army, air force, navy? He would be dashing in anything.

"I was a pilot. You were magnificent tonight," he says, and I allow him to continue complimenting me as we cross the dance floor. An orchestra replaces the string quartet and the new musicians strike up a waltz. He tells me about his family in London. I tell him about my time in Bombay. Then the musicians abandon Johann Strauss and begin playing a more scandalizing tune; I learned the accompanying dance my first week in Paris. The handsome aviator raises his eyebrows at me, asking if I'm willing to accept his invitation.

The floor clears and his chest presses against mine. I give him my hand and he stretches it out in front of me. "Ready?" he asks. I can smell the faint trace of soap on his skin and the musky scent of cologne on his shirt. In front of the baron's six hundred guests we begin the tango, stepping on half notes, dipping on counts three and four. He's a wonderful dancer, my aviator. I imagine he is equally graceful when he is dancing horizontally.

When our dance is complete the entire room erupts into applause. We make our way to Edouard and I tell him that henceforth all future engagements must come with dashing aviators. The man laughs. So does Edouard, as a blonde slips her slender arm through his in a proprietary way.

"Well done," she says to me, though I can't decide whether she's sincere or mocking me. Her hair is swept up into a pile of loose curls. She begins to steer Edouard away and I study the way she walks, how she holds her long cigarette between her forefinger and thumb.

As the evening progresses, half a dozen men ask me to dance. When the musicians begin their last piece, however, it's the aviator who returns. "May I have the pleasure of escorting you to your room?" he asks.

I search for Edouard and his sophisticated blonde, but they're nowhere to be seen. I notice that other couples are retiring for the night. "Yes," I say.

He walks me to the stairs. The thick red carpet feels like velvet underfoot; it's nearly black beneath the low light of the chandeliers.

"You're quite the dancer," I tell him. "So gentle yet so strong."

"As are you, my little mouse."

"Is that what you think I am?"

"Yes, and you should be careful before I pounce!"

He chases me up the stairs, pretending to be a tiger. And when we fall into bed together, I'm not even thinking about Edouard's blonde.

The next morning Edouard appears in my room without knocking, before I've had the opportunity to change from my dressing gown. "Pack your things," he says. "Quickly."

"We're leaving? I thought we were staying until—"

"The baron wants you to dance again tonight. But Mata Hari never repeats herself. You must always leave them wanting more, M'greet."

"You can't tell him no?" I'm imagining the Rothschilds' other guests, already downstairs and chatting to one another over orange juice and champagne. I'm looking forward to seeing my aviator again.

"This is the baron. He is relentless." He looks around my room, at all of my belongings—some hanging, some on the backs of chairs, some delicate pieces on the floor where they were discarded in haste. He sighs. "I'll come back for you in an hour. Be ready."

Edouard returns exactly when promised. He lifts my two cases and when I begin to protest, he shakes his head. "We're using the servants' stairs," he says.

A small thrill passes through me as I follow him into a stairwell reserved for the household staff. A butler on his way to the second floor scowls at us, but I borrow the tone of Edouard's blonde and say, "We're on our way to attend to Lady Brochard," and immediately he looks abashed and lets us pass.

Outside, the reporters are gone and Edouard's car is waiting. He starts the car and as we drive away I feel as light as a child; Edouard looks like a giddy schoolboy.

"You'd make a fine spy, M'greet," he says.

The car smells of freshly polished leather and smoke. The blonde must have been in my seat last night. We drive down the Rue du Cloître, passing under the shadow of Notre Dame. There are more cars on the road than carriages. I wonder if it's the same now in Leeuwarden. "Do people have more money to spend or are cars getting cheaper?"

Edouard frowns. "I suppose they're getting cheaper."

"How much do they cost?"

"Close to fifteen thousand francs."

The baron paid me twice that for Lady Godiva. I look at one of the rings that Guimet gave me and think that perhaps I will buy myself a car. We fall into silence. Finally, I ask, "So how was your night?"

He looks at me sidelong. "Excellent. Yours?"

I take one of the cigarettes the aviator gave me and light it the way

Edouard's blonde did, tilting my head back and letting the smoke out, slowly, sensuously, as I practiced in the mirror. "Wonderful."

He grabs the cigarette from my mouth. "Jesus Christ, what are you doing?" He flings it out the window and I'm shocked. "That's a nasty habit."

"Your blonde smokes!"

"Who?"

"The girl you left with last night."

"She smokes? Well, notice who's in the car with me. I don't live with her."

"You don't live with me either!"

We both brood for several long minutes. Edouard is the one to break the silence. "I have another engagement lined up for you," he says. "But this isn't like our previous arrangements. There will only be women in this audience."

"Wives want to see me perform?"

This makes him laugh. "I highly doubt it. You will be dancing for Comtesse de Loynes." He waits several moments before realizing I haven't heard of her. "Her literary salon is the most famous in Paris. She is in her sixties now; in her youth she had love affairs with half a dozen famous men, but she's not truly interested in the male of the species. If your desire is to gain social prominence and recognition, Jeanne de Loynes can offer both to you on a platter. Her connections in this city are unsurpassed."

I think of the reporters who followed us to the Rothschilds': What would they write if they knew I was engaged to perform nude for a group of women? They'd be trampling bushes to cover the story. "Is it already confirmed?"

"Awaiting your approval."

"Yes," I say swiftly. "Of course. Tell her yes."

Chapter 5

GLISTENS LIKE WATER

$\mathscr{S}$o this is the famous Mata Hari," Comtesse de Loynes says a few days later.

I have become an "overnight" sensation. *Le Petit Parisien* declares that I'm "the best-kept secret in France." *Le Figaro* calls my performance for the Rothschilds "astounding."

"Comtesse, it is a pleasure to meet you." I hold out my hand so she can see the rings Guimet has gifted me and she squeezes my fingers, inspecting each one. Nothing about the Comtesse de Loynes is what I imagined. I had thought she would be tall and sophisticated—an older version of Edouard's smoking blonde. But she's petite and a bit plump, with a head of unruly still-brown curls. She reminds me of the American actress, Maude Fealy.

"Please, have a seat."

She indicates a silk chair patterned with flowers. If the parlor reflects the house, her entire home is decorated in purples and mauves. The impact is slightly disconcerting. She may be famous for her salon, but I doubt she has ever been praised for her taste in décor.

"And please." She leans forward. "Call me Jeanne."

Immediately, the image of another Jeanne forms in my mind. But I refuse to allow it to come into focus; I simply won't allow myself to dwell on her. Not here. I focus on the heart-shaped face of the woman in front of me instead. "Jeanne," I repeat, giving her name a Malaysian lilt, and her hands go to the pearls around her neck, drawing attention to her face. It thrills men to hear their names spoken with an accent. Now I know it thrills her, too.

"You don't look like Isadora Duncan," she says. "If you don't mind my saying."

Yes, Isadora. The Dancing Nun. "My lawyer," I say, brushing Isadora aside, "has told me you desire a sensual performance, a piece that is provocative."

"Yes." She moves closer to me. "I read in *Le Figaro* that the most sacred festivals"—her voice is a whisper—"involve a snake."

I actually feel the color draining from my face. After I danced for the Rothschilds, Bowtie followed me all around town; I didn't notice him until he finally cornered me with Edouard as we were dining at Maxim's. I made up all manner of things to impress him. What else did I tell that man?

"If I arrange for such a creature, will you perform that dance?"

A servant lowers a platter of tea and sandwiches onto the settee between us.

"I . . ." I have never been near a snake, let alone danced with one. "I will have to consider this request."

"I understand. The dance is sacred. In ordinary circumstances it would be viewed in a temple." She indicates that the servant should pour the tea. "But as we do not have a temple . . ."

She has mistaken my reluctance for piety. I'm about to decline, to impress upon her the strict religious nature of a snake dance, when I recall how furiously Bowtie was scribbling. If he were to write about Mata Hari dancing with a living snake in Madame de Loynes's famous salon in front of an audience composed exclusively of "cer-tain" women . . .

"Please," Jeanne says. She is actually begging.

I take her hand. "For you—and only you—I will do it."

All throughout India men charm snakes. It can't be that difficult to dance with one.

I inform Edouard that my new dance requires extra time to rehearse and he has given me seven days. But I still have not solved the prob-lem of working with a snake. It has started to rain and the cream-colored walls of my apartment feel as if they are closing in on me whenever I think of reptiles. What am I going to do? My thoughts turn to the purse with the hundred francs. Perhaps I should visit the Champs-Élysées? I can shop, distract myself. I desperately need a new pair of gloves and also some boots for the winter. I look out the widow to judge how hard it is raining when the sound of the phone startles me from my daydreams. I hurry to answer it, feeling like an actress in a fancy movie. It is such a luxury to have a phone.

Guimet wishes to see me.

I watch from my window as the chauffeur opens the car door. As always, Guimet is impeccably dressed. Today he wears a long black coat against the rain and an expensive fedora. When he arrives at my door, I greet him with kisses and notice that he is wearing a new wristwatch.

"My God, I've missed you," he mumbles into my hair. And then he says, "I hear you are dancing for Jeanne de Loynes next week."

If my marriage to Rudolph MacLeod taught me nothing else, it schooled me in the ability to recognize jealousy in an innocent com-ment, to interpret a tone. When Rudolph asked, "Where have you been?" it always meant trouble. I could hear the tenseness in his voice as he sat at the table without his paper or drink, staring at the wall, waiting for me.

"I said, where have you been?"

"At the market," I hurry my words. *"At the market—"*

"I told you not to go there anymore, goddamn it!" He pulls his arm back and hits me. *"You think you can defy me? You think I don't see the way you look at the men I command?"*

"Yes. The performance is for a small group," I say, forcing myself back to the present, ignoring the tense quality of his voice by imagining the Buddhas of Borobudur calmly meditating their way to Nirvana. "The gathering is for women only."

"Jeanne will want you for herself, you know. Once she meets you."

I did not realize Guimet was the type of man to be jealous of a woman. "A woman will woo me away from you?" I tease. I don't like this ugly aspect of his personality.

"She's no longer a beauty but she can still be very convincing."

I want to ask if she has ever "convinced" him, but decide to distract him instead. "It's only a dance," I say. I lead him to my bedroom and we make love. Afterward, he isn't angry. But he's not happy, either, and he doesn't offer to take me to dinner.

I spend the night alone, feeling anxious. I am unable to sleep for the longest time, and when I finally do, my dreams take me to my darkest times in Java.

I'm in no mood to rehearse the following day. It is a clear day and I wander the boutiques along the Champs-Élysées with the money Edouard left for me. I can hear his voice in my head, scolding me. "Only for important expenses!" But today everything feels tremendously important: the hand-painted silk scarf in aquamarine, the stunning citrine ring and matching necklace, the bronze incense burner I discover in a shop run by an Egyptian man and his son. Nothing could feel better than this. Then I see a young girl begging outside of an expensive clothing shop and all of my happiness turns to dust. The girl has dark hair and wide dark eyes. Her arms look thin. She holds out her cupped hands and I tell her to wait while I go inside. When I come out, I wrap a new cashmere shawl around her shoulders. She begins to cry. "Thank you, madam. Thank you," she keeps saying.

"It's nothing, little one," I tell her. "Where are your parents?"

"Maman is gone." Meaning dead. "Papa is working."

"What does he do?"

She shakes her head. "I don't know."

I buy her a warm baguette and several slices of meat. When I return home, my purse is empty, but Guimet has completely vanished from my thoughts.

Comtesse de Loynes phones to tell me that the snake has arrived. Edouard is sitting across from me, looking completely at home in one of a pair of aubergine chairs he bought for my apartment. As soon as I click the receiver back into place, he wants to know why the wealthiest woman in France is calling me at home.

"Why isn't she calling me at my office?"

"Perhaps because you're not there," I offer. He doesn't find my answer humorous. I can see by the look on his face that he is concerned. "Don't look so grumpy," I say. "I've planned a surprise." Or a disaster.

He fixes me with his eyes. "I don't like surprises."

*   *   *

"Mata Hari!" Jeanne moves swiftly down the steps and kisses both of my cheeks. We walk arm in arm into her foyer, and for the second time in a week I am surprised by how little taste she possesses for furniture. The mirrors are ridiculously ostentatious. Her ornate chairs must have started life in Versailles; they look too complicated to sit on. She leads me into the foyer where the walls are frescoed with pasture scenes. Waiting for me is a man standing next to a crate. I smell straw and hear rustling. If I live to be a hundred, I vow silently, I will never boast about snake handling again.

"Mata Hari, this is Ishan," Jeanne says. "He comes to us all the way from Bombay, not so far from where you were born, I believe?"

His face registers surprise; I hold his eyes and he keeps his silence.

"I know you must be eager to begin your rehearsal," Jeanne continues, "so I'll leave you two alone." She shuts the door and the expectation on her face is almost embarrassing to witness. She should learn to better conceal her emotions.

I look at the crate. "The snake is inside?"

"You have never handled a snake before," he says.

"No. And I'm afraid of snakes."

He sighs. "The key is *not* to be afraid." He reaches inside the box and lifts out a glistening creature that is much larger than I anticipated. It must be at least six feet long and it's very muscular. Its forked tongue flicks in my direction. "Touch," he says, holding the snake out for me, one hand keeping the head firmly at a distance while the rest of the animal is winding its way around his body.

"Will it bite me? Will it *poison* me?"

"I am holding the head. And this snake constricts; there is no poison. Touch."

I touch. The skin is dry and cool like spun silk—not at all how it appears. I run my hands along its back and I feel a small thrill. This creature is powerful and elegant—and looks so dangerous.

"I will put her around your shoulders," he says.

"*She?*"

He drapes the python around my shoulders and smiles. "Yes."

I hold my breath as the snake moves its heavy body around mine, hugging my limbs, sliding over my breasts. The creature's weight is somehow comforting. "She is beautiful."

"She likes you."

I think he must be mocking me: Can a snake truly be partial to someone? But Ishan is the picture of earnestness. I watch as the snake slides her tail between my thighs, her skin reflecting the light. "She glistens like water but feels like silk," I observe.

Ishan's entire face glows, like a proud father. And for the next four hours he guides me, instructing me on how to hold her, where to place my hands so that she is supported, how to understand her body language.

"Treat her well," he promises when we are finished, "and she will never harm you."

Jeanne calls again, this time to tell me she has borrowed pieces from a friend's collection to transform her salon into a temple to Kama, the handsome Hindu god of desire. She calls a third time to ask if I have read the morning paper. Specifically, she wants to know what I thought of the article describing how Isadora Duncan is teaching young girls to dance and "share in her classic ideals."

"I have a surprise for you Mata Hari," she says, her voice full of promise. Then she says that she has hired eight girls to dance with me. "Perhaps you could come over this evening and rehearse with them?"

As soon as we disconnect I find the newspaper. I search until I find the headline.

DANCE ON THE SANDS AS IN ARCADIAN DAYS

PARIS—At Neuilly, near Paris, in that charming "garden city," where there are more trees than houses and where dwell more artists, musicians, painters, and sculptors than merchants, Miss Isadora Duncan, the American dancer, the priestess of Greek beauty, and her troupe of little girl pupils reside today in a pretty villa, and one can see all these young devotees of Terpsichore dancing on the sand of the shady paths or on the moss and amid the ferns of the grounds.

No picture could be more enchanting in its ideal charm and classic gracefulness than the dancing of these twelve little girls—the youngest is only 6 years old and the oldest 14—clad in light white or blue tunics, in the purest classic style, with their lasso hair held by a bandeau "a la Greeque," bare armed and bare legged.

Several times a day Isadora Duncan teaches the little nymphs. One by one, or all together, the happy pupils learn to be graceful and yet natural.

If Jeanne has hired six-year-old children to dance with me, I will have no option but to cancel. Surely she wouldn't have, almost certainly they'll be adults, but I skim the rest of the article.

As to how Miss Duncan evolved the idea of training children in her art, the story is best told in her own words:

"I sat once, on a bright afternoon, on the sands of Noordwijk, in Holland. I saw from afar my little niece, who was 'instinctively' dancing on the silver edge of the ocean, because the sun was bright, because the air was warm and cheering, because she felt happy to live. Noth-

ing could have been more beautiful than the little barefoot girl dancing with intense joy, with the ever moving
blue sea as the background."

I stop reading. I do not want to imagine little girls dancing by the sea.

"Mata Hari," Jeanne says, kissing my cheeks and ushering me inside
later that evening. "You are a vision!" She leads me down a number
of hallways until we are in a wide room that I have not seen before.
"Here are the ladies. They are yours to command."

I do my best to hide my relief. They are tiny creatures—girls as
thin and as pale as slips. But they are not children. I picture them
flitting around as light and nimble as fairies. Standing before them, I
feel like an Amazon. Did I look as eager and hopeful as they do when
I first arrived in Paris looking for employment? "Thank you, Jeanne,"
I say. I know exactly how I'll incorporate them into my dance.

"Anything you need, absolutely anything, all you have to do is ask,
Mata Hari."

She leaves us alone. There's a stage in the center of the room
and sitting in the middle of the stage is a large bronze statue of the
Hindu god Kama.

"Kama is the god of desire," I explain, gesturing for them to come
closer. "The dance we are going to perform is sacred in India. It happens only once a year—at harvest—when women gather before the
statue of Kama and try to seduce him."

"Why do they do this?" someone asks, a pretty girl with an
upturned nose.

"Because Kama can grant them whatever they wish. Whatever
desires are in their hearts. But he only chooses one girl. The one he
desires most. Each of you will be standing on stage." I arrange them

around the statue. "When I appear, I will be dressed in nothing but a thin white veil and a snake."

The girls look at one another. "Not a living creature?" one of them asks.

"Yes."

"Will we have to—"

"No. I am the only one allowed to touch the snake."

Their relief is visible. "And our dress?" another asks.

"I assume you're all familiar with Isadora Duncan?" I say benevolently. "You will all wear the kind of sheaths she favors."

Again, relief. Her sheaths are modest; they cannot be considered remotely revealing.

"I will be the only one undressed. Now in India, the girls approach the god with their hands outstretched. Here." I show them a pose of supplication and each girl imitates it.

I describe what the room will be like on the night of the performance. The lights will be dim. There will be incense and smoke.

"Each of you will entreat the god yet fail to move him. You will then glide to the edge of the stage, maintaining your arms in prayer, and form a semi-circle around Kama. After the last girl has attempted to seduce the god—you," I choose Upturned Nose, "I will appear."

Chapter 6

GIVE THEM A STORY

*A*re you sure there's nothing else I can bring you?"

Jeanne has delivered a cup of water to me. I'd desperately love a glass of wine as well, but I have to be clearheaded for this performance. Women are taking their seats in the salon and I hear them whispering to one another, asking about the statue in the center of the room. The only men here tonight are Edouard and Bowtie; I invited them both.

"I have everything I need," I tell her. I tighten the pair of gold vanki on my upper arms and slip heavy red bangles over my wrists. Both the vanki and the bangles are adorned with snakes, and I admire the gleam of their ruby eyes. I shake the bells on my anklets to be certain they are untangled and will sing while I dance. I touch the triangle between my breasts and feel the silver amulet that Mahadevi gave me one afternoon as we sat in her parlor in Java, sipping rum from frosted glasses. It is the only piece of jewelry I wasn't able to pawn after I arrived in Paris and I am glad I still possess it. Shaped like an eye, it is meant to ward off evil. Rudolph believed it was a sign of witchcraft.

"I have everything I need," I repeat. I wish Jeanne would take this cue and leave, but she lingers; now she is glancing at the amulet. "Were you born in India?" she asks. "Is that the truth?"

I'm tempted to say no. We're so very similar, Jeanne and I. She wasn't born into luxury and wealth; she was born Marie-Anne Detourbay. Bowtie told me she earned her title on her back. But I tell her what Edouard would want me to say, especially before this performance. "Yes."

The gamelan orchestra she's hired begins to play the piece I call "Seduction."

"It's time," I tell her.

"Good luck." She kisses both of my cheeks. Her hand lingers on mine. "You're quite the mystery, Mata Hari." And I can see this excites her.

She leaves and I allow myself a quick memory. *I am learning to imitate Mahadevi's hands; we are moving our hips together slowly and hypnotically, our arms raised. "Did you know," she asks me, "that my mother was Buddhist and my father was Hindu? It was a forbidden love." She sighs. "It should have stayed forbidden." Then she stops our lesson abruptly and says, "You must dance in public with me." She reaches out and touches my hair. "In yellow, you would be a goddess," she says.*

I am shocked. I've discovered that she is twenty-nine and has entertained many men. She understands men, the way they think. She is more than a dancer. This was why she owns such nice things yet has no husband. I envy her. I want to be able to look at a man and say, "He wants me for a week. No more, no less." I think about what it would be like to buy anything I want. I compare my life to Mahadevi's and decide I want that kind of freedom, even if it comes at the price of men who only stay for a week. I accept her invitation although I know there will be consequences. My error is in believing I will be the one to suffer them.

The night that I dance with Mahadevi, two hundred people sit in Rudolph's garden, dressed in chiffon and gold, laughing with one another.

The women wear silk and pearls; the men look dashing in their uniforms and brass. When Mahadevi and I finish our performance, the wives of my husband's subordinates, not knowing whether to be awestruck, scandalized, or both, finally stand and applaud. Their husbands' admiration follows, and I bathe in their sun as Mahadevi kisses me on the lips, her taste like saffron; our sarong-clad bodies melt together like molasses in the warm island moonlight.

I look at myself in the mirror. What is the difference between those men in Java and these women in Jeanne's salon? "None," I whisper. They both crave a spectacle.

In a small room outside the salon my eight dancers are listening for their cue. Ishan is with me backstage, minding the snake. The guests are all seated and now the first of the eight doomed to fail the god Kama enters the salon. Through a small opening in the curtain I watch her dance: She is faithful to everything we've rehearsed. She finds her place, and the next dancer begins. She, too, positions herself around the god of desire. There is absolute silence in the room. As the next girl appears, Ishan drapes the python like a stole across my shoulders, its diamond-shaped head resting between my breasts. I adjust my posture to accommodate the weight, and I anticipate what is to come. Soon, Upturned Nose has joined the ranks of the others who could not win over the god. I step from behind the curtain and take the stage wearing only a sheer white veil and the snake. The women in the audience gasp collectively.

The lights dim and I let my veil fall. I am shaved, a nubile virgin gifting herself to the god of desire. In the flickering candlelight the girls join my veils on the floor, watching as I make love to Kama. They chant as I begin to writhe and moan. I think I hear a woman in the audience invoke God's name. As I reach my climax the girls rush from the stage as a scarlet curtain falls: I am no longer a child, but a woman.

Backstage, I quickly return the snake to Ishan, and he gently places her in her crate. We both can hear that the audience is ecstatic. After I slip on a simple black wrap and place camellias in my hair and around my neck, I rejoin the salon. Some of the women are fanning themselves with their hands. I go directly to Jeanne and kiss her lips, knowing how much it will shock Bowtie and Edouard. For a moment, she's stunned, and I wonder if maybe I've presumed too much. Then she takes my hand and raises it with hers. "The beautiful and alluring Mata Hari!"

Everyone wants to meet with me. To shake my hand or kiss my cheek or to ask me questions about India. Bowtie is busy snapping away, alternating between writing and taking photos. But Edouard remains at the back of the room.

"A moment?" Bowtie asks, interrupting a woman who is standing too close and telling me about her trip to Bombay.

"There is an intruder in the house!" I tell her. "A man!" In truth, I am so happy to be rescued from her company that I am tempted to kiss him. Instead, I follow Bowtie to a quiet corner where he can interview me in peace.

"That was quite a show you put on. Was it truly an authentic temple dance?"

"Of course. I believe I already told you—"

He waves away my response. "That's part of the act. I get it. I'm merely curious." He bends his head toward me. "Off the record."

He is wearing a dapper chartreuse bow tie with a plain gray vest, but it is his baby face that tempts me to confide in him. I resist and honor my promise to Edouard. "Yes, this is precisely how this dance happens in India. Once a year. At harvest time."

He nods. "Good. Now give me something new to work with.

Readers already know you come from India. They read all about it after Guimet's soirée. Give me something exclusive that I can tell them now."

I laugh self-consciously. What does he require from me?

"Tell me about the snakes in the temples. Do you sleep among snakes if you dance in the temple?"

"Snakes—"

"Fantastic! They sleep with you to keep warm. And it's dangerous, isn't it? But young women like you believe the god will protect you. Is that right?"

He's practically feeding it to me. "Yes."

His pen is moving faster than I can speak. "And have you always lived in India? Is Paris the first city you've lived in since leaving the country of your birth?"

"I've lived in Java," I reveal, wanting to remain as close to the truth as possible. Those are always the most believable lies.

He looks impressed. "And what did you do in Java?"

"Dance. And fall in love," I say, warmed by his enthusiasm.

He looks up sharply. "Any man in particular?"

I look at him slyly. "All men, of course."

"But there was one man in particular. You were married, am I right?"

I am not prepared for this question. How does he know about my marriage? I've told no one. Not even Edouard. "I'd prefer not to talk about—"

"Was his name Rudolph MacLeod? Was he in the Dutch army? He was much older than you—"

"I'd rather *not talk* about it," I repeat. I can hear the shrillness in my voice and lower it immediately. "Ever."

"Do you still love him?" Mahadevi asked me before I left. She watched me closely under her thick, black lashes.

I avoided her question. "He's old. He's sick. He has rheumatism, and a bad heart. He's going to die soon."

"A man like him? He will live to be a hundred and four. Men like him live forever."

"All right, all right." Bowtie flips his notepad shut. "They're going to love this. Thank you," he says. "I'm off to file this and then have a drink at the bar in the Grand." He tips his chin and leaves with his story. The room has largely cleared; Edouard is waiting for me near the door; he's been standing there for at least half an hour.

"Are you ready, Mata Hari?" he asks. "Shall we get your cloak?"

Suddenly Jeanne is at my side, her arm linked through mine. "Oh, it's early yet! Mata Hari is welcome to stay."

"I don't think that is advisable—"

"Would you like to stay, Mata Hari?"

I glance at Edouard. "Very much."

I expect him to object; instead he leaves without saying goodbye.

Jeanne takes me by the hand and leads me to a room that is unbelievably overdone in florals and gold. A pair of Chinese lamps flank her bed, along with matching chairs in an aggressive pattern. But the bed! I have never seen one like it. It's the size of the stage I performed on tonight. I look at Jeanne and think I know what she wants. Another performance. Instead, she leads me to the edge of the bed. Then she sits next to me and says, "That was extraordinary. Truly, Mata Hari."

"Thank you." In the way she looks at me she reminds me—for a fleeting moment—of Mahadevi. She could gaze with eyes like black fire. The heat of Mahadevi's stare was sometimes too intense. Many times I looked away, embarrassed.

"I've never met anyone like you in France. Or anywhere else."

"That's what Edouard says," I answer, looking her straight in the eye.

"He's more than your lawyer, isn't he?"

I don't know why I'm blushing. "No. It's strictly business between him and I."

I can see by Jeanne's face that she's surprised. "I had thought you were lovers."

"No," I scoff. "He'll never settle with one woman."

"Men don't have to. That's how women like us stay alive, isn't it?" I had thought she would be embarrassed by her past. "Thank you for agreeing to stay," she says.

"I'm risking a great deal to be here."

"Not with Edouard?"

"No. His client, Guimet."

"Ah, yes. He won't be pleased. Men like him never are when their 'discoveries' grow wings and fly away."

I enjoy thinking of myself as a discovery.

"Come," Jeanne says, with a mischievous look in her eyes. She takes my arm and I follow her to the window. "You see them?" she asks as we look out into her gardens.

In the silvery light of the moon, I don't see anything but shadows and shrubs. On closer inspection, however, the shrubs begin to move and look like men. "*Reporters?*"

"They're waiting to see what happens tonight. *Late* tonight."

I cover my mouth. "I can't believe it."

"They know you didn't leave with Edouard." She pauses. "You do realize that we're silhouetted against the light? Shall we give them a story?" she asks.

I throw my arms around her neck and say, "Why ever not?"

The next day Jeanne takes me to lunch at Café de la Paix. It's my first visit and I am completely taken with the frescoed walls and ornate ceilings. Jeanne orders champagne and our heads bend together as we read from Bowtie's column in *Le Figaro*.

> No woman in France has ever put on such a perfor-
> mance as Mata Hari. To see her last night was to see
> Salome as she danced before King Herod, to watch
> Cleopatra as she sailed, ethereal, along the waters of the
> Nile. But even those women could not have held such a
> sophisticated audience as entranced as this mysterious
> siren hailing from the East.

Jeanne looks up and raises her glass to me. "To the most beautiful woman in Paris," she says.

I raise my own glass. "*Women*," I correct.

We dine on buttery gratinéed shrimp, sautéed mussels, and clams steamed open with garlic and wine sauce. Nothing has ever tasted so delicious. The staff knows Jeanne and when we're ready to leave, they simply add our meal to her tab.

"I'm taking you to meet someone with tremendous talent," she says.

"A dancer?"

"No, a fashion designer for Callot Soeurs. You've heard of them?"

The four Callot sisters are as famous in the fashion world as Jacques Doucet and Paul Poiret. "Of course I have heard of them. Even in India," I add, "they are admired."

Jeanne's chauffeur lets us into her car. As we ride through the city, Jeanne tells me more about her plans.

"There is no one in Paris like Madeleine Vionnet. I'd go so far to say that there is no one like her in all of France. At the moment, she works for Callot Soeurs, but that will change, and soon, I'd venture. She's going to have her own fashion house one day."

"Is she young?"

"Only thirty. But thirty very difficult years."

I am intrigued. "How were they difficult?"

"She lost her child. After that she divorced her husband. Two devastating losses in very short succession."

I glance away. She could be talking about me.

Jeanne doesn't notice my discomfort. "However, to meet her you would never know any of this. There's a wonderful energy about her. When Madeleine creates, it's as if a personal muse is guiding her hand."

I am eager to meet this woman who has reinvented herself after so much tragedy. Surely, though, Jeanne is mistaken: There must be some sign of her past in her eyes, on her face. We stop in front of a beautiful shop on the Rue Taitbout and Jeanne's chauffeur announces our arrival. He opens our doors, first Jeanne's, then mine. I step into the sunshine and before we reach the shop Jeanne and I are already surrounded.

"Jeanne!" someone cries as I step into the sunshine.

Then another voice summons her from the doorway, and finally four women appear to greet us, and all of them are excited to see her. They usher us inside and Jeanne introduces me to the Callot sisters: Marie, Marthe, Regina, and Joséphine. It is plain to see they all bear a striking resemblance to one another, with oval faces and thick, dark hair. They're dressed in simple white blouses and black skirts, yet all around us is evidence of their genius. Gowns made of gold and silver brocade, silks decorated with metal embroidery, dresses so exquisite I hold my breath to look at them. I want to own everything I see.

"We've heard so much about you," Marie says to me. "We were terribly disappointed to miss your dance at Jeanne's soiree."

"We were all out of town," Regina explains.

"Hopefully there will be more dances," Jeanne says, glancing sideways at me.

There are quite a few customers in the shop watching us, wondering who we might be. Regina guides us toward the back, to a small kitchen.

"I expect you're here to see Madeleine?" she says knowingly.

"You know me well," says Jeanne. "Is she available?"

On cue, a woman appears. She's tall, with short hair and very large hands. As soon as she sees Jeanne, her face lights up and I realize that Jeanne is right: I can't read this woman's past on her face. She greets Jeanne with kisses on each cheek, tells her she looks wonderful, and then both women turn to me.

"And this is Mata Hari," Jeanne says. "Mata Hari, Madeleine Vionnet, a dear friend and one of the finest dressmakers in Paris."

Madeleine steps back to take a better look at me. I'm not wearing one of my Javanese sarongs, but I can see that she's heard stories and she's imagining me in a sheath of silk. "Very pleased to meet you," she says.

"The pleasure is all mine," I assure her.

"Shall we take some coffee?" Regina asks, and when we are all seated at the kitchen table, I ask her how Callot Soeurs came to be and she tells me the story.

"Our mother taught us lace making," Regina says, "and then Marie trained as a dressmaker with Raudnitz and Company. We started off small. Adding lace to lingerie, that sort of thing. But as we became more skilled our clientele grew and soon enough we were able to establish this shop."

"Was your mother ambitious?" I ask.

"Yes." Regina sips her coffee thoughtfully. Then she adds, "She pushed us. All of us."

Her sisters nod.

"It all began with her," Marie agrees. "A few years ago, Madeleine came to us, and I can only hope we get to keep her for a little while longer."

"We all know she's biding her time and that one day she will become one of our fiercest rivals," Regina says.

Madeleine blushes, but there's no malice in Regina's statement.

"I expect that's how you must feel about Mata Hari," Regina adds, addressing Jeanne. "You discover a wonderful new talent and then—" She snaps her fingers. "Someone else wants to take it away."

Jeanne wraps her arm around my shoulders. "No one is stealing Mata Hari," she declares. Her tone is light.

Regina wags her finger. "Just wait."

"I suppose it's inevitable, isn't it?" Jeanne sighs and the sisters look at me.

"We were hoping that Jeanne would bring you," Marie admits. "Ever since *Le Figaro* photographed your debut at Guimet's, Madeleine has been wanting to sketch you. I think she was expecting you to show up wearing one of your sarongs."

"I save them for very special occasions," I say.

"I understand." Madeleine waves away any concern, looking, perhaps, slightly embarrassed. "But perhaps—if you don't have any pressing engagements—you would be willing to model for us today? It won't take much time," she assures me.

"And you can wear one of Madeleine's exotic creations," says Marie, as if sweetening the deal.

I look at Jeanne. What are our plans for the rest of the day?

"Of course she can," Jeanne says. "That's why we're here."

I feel a surge of gratitude toward her. Why is she so kind to me? Perhaps she sees in me a younger version of herself?

Madeleine rises and asks us to follow her into a brightly painted room filled with bolts of fabric and a dozen sewing machines. Several chairs are arranged around a soft white rug where I imagine previous models have stood.

"If you could take off your gown and gloves, I'll get the materials for the design I want you to wear," Madeleine says and leaves for a moment. Jeanne seats herself to watch as I undress. I smile at her in my undergarments.

"It's going to be such a great shame to lose you," she says.

I keep the mood light. "I don't think you will lose me to Madeleine."

"Then it will be to someone much more infuriating. And I dare say a man."

Madeleine returns with an armful of nearly translucent fabric in a soft mint green. "Have you ever modeled before?" she asks, as she arranges a loose sheath around my body, tucking it in here and pinning it there.

"I haven't." The material is soft as a whisper.

"It is the opposite of dancing. Simply stay still."

It takes nearly an hour for Madeleine to create her vision, and when she's done, I'm standing barefoot on the carpeted floor wearing a stylized version of an Indian sari in loose tulle. It's exquisite, unlike anything I've ever worn before. I stand still while she sketches me, first my front and then my back. Jeanne talks while Madeleine works.

"I want to hear all the gossip at Callot Soeurs. What tidbits do you have for me?"

"Absolutely nothing." Madeleine continues drawing. "It's incredibly boring right now. No infamous customers, no shocked matrons, no scandalous women." She nods at me. "Until today."

We all laugh.

"I was telling Mata Hari how successful you've been, Madeleine."

"Have you? I suppose mine is an underdog story."

"I can appreciate that," I say, and something in my tone of voice makes Madeleine look up from her paper. I've been too honest. "Similar past. Similar triumphs," I admit.

"I didn't know that," Jeanne says, looking at me expectantly, wanting more.

"I don't talk about it," I say. Perhaps I've talked too much.

"Women like us prefer to forget we had a past. Too painful," Madeleine says, saving me. "We'd rather create."

She has no idea how true this is.

Madeleine puts some finishing touches on her sketch and shakes her head. "You're striking," she says, speaking as though to herself. "But of course, you already know this."

The compliment feels significant coming from her. She's seen so many beautiful bodies and women. And she's made a great success of her life. Tragedy didn't force her to live in the ashes of her burned-out former life.

"This sketch"—she holds it so that I can see it—"will advertise this sheath dress in the Sunday papers. Look for it next month."

I can't wait to tell Edouard. Of all the things! I'm a model in the Sunday papers!

"So where are the two of you going next?" Madeleine asks.

Jeanne looks at me. "I don't know. Are you tired?" she asks.

"Not at all." I feel invigorated.

"Have you stopped by Paris Nouveau?" Madeleine asks. "There are some truly beautiful pieces there right now."

So that's where we go, passing by a line of fancy boutiques with glassy storefronts and heavy oak doors. At Paris Nouveau Jeanne buys me a cashmere sweater in baby-doll pink, a muted gray dress, and a simple black coat. From the shop, she places a phone call to someone to collect our bags. I can't imagine who the operator is connecting her to, but five minutes later her chauffeur appears.

Outside, horses still amble down the cobbled streets, but it's the cars that dominate, at least today. They make nearly as much noise as the carriages, yet I prefer their smooth, glossy exteriors and how they make moving seem effortless. I note that many pedestrians don't like them but I still want one. I wonder if Jeanne has a carriage as well, or whether the car is her only vehicle now.

She takes me to the restaurant Le Grand Véfour and we slip into the padded leather booths. Then she whispers to me about all the famous people who have dined here. Apparently, all of Paris has been. Even the Callot sisters.

A young man approaches our table. I have never seen anyone with eyes like his—so clear and blue. They are hypnotizing.

"Jeanne, I haven't seen you here in months," he says.

"I've been keeping far too busy, Marquis."

She offers him her hand and he kisses it slowly. Then he steps back to look at me.

"Mata Hari," Jeanne says, "may I introduce you to the Marquis de Givenchy. The most charming *and eligible* bachelor in France."

He leans forward to bring my hand to his lips and inhales my perfume as he does. "What *is* that?" He is still holding my hand. He closes his eyes. He inhales again.

"The scents of Java," I say. "Tobacco," I tell him. "Vanilla, cedar wood . . ."

"Stunning." He opens his eyes. "Jeanne, how long were you planning to keep this creature from me?"

"As long as possible." She winks at me.

"You are terrible. A woman this beautiful should never be hidden." He's still holding my hand. I take it back and Jeanne offers him a seat, but he refuses.

"I'm afraid I am meeting someone," he says. I wonder if it's a woman. "Another time. Where are you staying, Mata Hari?"

"With me." Jeanne smiles, and I know what she wants him to think.

"Oh."

"It's temporary," I say. "I have an apartment."

He reaches into his pocket and hands me a card. His name and address are printed on the front. There is also a number. I have never been given a card with a number. I thought that only lawyers used these.

I don't call Givenchy. When I return from my stay with Jeanne, I call Guimet instead, knowing that's what Edouard would want me to do. He is hesitant at first, but I am all sweetness and honey with him on the phone. "I will make it worth your while," I promise.

As soon as he arrives, I regret this decision. He's dressed in an overcoat and hat. He removes neither one when he takes a chair in the salon.

"So tell me about your performance," he says.

I sit opposite him, crossing my legs so that the silk of my dressing gown parts along my thigh. "It was nothing like the performance I gave for you."

"That's not what I heard."

I try to turn the situation light. "It's true. There were only women in this audience. How boring! Can you imagine?"

"No. I cannot. Why anyone would want to spend time with the *Comtesse* de Loynes I cannot imagine." He emphasizes the word *comtesse* to indicate he knows how she came by the title. "I thought you had better judgment, Mata Hari."

"No. Apparently not. Good night, monsieur," I tell him.

Guimet stands, affronted. No woman, I'm sure, has ever spoken to him this way.

"Perhaps I will see you when you're in better spirits," I say. I don't see him out. I disappear into my room and when I hear him shut the door, I call Givenchy.

"I'll send a car for you," he says.

The marquis is similar to my aviator at the Rothschilds': slow and tender. He makes love as if the two of us have all the time in the world and nothing is more important than my pleasure. I know he has had women hundreds of times before, but there is something in the way he holds my gaze that lets me believe that none of his other women have mattered. It is us—only us. This is why he's the most eligible bachelor in France. By the time we have finished our last glass of wine the sharp memory of my fight with Guimet is only a dull recollection; it means nothing.

Perhaps Guimet senses this. The next evening before I'm finished dressing for the night a large package arrives.

"Mata Hari?" the delivery boy asks.

"Yes."

He holds out a box with a familiar logo and a single printed word: HERMÈS. I take it inside and unwrap a cashmere shawl and gloves. The note inside is signed by Guimet. "I'm sorry," it reads. I am trying on the gloves and wrapping myself in cashmere when there's a knock at the door. Guimet! I open it at once but Givenchy is outside.

"Not a good time?" He looks past me, thinking he's caught me with some other lover.

"No. Come in." I take him into the salon. Guimet's note and the box from Hermès is still on the table.

"A gift?"

I shrug. "They come sometimes."

"I imagine it's more than sometimes."

I see he's carrying a box as well. It's small. Jewelry? He holds it out for me and I unwrap it slowly. A sapphire ring encircled with diamonds. How many nights of rent would this have paid for those first months in Paris? I take it out and slip it on my finger, showing it off for him. "It's beautiful."

"Enough to convince you to stop taking gifts from anyone else?"

"I can't help it if friends want to send me gifts."

His blue eyes meet mine. "*Friends?*"

Three months later—after a war of gifts—Givenchy gives me 3 Rue Balzac. He declares that the apartment is mine for being "the most exquisite woman on earth"—but we both know it is also the best way to rid himself of reminders of Guimet and to keep me to himself. It's not in my name, but I am in love with the gorgeously wrought iron doors and the elaborate window boxes. It is on an elegant street and now I can live among the fanciest buildings in Paris. The décor will not be to Edouard's taste. Even Guimet will probably be offended by how modern it is. But it's new and chic and I think it is tremendously elegant. I call Edouard to give him the news.

After a chilly pause he says, "Let me understand. You are breaking my lease and deserting one of my most important clients."

It never occurred to me to think about the lease on my current apartment. "I thought you'd be happy for me," I say.

There is another pause on the phone.

"I'm sorry." And I really am. "It's bigger, Edouard. And closer to Givenchy."

"Is that all that's important now?" he says.

"Why don't you come over? Let me take you to dinner."

"I've already eaten."

*   *   *

That night I dream of my father. Dressed in my best suit, a cream silk trimmed in green with small pearl buttons and looking like a genuine baron's daughter, I walk quickly along the streets of Amsterdam, stepping over the fruits of the spindle trees that litter the sidewalks. My heels crush them into the ground, turning them into stains of red.

I follow the canals to the center of town. Here the ginkgo trees hang heavy in the heat. I arrive at the bottle-making factory. I stare up at the blackened brick building. I walk up steps covered in soot. Inside, the lights are dim. I adjust my hat and immediately a man appears to greet me. He is dirty, with stained trousers and grease on his face.

"May I help you?"

"Yes, I'm looking for a man. Mr. Adam Zelle."

"Oh ma'am, I'm sorry."

"He's dead," I whisper, feeling it in my heart.

"Dead? The last I saw him he was fit as an ox."

"Then what are you sorry for?"

"He left six months ago to take another position."

So he is alive. My papa is alive! "Do you have any idea where he went?"

"I can tell you exactly: 148 Lange Leidschedwarsstraat. I was there last night. His new wife cooks up a feast every Sunday."

I awaken gasping for breath.

Chapter 7

CAN MADRID APPRECIATE
A FRENCH SENSATION?

*E*douard lets himself in to my apartment on Rue Balzac as if he's the one paying the rent every month. "How would you like to move up from private shows to theater performances?" he calls to me.

"Like La Madeline?" I answer from the kitchen. That would be wonderful. They rejected me before Edouard discovered me at L'Ete. "Why not?" I take the flowers I've been arranging and join him in the living room; he is on my couch lighting a cigar. "We could charge five thousand francs," I suggest, "for a single performance." I think of the owner's smug face and imagine the pleasure of telling him what a performance from Mata Hari now costs. Enough to buy a car for each day of the week. Although when I would find time to drive it would be another story . . .

"No, not in France." He snaps his silver lighter shut with his thumb.

I stop fussing with Jeanne's flowers.

"Madrid," he says. "The Kursaal."

The Central Kursaal in the Plaza del Carmen? It's one of the most beautiful buildings in Spain. "Will they want me?"

"Of course. It's time we build Mata Hari. You are a 'French sensation' right now," he says, and I realize he is quoting someone, "but destined to be an international one, M'greet."

He pulls a clipping from his breast pocket. It's Bowtie's latest article and now I understand. We met for dinner last week at Maxim's. He told me our last interview had sold out *Le Figaro*. *Tell me something sensational*, he said, as if we might trade gossip of any other kind. I hesitated before giving him Givenchy; I did not want to make the marquis angry. Then Bowtie bragged about his interview with Isadora Duncan—how *her* latest lover is Paris Singer, of Singer sewing machines. I knew he was casting a line, but I bit. I gave him details. I told him where he could find us the next afternoon, at Longchamp betting on the horses. He waited with his camera and notepad. I pretended to be shocked by his sudden appearance; he pretended to be shocked by his good fortune. Now I read the headline: MATA HARI AND HER MARQUIS: WILL THEY MARRY? Beneath the headline is a photo: I'm wearing a walking skirt with a matching parasol and wide-brimmed hat. Givenchy, in his linen suit and straw boater, looks dashing.

As soon as Bowtie started snapping photos Givenchy became angry. *Is that the man who interviewed you last month? I recall that bow tie.*

I don't recognize him, I claimed.

But he saw through my lie and hasn't called since. Maybe it doesn't matter now. "Do they sell *Le Figaro* in Amsterdam?"

Edouard raises his brows. "Someone there you're hoping to impress?"

I shrug and tuck the clipping into my pocket. Another victory to put in my scrapbook.

"The Kursaal," Edouard says, "is a venue that requires something extraordinary. Not an Indian dance. An exotic character the masses will identify with. I don't want you to repeat Lady Godiva—"

"Cleopatra," I say.

"Perfect." Then his eyes grow distant. "We will book you in Madrid, Berlin, and after that, who knows?"

"In Berlin," I say, "I want to dance Salome."

That evening I leave messages with both Givenchy and Guimet to let them know that I will be leaving Paris shortly. It's been so long since I've seen Guimet that I'm not sure if he will care. But he calls a few hours after Givenchy—who expresses dismay that I'm abandoning him.

"And that gives that lawyer a reason to abscond with you? What about my needs?"

We are sitting in the restaurant of the Hotel de Crillon. He's dressed in a blue suit and I realize I could search a dozen cities and never find a man as good looking as Givenchy. But the man is in love with himself. Whomever he marries must be willing to worship him.

Before the wine has even arrived Givenchy is asking why I must go. I remind him that I'm performing at the Kursaal and he talks over me as if this doesn't matter. "What can Madrid offer that Paris doesn't? Can Madrid appreciate a French sensation? I ask you again, what about my needs?"

His self-absorption is both exasperating and comical. I imagine his childhood. Nannies tripping over themselves to give him toys, sweets, pony rides. "I'll send you telegrams," I promise.

We eat our dinner in silence.

Guimet, however, is practically joyful. We sit across from each other in Maxim's and over roasted duck he tells me what to expect in Madrid.

"The Spanish are not like Parisians. They run hot, like the Italians," he says. When I ask him to explain, he tells me, "It's the way they dance, the way they talk. It's in their blood. Or maybe it's in their food." He laughs.

"It sounds like you enjoy Spain."

"More than any other country in Europe."

I imagine being as well traveled as him. Where would I want to go if I had already seen everything? Back to Java. To the beaches and hills and my friendship with Mahadevi.

"If you have time, see the museums," he suggests. "The Prado especially. Edouard is going with you, correct?"

"Yes."

"He'll know where to take you."

"He's been to Madrid?"

"A dozen times, I should think. His business takes him everywhere." He sips his wine and watches me thoughtfully. "He likes you."

"Of course he does. I make him money."

"It's more than that." He puts down his glass. "He enjoys your company, Mata Hari. If I had the time to return to Madrid, I'd go with the both of you."

I try to picture it. The three of us traipsing across Spain. It would be museums and fine dining and the theater every night. I wouldn't even have time to perform!

"Perhaps when you return, we'll go on a trip."

"That would be lovely."

"I've always wanted to go on safari," he admits. "I have friends who have been. They tell me that the savannah is unlike any other place on earth. It gets into your soul. It's a very long journey, but I've never known anyone to regret it."

I can't imagine traveling so far away from the people I love. Even if Edouard came with me, I couldn't do it. But I smile, because I know it will never come to pass. Guimet may go, but he won't take a woman he hardly knows so far away or for so long. A trip like that is an investment. You take a woman you want to marry. Not some casual lover.

"But why don't we talk about that when you return?" He raises his glass to me. He isn't distressed at all that I'm leaving. Instead, he's excited on my behalf. "The world deserves to experience rare things of beauty," he says, and at the end of the meal he hands me a gift. It's an Egyptian necklace. Perhaps he's glad I'll be away from Jeanne and Givenchy. "The scarabs in the center are three thousand years old."

He fastens it around my neck and I feel like Cleopatra. I tell him this.

"I doubt she was as exquisite as you."

The next morning at the train station I show the necklace to Edouard. In the bright spring light the scarabs, set in gold filigree against agate and jade, appear brilliant. He looks from the necklace to me. "He must like you," he says drily.

And even though he is being blasé, I feel delighted. Rudolph wanted me, but he never liked me. He never liked anyone, including himself.

The train pulls into the station and Edouard rises. "Our adventure begins," he says.

A porter takes our luggage and my pulse races as we pass by coach and enter the first-class car. Edouard sinks into one of the oversize chairs—I have never seen seats this large on a train—and takes a newspaper from a stand, looking as comfortable as he does in his own office. I notice that a few of the women in first class are glancing my way; they recognize me from the papers. Several minutes pass before the sound of a whistle tells me we're about to leave. Slowly, the train pulls away from the Gare de Lyon and I'm so excited that my nose is practically pressed against the glass.

Edouard lowers his newspaper. When I catch him watching me, I take out my compact but he doesn't look away. "Have your parents tried to contact you?" he asks.

I snap my powder case shut and study my reflection in the window. My hair is pulled back beneath the veil of my hat, and in my yellow dress chosen by Jeanne de Loynes I feel like I actually belong in first class. Thinking of Jeanne pricks me with guilt: I should have returned at least one of her calls. "My parents are gone," I tell him.

"Gone where?" he prods.

"Gone out of my life. Why? What does it matter?"

"It matters a great deal. They will to try to contact you," he says. "Sooner rather than later. This applies to anyone you've ever owed money to. Anyone you've ever considered a relative. You've gained considerable fame, M'greet, and people will start to come out of the woodwork. I've seen it happen."

"That's absurd. How would they know me? I'm Mata Hari now."

He looks at me as if he isn't sure how a person can be so foolish. "Your picture is in every paper. Every word you speak is published alongside your photo. You believe your own blood won't recognize you?" He tips his newspaper at me. "Prepare yourself."

"You make it sound as though I'm going into battle," I say. Then I think of Rudolph and just as quickly shut him out of my mind. "So what is the name of our hotel?" I ask.

"La Paz." He opens his paper and my photo is there next to Bow-tie's article: MATA HARI ABANDONS FRANCE.

I open the doors to my balcony at La Paz and inhale the scent of saffron. Guimet was right. The food, the people, even the weather—all of it is marvelously different from France. "This is exactly what I need." I toss my hat on to my bed, feeling exuberant. "Let's go out tonight, Edouard!"

"Sorry. Other plans. And you have a contract for fifteen performances. Get some rest." He leaves and I wonder if she is blonde.

Fine. I will enjoy the city alone. I have never seen Madrid, and why should Edouard be the only one to have fun? There must be handsome men in this city. Perhaps some Spanish officers. When I tell the hotel concierge what I'm looking for, he grins. "There aren't many women as truthful as you are." He directs me to a part of town lined with jewelry stores and bars: an ingenious combination.

The cabdriver takes me through the Barrio de Salamanca to Serrano Street. It's the most exclusive part of the city. "No poor people here," he tells me. I can see why. Everything seems costly and reserved, like old titled men. The area doesn't have the same feeling as Paris, where everything feels sharp and modern. Old growth trees line the roads. There are more carriages here than cars. But the wealth is unmistakable. It's in the cut of people's suits as they pass and the dark beauty of the horses as they trot through the streets. The chestnut trees are in bloom and everything smells wonderful.

The cabdriver lets me out on Serrano Street. There are businesses and bars, as the concierge promised. I walk a little ways, taking in the feel for the city. There are very few women here. But there are a number of single men.

I see Eliodoro before he sees me. Leather boots, gold watch, three gold rings. He's not an officer, which is disappointing, but there's something about him I like when our eyes meet.

"Señorita." He tips his hat to me.

"Señor."

We spend the evening together, drinking, dancing, then drinking some more. When he leans across the table at Las Noches to kiss me, I don't stop him. On the dance floor behind us, women are doing far more scandalous things.

"Come home with me," he says.

I refuse. "I don't even know you."

"Then let's at least enjoy the night air."

I agree to this and as we walk the streets he tells me about his life in Madrid. His ornery wife, his three difficult children, his business trading oil. He has no interest in my life or in knowing anything about me. He simply wants to talk and I let him. When I return to La Paz at six the next morning, Edouard is pacing outside my room.

"Where have you been?"

I turn my key. "Out." I give him a sly smile and hope it infuriates him.

"We leave in ten minutes," he says. "I'll be waiting in the lobby."

From the passenger seat of our rented car I roll up my knee-high stockings and yawn. "Have you ever been to the Kursaal?"

"Yes." Edouard glances at me and his eyes rest on my necklace. "Something new?"

I touch the cold stones; they feel solid, permanent. "You like it?" A small keepsake. "From last night."

He doesn't respond, and I don't make further conversation. When we arrive at Tetuan Street, Edouard parks the car; there is no valet.

The Kursaal is more beautiful than I imagined, with towering Greek columns and laurel designs. We enter the building and I am swept away: the high ceilings, the chandeliers, the dramatic scenes from Spanish literature decorating the walls. I move closer to one of the paintings to see if I can recognize its source but am interrupted by a man who steps directly in front of me.

"Mata Hari? It *is*! Welcome, welcome!" He embraces me with kisses and I laugh.

"Mata Hari, this is Ramón," Edouard says. "The owner of the Kursaal."

"Ramón," I say. "So lovely to meet you."

Ramón kisses Edouard's cheeks and tells us both how excited he is. "You have no idea, the anticipation. No idea! Come, I want to show you the theater. Then we can meet the dancers."

He takes us on a tour of the Kursaal. Everything about it is enormous—the chandeliers, the ballroom, sweeping flights of lushly carpeted stairs. Nearly every wall that isn't painted is mirrored. When the sun sets, I think, the chandeliers will be absolutely dazzling. In a mirrored hallway carpeted in red velvet a long line of dancers are waiting. "Two dozen of the most beautiful women in Spain." They are taller than Jeanne's dancers, and though I wouldn't think it possible, even more beautiful. They press around me, telling me their names, hoping to make an impression, eager for me to remember them. "We've heard so much about you," they say. And, "Everyone in Madrid is in awe of your talent."

I look at Edouard, overwhelmed by gratitude. "I hope you will all help me make this two of the most memorable weeks in the history of the Kursaal. It's an honor to be here."

On opening night, I am Cleopatra, queen of the Nile. The female dancers Ramón has given me are dressed in Grecian sheaths and golden breastplates. The male dancers wear nothing but short, white kilts. On stage, in front of a thousand people, I dance her agony with Caesar, her ecstasy with Antony, her untimely death. I wear more jewels than the queen of England and a constricting snake (it seemed unwise to wear an asp). I don't wear anything else. The next morning I am front-page news in every paper.

"You see this? You see this?" Ramón holds up a copy of *La Van-guardia*. He is waiting for me in the lobby of the Kursaal.

I look at the front page. There I am. And next to me, all teeth and lace, is Ramón. Beneath us is the headline: MATA HARI TAKES THE CITY OF MADRID BY STORM.

"You are a gift! The most exciting thing that's ever happened to the Kursaal," Ramón says. "Thank you for coming here." He takes my hand.

"Ramón—"

"No. *Thank you.*" He's weepy eyed and sentimental. "Is there any-thing I can do? Anything I can get you?"

"Nothing, Ramón. I don't want to keep you."

"Take this," he insists, pressing the newspaper into my hand.

"Thank you." I will keep it for my scrapbook. "I should go and rehearse."

But when I get to the ballroom, everyone is standing in a circle around one of the musicians—I believe his name is Jean Hallure. He is sitting on the floor. "Encore, encore. Will it be like that every night? Mata Hari is going to exhaust us!" he is muttering.

The circle of dancers and musicians breaks up as I enter. Jean Hal-lure has his head in his hands and is very drunk. When he sees me, it appears as if he believes he has summoned me. "Mata Hari, I've never seen anyone as beautiful as you!" he bellows. Then he blanches and makes a pathetic attempt to rise and ends up lurching back to the floor. The other performers are shaking their heads in disgust.

"I don't think you're in any condition to rehearse," I say. I turn to the others and nod to one whose name I don't recall. "Could you take Jean someplace quiet?"

One musician offers Hallure his arm. "*I* wouldn't take advantage of you!" Hallure exclaims, struggling to his feet.

"Thank you, Jean." I nod and Jean Hallure is escorted away.

Everyone looks at me. The orchestra can't rehearse without Jean. They are waiting for me to make a decision.

"Let's take this morning off," I say. "Rehearsal is canceled." I can see the relief on everyone's face. The truth is, we don't need more practice.

Back at La Paz I find Edouard in his room, relaxing. "Let's go out," I suggest. "To a museum. I want to see the Museo del Prado. Did you know it was built by Charles III?"

"I had no idea."

"He wanted to prove that his was the period of Enlightenment."

"Thank you for enlightening me. Let me get my hat."

The Museo del Prado is spectacular: all tiled roofs and floors, marble fountains, and lovely rotundas allowing light to filter in and kiss statues of military leaders. My favorite kind of men, my husband the only exception. We spend the day looking at art. It is peaceful; the quiet click of heels on smooth orange tile and the soft, still paintings of Goya and Titian. We find ourselves in front of a Rembrandt, on loan from Paris. I stand in front of the Dutch artist's painting, *Bathsheba at Her Bath*, and I am remembering my father.

"What are you thinking?" Edouard's voice is soft.

"Me?"

"No, the woman across the gallery."

I tell him the truth. "Sometimes my father would show us these paintings in books. My brothers and me. He'd tell us stories. But that was a long time ago."

Edouard nods. I can feel he wants me to say more, but I don't want sympathy. Fathers abandon their children. Mine wasn't the first. "Tell the truth now," I change the subject. "All of your pretty little blondes . . . they wouldn't know a Goya from a Rembrandt, would they?"

We stay in the museum for hours, sitting on the marble benches, wandering in the gardens, watching the people. Edouard stands in front of a statue of Charles V holding a spear and assumes the same pose. It is my favorite moment of the day.

We are the last visitors to leave.

"Shall we dine?" Edouard asks.

"We shall," I say, taking his arm. We stroll to the Plaza del Angel, pass beneath the yellow and blue tiled walls of Ramón's España Cañi, then go to a café near La Paz. We order salmorejo with fino sherry. Edouard tells me that his last trip to Madrid was with his sister. "She insisted on seeing the Running of the Bulls in Pamplona. *The Encierro* they call it. So we traveled there by train, not knowing that the opening ceremonies were underway. We stood in the Plaza Consistorial, wondering where the bulls would be running."

"You didn't!" Even I know this was a foolish move.

"We did. The San Saturnino clock struck eight. Suddenly everyone was moving."

"How could you not know the bulls go charging down that street after everyone?"

He laughs. "We ran for our lives. It was madness. Finally, we hid in a doorway."

I imagine Edouard cowering in a doorway. I imagine him having a sister.

"God, M'greet, it's so refreshing to get out like this."

I know what he means. We toast to each other. And for the first time in many years I feel content. It's almost unsettling.

And when we finish the first bottle of wine, we order another.

*   *   *

"Would you like to come in?" We are at the threshold of my room at La Paz, both a little drunk.

"I'm not a diversion, M'greet. When you're more serious, ask again." He starts to say something else, then pauses, changes his mind. "Men become obsessed with you," he says at last. "I don't know why. But they do. If we start something, it won't be for a night."

"That's fine," I promise. I pull at his jacket, trying to sway him. He resists. "This offer doesn't stand forever," I warn him.

He tips his hat to me. "Good night, M'greet."

I stand in the empty hallway, alone, burning with shame.

Thousands of people come to the Kursaal to see *Cleopatra*. They come from cities as far away as Copenhagen and Cologne just so they can say they've seen Mata Hari dance. After each performance I mingle with the elegant and the powerful. The prince of Sweden, a princess from Germany, a colonel from Germany by the name of Braun. Over the course of fifteen evenings I conquer Spain. I send telegrams that keep Guimet and Givenchy longing for my return. But Edouard is another story, and we don't discuss what happened between us after opening night.

On *Cleopatra*'s closing night, Edouard lets himself in to my dressing room. His hair is perfectly combed and in his black suit he's more distinguished looking than any prince in Europe. He's holding a small velvet box. He offers it to me as I take off my wig.

"A peace offering?" I joke.

He nods. "Something like that."

I take the box and open it. Inside is a thin gold necklace with a dragon pendant. "It's beautiful."

"From China."

"You've been?"

He makes a small gesture I interpret to mean yes. Why haven't I ever thought to ask Edouard about his travels? I let him fasten the necklace around my neck and admire the pendant in the low light of the room. It gleams.

"You were stunning tonight. They'll be talking about it in all of the papers."

"Do you think so?"

"Yes." He takes a seat on the padded bench and watches me. "Anyone coming tonight?"

He means men. "No. Only you."

"Then why don't we go out? To celebrate."

"A last night in Madrid?"

"It might be a while before we come back, and who knows if it will be together?"

For some reason, the idea stings. I wouldn't want to return to Madrid without Edouard. It wouldn't be the same. "You're always so pessimistic."

"You're always so optimistic. That's why we make a good team. Get dressed. I have a special invitation for tonight."

He won't tell me what it is. I put on my favorite piece from Callot Soeurs, a satin dress with lace worthy of a princess. Outside the theater, Edouard's smile tells me I've chosen right. We drive toward the Royal Palace, and when the car turns at the gates, I catch my breath. "Is this where we're going? You are taking me to the palace?"

"Wait and see. Patience."

We stop at a guardhouse and the soldier inside consults a register. Incredibly, our names are on his list, because he waves us through. When a man in a black tuxedo escorts us from our car, I tell Edouard, "I have to know what this is. What have we been invited to?"

"The king's gala dinner."

I stop walking. "How long have you been keeping this a secret?" Then a thought occurs to me. "Were you always going to take me?" I ask him.

Edouard pulls me along. "It depended."

"It depended on . . . ?"

"I don't know. How I woke up feeling this morning."

I slap his shoulder gently, too excited to be insulted. I have never been to a gala dinner. Above us, the stars look like small chips of ice. It's a magical night.

"Shall we?" he asks.

We're at the steps of the palace. Inside, music is playing and I can see the lights of magnificent chandeliers. The high, sweet laughter of the women floats down the steps to us.

It's as if the king decreed only the most beautiful people in Spain could be invited. We dine from a table that's impossibly long, set with crystal and china on brocade tablecloths. There is electricity in the palace, but our dinner is served by candlelight. We are seated near a couple who boast that they arrange the king's meetings: secretaries of the most glorified kind. They inform us that the gala is held each year and that china and linens are never used twice.

"Can you imagine?" I whisper to Edouard.

"You'd need a house just for the china."

We dance together when the dinner is through in a space that's so large you can't see from one end to the other. The musicians are arranged high on a stage. Midway through the evening new players come in to relieve them. Around midnight, I follow Edouard to a table where drinks are being served and a man in a crisp black military uniform approaches him. They speak, laughing at each other's jokes, and it is quite a while before I realize who he is. Both men turn to me, and King Alfonso says, "Ah, and you must be Mata Hari."

I stare at Edouard, trying to fathom how he could possibly be acquainted with the king of Spain. Obviously, there's a great deal I don't know about him. "Yes," I say, at a loss. Do I bow? Curtsy? What were other women doing? Before I can puzzle it out, the king is already speaking.

"Your dancing has made news all across Madrid. I was hoping to see some of it for myself. Will you be returning someday?"

"I certainly hope so."

"Most definitely," Edouard says.

"Good. You are always welcome in Spain."

He leaves and I look at Edouard. "The king of Spain?"

"You think you're the only one who dines with royalty?" he says, with a studied air of mystery.

Chapter 8

WILL YOU DANCE
NUDE IN BERLIN?

*B*erlin is a blue-gray contrast to our red-hot days in Madrid. Le Metropol is a towering structure, as beautiful as the Kursaal, but it lacks the same heat and passion. The outside boasts five enormous pillars draped with fifty-foot green swaths of cloth that advertise the latest shows. Today SEE MATA HARI AS SALOME! waves in the breeze. I catch Edouard's eye and we share a smile.

Inside, we are taken to a dressing room. I find wine, flowers, and chocolates waiting for me. There is also a white bathrobe, my name embroidered in black lettering. I whisper, "Do they think I won't know it's mine if it isn't labeled?"

Edouard laughs. But before he can reply, Hilda Schweitzer appears to take us on a guided tour. She is the owner's wife, but I'm disappointed that Heinrich Schweitzer isn't escorting us himself. On the train, Edouard told me that Heinrich Schweitzer had invested his entire life's savings in Le Metropol. I admire his passion.

As we follow Madame Schweitzer, I realize that Le Metropol is more of a resort than a theater. She points out cafés, a luxury spa, and a three-story ice arena within the building.

"It is the only indoor ice arena in Germany," she says with pride.

"An indoor ice arena?" Edouard whispers to me. "Is there a short-age of cold weather in Germany?"

Finally, she takes us into the theater, a circular room with sev-eral hundred seats and a gilded ceiling painted with angels. A dozen women are waiting for us on the stage: my dancers. They are tall, like me, but blonde, and many of them have blue eyes. I will stand out. Even if we are all dancing together, no one will ask which is Mata Hari.

I'm in high spirits when we arrive at the Hotel. It is icing on my cake to learn that the crown prince of Prussia is also a guest. And that he has requested to meet me. "The future kaiser," I crow to Edouard as we make our way across the lobby.

"Don't gloat; it's unbecoming. He's too young for you and engaged to be married."

"I have an official summons." I ignore his lack of enthusiasm. "Do I have time to change? What do I wear to meet a prince? I think a—"

"Mata Hari!"

I cover my chest with my hand as a reporter appears from behind a potted plant. "My God, you scared me."

"Are you here to meet the crown prince of Prussia? Will you dance nude in Berlin? How long will you be here?"

I say, "Go to the lounge in forty minutes."

The reporter looks at Edouard, but he is stone-faced. "What hap-pens in forty minutes?" he asks me.

"You'll see."

I make my way down to the lounge within the hour, wearing a cream Paul Poiret dress and white pearls, feeling invincible. The prince is young, but he is also tall and confident. He greets me in German and I reply in kind. This pleases him immensely and he gestures toward a sofa. As soon as I sit we are surrounded by handsome men in uniform. A hotel employee is summoned and wine appears. The prince offers to pour me a glass and as soon as I raise it to my lips we are photographed.

"Get them out of here!" the prince shouts, but it's too late. The photograph has been taken. "Always these journalists." He is shaking his head. "Don't you tire of them?"

I feign exasperation. "Absolutely."

"I can't go anywhere without being spied upon."

"I hope you will come to my show," I say.

"Oh, you may be certain of it."

But the prince doesn't come that night. I don't see him until my third performance. And that presents a problem, because Alfred Kiepert is already waiting for me in the hall. He is dressed in his officer's uniform and looks irresistible. I've invited him back twice since my opening, when I spotted him in the audience. It's a shame I have to turn him away tonight. But there is no question of disappointing the heir to the German throne.

There is no other way to see Berlin than on the arm of a crown prince. I am convinced of this as he accompanies me to dinner at the Hotel Kaiserhof. It's the grandest hotel in all of Europe. Over two hundred rooms and a ballroom so beautiful that it will hurt to leave it. But we have not come to dance. After a long day of shopping and sightseeing, the crown prince wishes to eat.

We sit across from each other in the hotel's glittering new restaurant and I worry that I'm a fraud among so many wealthy people. Though surely some of these women with their long cigarette holders and heavy furs must have married into their money. All of them can't be titled heiresses. I look around the room and try to pick out which ones might be like me. Definitely the blonde with her low-cut dress—if not, why would she wear such a thing? Perhaps she's a mistress. Or maybe she's made herself into a second wife? There's a man with a woman who wears rings on each finger and a diamond necklace that dips into her cleavage. She wasn't born into this world—I'd stake money on it. So I'm not the only one.

"What do you like best about Berlin?" the prince asks.

There is so much I have enjoyed I have to weigh my answer carefully. We did so many things today. I have now ridden on Berlin's electric trams and taken coffee in the most famous of shops. I'm the owner of a new fur hat and three rings, one diamond, the other two emerald. Everywhere we went, on nearly every street, I saw billboards using electric advertising. "Berlin is the city of the future," the prince said. If this is true, then the future is all moving type and flashing lights. "I believe I liked the Esplanade best," I say.

He grins and it makes him look so youthful. "Me, too."

I order the pot roast. He orders the pork. When Bowtie finds us again, we're toasting to the wonder that is Berlin.

On the train back to Paris, I finish reading a review aloud to Edouard. "'Mesmerizing Mata Hari was a most entrancing Salome. Her interpretation was bewitching.'" I hold up the *Berliner Tageblatt*. "And here is the best part." There is a photo of the prince and me in an expensive shop on the Unter den Linden. "For the scrapbook." I fold the paper carefully. "Isn't it wonderful? I love Berlin. And Berlin loved me."

"It isn't wonderful for him," Edouard says. "Or, I imagine, his fiancée."

"Why are you so sour?" I hug my fur stole closer to me, comforted by the warmth. "Are you jealous?"

He ignores my question. "I've arranged a contract for you to perform *Samson and Delilah*. Three weeks. At La Cigale."

"Excellent. I want to buy another fur coat. Givenchy would buy one for me but he was so terse in his last telegram that I want to make him wait—"

"M'greet, are you saving any money?"

"Why? What for?"

He is so astonished that it takes him several moments to reply. "For when this—all of this—is done."

Now I'm the one who's shocked. "Why should it be done? This is my life, Edouard."

"Be serious, M'greet. The public is fickle. Novelty wanes and someday this will all be over."

"Fine. Then I'll take a lover," I say, and watch his expression.

We don't speak to each other for the rest of the trip.

Chapter 9

JEANNE LOUISE

*E*douard sends his secretary with the contract for La Cigale. When I open the door, she appraises Givenchy's apartment with a cool sweep of her lashes, the polished floors, the marble staircase. In the curl of her lip I can read her thoughts: *Mata Hari is nothing but a grande horizontale.* She hands me the envelope and turns on her heel without the courtesy of a single word.

I stand on the Champs-Élysées and think about what a fool Edouard is. I have nothing to save for. No reason at all to be careful about what I spend or what I do. What's the difference if I buy one diamond ring or ten?

I go into E. Goyard Aîné, one of my favorite shops on the Rue Saint-Honoré, and ask the salesman about the steamer bag, designed to be taken on long trips abroad.

"Madam, you understand this piece is four thousand francs?"

"Wonderful. I'll take two."

Purses, scarves, silk blouses, cashmere shawls. Everything comes home with me that day. I'm never supposed to repeat an outfit twice.

Isn't that what Edouard said? And now I'm one of the fashionable women in Paris. Bowtie thinks so, and the admiring gazes of other women tell me he's right. The next morning I do it all over again. That afternoon I make a purchase I've been longing for since the day Edouard arrived at my vile little apartment in Montmartre: I buy my own car. A blue Renault. Louis Renault himself drives it home for me when I tell him that I will be finding a chauffeur, since I don't know how to drive. I slide into the passenger seat and enjoy the stares of the people we pass. The blue of the car is bright, electric. He parks in front of my apartment and when my neighbors see Louis hand me the keys, I feel absolutely giddy.

La Cigale is filled to capacity. I drop my veils and men rush the stage, flashbulbs popping as women take out binoculars. It's a stupendous opening.

A little mustached man crowds the door to my dressing room after the performance, trembling with rage. "It is illegal in this city to perform in the nude," he threatens. "I can have you arrested!"

"But you won't."

He draws himself up to full height. "I am Sergeant Bouchardon, the head of the French—"

I hold up my hand. "Take your concerns to my lawyer, Edouard Clunet."

His face turns red. I watch it in the mirror. "I will have you arrested—"

"But you won't, monsieur. If you do, your superiors will be most displeased."

As if on cue the chief of police appears, so handsome in his uniform that I catch my breath. His sergeant cannot leave quickly enough.

*   *   *

People now recognize me wherever I go. At Longchamp, at Maxim's, even on the Champs-Élysées they call out, "Mata Hari!" The public loves me, but Edouard is still angry. He doesn't visit me for the entire three-week run of *Samson and Delilah*. Just as I start to think that maybe I don't need him anymore, horrible news comes and he is the only person I want to speak with. I go to his office in tears, my makeup running in dark lines down my face. When his secretary sees me, she actually recoils.

"Where is Edouard?"

"Upstairs. But ma'am—"

I go to his office and fall into his leather chair. "He's divorcing me."

Edouard gets up quickly and shuts the door, a quiet click. He hands me a handkerchief and I wipe my eyes. Then I weep into the handkerchief.

Edouard waits. When he speaks, his voice is calming. "Who is divorcing you, M'greet?"

"My husband. I hate him. I left him. He was a captain. In the army."

"The Dutch army?"

I nod.

Edouard lets me cry, trying to piece the puzzle together in his mind. "On what grounds, M'greet?"

It is too much to bear. "Adultery and debauchery."

His eyes go wide as I hiccup into the handkerchief.

"He's the one responsible for the death of our son and now he's calling *me* debauched." I can't bear it. The memories are actually cutting me open. "Oh God, Edouard, what should I do?"

"Nothing."

I think I must have misheard him and look up. "What?"

"You say you hate him. Do you want to be independent of him?"

"I already am! But Edouard—"

"Why didn't you tell me you were married?" He stands and I can see the hurt in his eyes. "You had a son?"

"Norman John." Edouard's office is suddenly oppressive. "I need air." He opens a window. "M'greet—"

I hold up my hand. "Don't ask me to tell you any more. I can't."

"I could have had you divorced in a day."

"I didn't think I needed it. We were living separately. I never considered he'd find another wife. I wish he was dead." I bury my head in my hands. Of course Rudolph was going to divorce me. Why didn't I see it? "And now my daughter—"

"You have a living daughter?"

I whisper her name. "Jeanne Louise." I miss her so much I can't bear it. Sometimes, I imagine I see her in the street, so much bigger and yet still my sweet girl—but of course it's always someone else's child. For a moment I thought I saw her in Berlin. "I never wanted to leave her. But Rudolph said he'd kill us both if I tried to take her. And he would have killed me if I'd stayed."

For several moments, Edouard is silent. "M'greet, how much money do you have? Can you live for the rest of your life on what you've earned?"

"Never." I wipe my eyes. "Why?"

"It's possible to get your daughter away from your husband. But you need money. A great deal of it. Forget your goddamn furs and trinkets. I know people who handle this kind of thing. Recovering the girl is one hurdle. You also need to be granted custody, and to do that you need to prove that you can provide stability."

"Edouard—"

"Tell me about your daughter."

I dab at my eyes with the sleeve of my dress. "I called her Non." My chin begins to tremble. "It means little girl. I don't know where to start—"

"At the beginning."

"On the morning of my mother's funeral, then. I was thirteen years old."

If he is surprised at the start of my tale, his face doesn't betray him.

"My two aunts arrived—my mother's sisters. They weren't close to our family. I couldn't remember meeting them before. They were strangers to me. And all they had to say about me was, 'Look how dark she is,' and 'So tall.'"

"Your father was still alive then?"

"My father had deserted us. I thought he would come back as soon as he had word that his wife had died and his children were alone; I asked my aunts about him and my Aunt Mina told me that he was *kloten*." I whisper the word.

"What does that mean?"

"Good-for-nothing. 'You are an orphan,' she said. She told me that she was willing to take my brothers. But they didn't want me. Boys go to factories and collect paychecks. But a girl is a burden."

"You had no other relatives?"

"An aunt on my father's side in The Hague. I asked about her and they pointed out that if she couldn't afford to attend a funeral, then she certainly couldn't afford an extra mouth."

"So where did you go?"

"A school for teachers. They put me on a train with my aunt's husband. He was in his thirties and owned a shoe shop. They had the means to take me in."

Edouard is shaking his head. "One isn't always blessed with relatives," he observes.

"On the way to Leyde," I say, "my uncle told me that the city was as old as The Netherlands herself. Beautiful. He thought I'd like it there. When I arrived, I was still dressed in the mourning clothes I'd worn to my mother's funeral."

"M'greet—"

He pities me. He sees me as pathetic Margaretha Zelle now, the girl whose father abandoned her. Whose entire family refused to take her in. "That was the last time I saw him." But I correct myself. "The last time I saw any member of my mother's family."

"That's a terrible story."

"Everything that happened after my mother died was terrible." I don't know why I'm exposing myself to him, laying everything in front of him like an offering. I blink quickly so I won't start to cry again.

"M'greet, you are going to get Non back."

"It's impossible—"

"Listen carefully to me." I have never seen his face look so serious. "First, we will find out exactly where she is. Where she lives, what school she attends, where she goes to church. During this time—and this is going to take time—you are going to save your money. I will make calls and we will gather information. But after that we will need to secure someone trustworthy who is willing to take her away from her father and out of The Netherlands. That requires a great deal of money. More importantly, M'greet—and this is the part you must understand—it takes additional time. From this point forward, there are to be no more frivolous purchases and lunches at Maxim's unless someone else is paying the bill."

I am nodding. "Of course. Yes."

"We can do this. We can bring your daughter to live with you, here, in Paris."

Back in my apartment I can't sleep. I'm excited and happy, yet I can't keep my mind from digging through the past. I was so young. Leyde had felt so big: three churches, two dozen shops, canals that were wider than any in Leeuwarden. My uncle had put me in a carriage alone and the ride to the school had seemed endless. When at last the driver stopped at a coffee-colored building, I couldn't move, I could barely breathe. I just stared out the window as he took down my luggage and watched the cobbled streets until the tears in my eyes turned them into a sea of raised bruises.

Chapter 10

THE HAANSTRA
SCHOOL FOR GIRLS

*T*he next morning, sitting in the warm sunshine outside of the café Les Deux Magots, I tell Edouard everything. The light is extraordinary—soft and bright and perfectly golden. I see it, but I don't feel it; in my mind I'm in Leyde and the weather is dark and ominous, threatening rain.

"The Haanstra School for Girls was where I learned to reinvent myself," I say quietly. I think of the director, Heer Haanstra. A large sweaty man with fleshy jowls. His long mustache looked like two ivory tusks. I thought of him as the "Walrus." On my arrival, he studied me, trying to make out the shape of my body beneath my mourning dress. And although my aunt had telegrammed in advance, he gave me the impression that he was unaware that I was meant to join his school. "I was afraid that if I didn't impress him, he would put me out in a strange city, so I told him I was born in Caminghastate."

Edouard frowns.

"It was a game my father and I used to play: Papa would pretend that I was born in the castle, to nobility. That we both had power and status."

"Your father taught you this?"

"My father was full of dreams. I loved them, once."

I think of how my father used to call me his Scarlet Princess and how, on my sixth birthday, he built me a miniature bokkenwagen. He painted it red and bought two goats and two shiny gold harnesses to pull it. My whole family stood outside to watch as I flipped the reins and the goats took off, charging out the arched gates of 28 Groote Kerkstraat. "Before he abandoned us, he owned a shop that sold the finest hats in Leeuwarden." Edouard is nodding and I wonder if he can see it the way I can. The largest shop on the nicest street in town. "But the September when I was thirteen," I say, "he invested in the stock market. By that November we had nothing."

"And then your mother passed away."

"Yes. She died of a broken heart." And so, I think, did Margaretha Zelle. "I was sent to Leyde and—reluctantly—the school's director agreed to take me on."

I'd followed him down a whitewashed hall and my heart beat so loud I could hear it in my ears. There were children crying and little boys chasing after girls with paint on their hands. He took me to a room with fifteen beds. White sheets, white walls, white curtains. As if the school wanted the history of their girls whitewashed right out of them. He told me to put my things away and that I could join the other girls for dinner. "I owned so few things that they fit into an overnight bag. I had the outfit I was wearing, a worn birthday dress, a photo of my family, and a silk scarf my father brought me from the Indies."

"And you think buying things now will make up for that time of deprivation."

I stare across my coffee at Edouard.

"It's not unusual," he says softly. "You're not the first and you won't be the last. But all the spending in the world—it can't bring your family back."

"No." And it can't change the past, I think. As soon as the Walrus disappeared the other girls came upstairs to change out of one black dress into another.

"What's your name?" one asked. She had porcelain blue eyes and soft blonde ringlets. A daughter my aunts could have loved.

"Margaretha Zelle. But I am called M'greet."

"Adda Groot. Nice to make your acquaintance, M'greet. Have you met Mrs. Van Tassel yet?"

"Who is Mrs. Van Tassel?"

"She's the one who trains us." She looks me up and down. "She doesn't like girls who are untidy or idiots." She leans closer and speaks in my ear, "That's why she doesn't like Hendrika Ostrander." Adda nods slightly, indicating a heavyset girl across the room who is wearing a dirty cap. "They get the worst jobs."

I don't want to ask, but I have to know. "What are the worst jobs?"

"Washing down the toilets," she says, without hesitation. She grimaces. "After twenty-five children have used them." Then she says, "Most of us have been here for two years, except for her." She flicks her eyes to a girl at the very far end of the room. "Clara's only been here for three months. She didn't like the man her parents wanted her to marry, so she was sent here. As punishment."

If my aunts had found me a husband, I'd have married him. No matter who he was.

"Did the other girls treat you well?" Edouard asks. "Were they welcoming to you?"

I think back. "They were. I wanted them to like me—I wanted to impress them. I told them I was born in Caminghastate and that my mother had died giving birth to me. That one day my beloved papa and I were out riding when he grabbed his chest and collapsed. The doctors did everything they could, but he was gone. The last part was true, at least."

Edouard looks sad and I'm not sure if it's me he pities or my lies. "How did you explain your poverty to them?"

"I told them that men came after my father died and took everything away. The paintings, the silver, the china. I said that there were debts that had to be paid off. The tale wasn't so different from the real reasons some of the other girls were there. Adda's mother was widowed and could no longer afford her. Adda's dearest hope was to get married. Another girl, Naatje, wanted to travel the world. Whenever she and I talked, I conjured all of the faraway locations I'd dreamed or read about with my father. I reminisced about the Indies, France, England. I was poor but my stories lifted us all out of that awful school. Some days we were able to forget we were there, in service, unlikely to ever get married and have children of our own."

"Your father was alive. Did he ever try to contact you?"

"No. I wrote to him. I described the school and what my life had become and I believed he would collect me and my brothers and bring us all home."

"How many brothers?"

"Three. Ari, Cornelius, and Johannes. For months and months I held on to the dream of my father's return. It became a precious gem, one I polished into different visions of reality. Outside of my fantasies, every day was the same: up at six, greet the children at seven, read to them for an hour, take them for a walk. Paint with them. Take them to lunch. Nap time. Clean up after them as they sleep. Songs followed by more stories. Then the children go home. Then preparing for the following day. Then dinner." It was an endless cycle: endless whining, endless crying, endless runny noses. The school said it was good for children to have fresh air. No matter the weather. I didn't have a warm coat."

"And now you have half a dozen furs."

I see what he's implying. He's suggesting my outrageous spending is related to my wretched past. "There are times when it's very cold here," I say defensively.

"And your father . . . He never came for you?"

"Of course not."

A waiter comes and asks if I would like a second cup of coffee. Edouard isn't halfway through with his first. I tell him yes. Then I close my eyes briefly and concentrate on the warm scent of spring. I hear the bells ringing at St.-Germain-des-Prés and am instantly reminded of my church days in Leyde.

"The newest girl always sits next to me," the Walrus said the first Sunday I arrived. But there wasn't any room for him in the pew where I was seated. He hooked his thumbs around his suspenders and stared at Naatje, who was sitting next to me.

"I'm sure we are as tightly packed as we can be," our head instructor, Mrs. Van Tassel, said primly.

"Did your family take you to church often?" the Walrus asked me, ignoring Van Tassel.

"Every Sunday," I told him. I didn't like the way he focused on me. He was paying me too much attention, often following me during school hours. He squeezed my shoulders. "A good girl," he said, and sat behind me.

Naatje narrowed her eyes and Mrs. Van Tassel hissed in my ear, "This is *church*, Miss Zelle. I suggest you stop encouraging him."

I looked at the headmistress with her gray hair wrapped tightly in a small, neat bun, and I was mute with outrage. The preacher was talking about Jonah's sins and I was thinking that if there was a God, he would have sent my father already. He would have told my brothers to answer my letters. I had already written to them five times. As I knelt to pray I could feel the Walrus's heavy breath on my neck.

"I'm sorry to learn that your father behaved so terribly toward you," Edouard says, interrupting my thoughts, and I'm in Paris again, not Leyde. I'm safe in Les Deux Magots. "I have some news that I hope will make you very happy. I've made contact with several men in Amsterdam. They will help us get your daughter, Jeanne Louise."

My hands knock into my empty coffee cup and it shatters on the ground. "When? How?" A waiter hurries over to clean it up. *Non.* My tiny angel, Non. Or maybe not so tiny. She was six years old when I left her.

"The when remains to be seen. We must be patient. As for the how, we have verified that she is still in The Netherlands and still living with Rudolph MacLeod. My men are observing his daily routines and her daily habits. As I've told you, getting a child out of a foreign country requires a great deal of planning and coordination."

"How does she look? How tall has she gotten?"

"I am happy to see you so excited, M'greet. You deserve to be happy. I will ask for photographs. In the meanwhile, as we wait, you must earn. I've secured you a contract here in the city to dance as Salome at the Odéon."

"I danced *Salome* in Berlin. I thought I didn't repeat performances?"

"Let's agree that you never repeat the same performance in the same country. This is France. And the pay is extraordinary."

"How much?"

"Seventy thousand francs."

My God, that's triple what the Rothschilds paid. It's an absolute fortune.

"But you will have to save everything, M'greet. These men I've contacted have the experience required, and they do not come cheap. This is a difficult case. It will cost."

"They are discreet—they won't alert Rudolph, will they? If he finds out that I'm trying to get my little girl back . . ." I whisper the truth: "I'm afraid he'll kill her."

I see in his expression that Edouard believes I'm being overly dramatic. I don't want to dwell on Rudolph MacLeod. But I can still see him at the train station, gripping Non's hand in his while I boarded, my face streaked with tears. "Because he told me he would."

Edouard takes my hands in his. "Rudolph MacLeod will have no inkling that he is being watched; my men are professionals." There is steel in his voice as he says, "When the time is right, they will snatch your daughter from him and Jeanne Louise will be escorted safely out of The Netherlands so quickly that MacLeod's head will spin. He will not be aware of anything unusual until after she's gone, when he is powerless to do her any harm."

I have revealed so much to Edouard about myself. But I have never told him that I found my husband through a personal ad. I was seventeen years old; I had no job and no money. Then I saw a paragraph in the paper:

> Captain from the Indies, passing his leave in Amsterdam, seeks a wife—preferably with a little money.

I wrote to him immediately. We agreed to meet at the Rijksmuseum, in the glass-domed building that houses the museum's military collection. I made my way to Amsterdam. I expected the city to have changed while I was gone, but as I walked along the narrow green canals and past the same brightly painted buildings, it became clear that the only thing that had changed was me. Was my brother, Johannes, still working in the same garment factory? All of my letters to him had gone unanswered. Perhaps the owners had kept them—perhaps he had never received my letters. I looked for signs along the canal that I should visit him, making little tests for the universe. If two ducks landed in the water before I reached the church, I would go and see him. Two ducks landed. I thought up another test. Then another. By the time I was finished I was standing in front of the dreary-looking building where my brother had been sent to work four years earlier. I mounted the steps and went inside. The chemical scent in the air was so strong I had to cover my nose with my hand.

"May I help you?" a man asked. A manager of some sort. I could see by his suit.

"I'm here to see a worker. Johannes Zelle."

"Stay here and I'll get him."

I waited by two chairs and a very old couch. Beyond a pair of double wooden doors I could hear the sounds of a busy factory. Several minutes later the doors swung open and Johannes appeared. He lingered in the doorway for several moments. And when he finally spoke, all he had to say was, "Why are you here?"

It was as if someone had stolen the air from my chest. "To see you," I said. I knew I had changed, but I barely recognized him.

He brushed his hands against his overalls. "So? Do you like what you see?"

I moved forward to embrace him and he moved away.

"Don't. You'll dirty your dress."

"Have you been getting my letters?"

"About your hardships in Leyde? Your terrible time at school?"

This wasn't the boy who sat next to me in class and giggled at the teacher. Even Johannes's voice was unrecognizable.

"I didn't feel like writing about my happy days soaking my hands in chemicals, dyeing women's clothes. Or maybe you were hoping to hear how Ari enjoys the mill?"

He turned to leave.

"What about Cornelius?" I called after him.

He stopped and turned. "He's no happier than the rest of us."

"And Papa?"

He covered his mouth with a dirty hand, as if he wanted to keep something truly vile from spilling out. "He has forgotten about us, M'greet. Take a lesson from him and forget about us as well."

I met Captain Rudolph MacLeod in front of a glass case filled with rifles. He was tall and bald, with a white mustache and a sunburned face. He was holding a polished cane and looked old enough to be my father. But he wore the dazzling uniform of the Dutch colonial army.

"Captain MacLeod?"

"Lady Zelle." I watched his face transform. He held out his hand. A bear paw. I felt the heat of tropical suns.

"Please, call me M'greet."

We strolled arm in arm around the museum. I wondered what his house in Java looked like; I imagined bamboo floors and fans turning slowly on hot afternoons. With each step we took I left The Netherlands behind. When he asked for my hand, I'd known him for six days. We were married on July 11, 1895, in city hall. My wedding dress was yellow tulle. I bought it in the most elegant shop in Amsterdam. "In yellow, mademoiselle?" the French dressmaker questioned. "You can't possibly desire yellow. Cream, perhaps?"

"Yellow," I insisted. Like saffron. And curry. And tropical suns.

Before I could leave Amsterdam behind, I climbed the seven steps to 148 Lange Leidschedwarsstraat and knocked. A blonde woman answered the door and I was surprised by how young she was, a thirty-year-old version of my mother, but not as pretty.

"Is Adam Zelle here?" I could smell *hutsput* cooking. My mother made *hutsput*.

"May I ask who's calling?"

"Tell him his daughter has arrived."

Her hand moved to her chest. "*Daughter?*"

I wondered if he hadn't told her, or if she simply believed I'd never intrude on his new life. I saw him in the kitchen and my chest constricted; he turned and I would have forgiven him anything at that moment. But then a terrible thought occurred to me. What if he wouldn't let me in the door? What if he denied knowing me, his black orchid? "Look at her. Could a girl that dark belong to me? No, my children are lilies, pale as snow."

"Margaretha, you've come back!" He rushed over to embrace me but I backed away. I glanced at his wife as I said, "You were the one who left me. You left us all."

"No." He shook his head. "No, come into the parlor."

I let myself be led into the parlor. I watched him. He was happy. No tears, no regret. He sat in a straight-backed chair, still the baron of Leeuwarden, now with a wife named Catherine. He sat forward in his chair. What had he been telling people all these years? That his children had abandoned him? That our mother had run off?

His wife sat next to him, pulling her chair close to his.

"I'm getting married," I said, my voice flat. I couldn't accept that he was married to another woman, letting her cook for him, sleep with him. Had she given him children?

I held my purse tighter, watching my knuckles turn white on the clasp. "Will you give me permission to marry?"

"Oh." He sat back. "So is that what this is about? I thought you had come to visit."

A wave of anger swept over me. I felt a new M'greet blooming in place of the old, something darker. I stood, enraged. "Are you not the least bit curious to know what happened after you abandoned my mother? Aren't you interested to know why I was thrown out of Leyde's school for teachers? I *waited* for you," my voice was shrill. "In Leeuwarden, in Leyde, in The Hague. You never came! Where were you?"

Catherine pulled a handkerchief from her pocket, giving it to me. I hadn't even realized that I was crying. "It's all right."

She patted my hand as if I were a child, making a fuss over nothing.

What had he told her? That I had left? "Where are my brothers?" I demanded.

My father hesitated. "In the factories. They're doing well."

No one did well in the factories. Grief overwhelmed me. This was not the man I remembered. My father really was dead. "Do you give me permission to marry?" I asked, moving toward the door. My body felt like lead.

My father hurried to his feet. "You're not leaving?"

I didn't answer him.

"Of course you can marry. As long as he comes to me to ask for your hand."

I stopped. He hadn't cared what happened to me for years, and now he wanted a formal visit?

"He must come to ask for your hand." The idea was blossoming in his mind. He was thinking of all the fruit it could bear.

My cheeks flushed. "How *dare* you ask this." He was living in his own world. I wasn't his daughter. I considered telling him about fending off the Walrus. How would he react when I told him that I'd had half a dozen men at the Grand Hotel? I wanted him to see what he'd created, to feel the sharp edges of my pain.

"Margaretha," Catherine interjected. "A formal proposal is only right."

I turned around, prepared to give her a lesson on what was right. But I stopped myself. A woman can't marry in Amsterdam until she's thirty without her father's permission. It was either comply with my father's wishes or lose a husband, and I wanted Java too much to lose Rudolph.

I set my jaw, cursing him to hell. "Tomorrow, then."

Chapter 11

A GIRL'S PRIVATE LAUNDRY

I'm changing my clothes after an exceptional opening night when Edouard lets himself into my dressing room at the Odéon. "Did you see the prince of Schwarzburg?" I ask. "He was in the second row tonight. I have to hurry. He's waiting for me in the lobby."

I look up and notice Edouard's face. It's serious. He sits down across from my dressing table and I realize that he's holding something. "M'greet, I want you to be calm."

Immediately, all calmness drains away. "Has something happened to Non? Has something happened to my daughter?"

He holds up the book he's carrying and I'm shocked. There's a photo of me on the jacket. I am nine years old, dressed in a ridiculously expensive outfit my father had indulged me with. I remember the moment it was taken clearly: I was standing in front of Leeuwarden's fountain, imagining I was a queen. It was summer and the air was heavy with jasmine blossoms.

"Who found that photo?" I reach for the book but he pulls it back.

"This book is going to make you very, very angry," he warns me. "It's a biography," he says. "Of you. Written by your father."

Rage, white-hot, burns through my body. "You aren't serious!" But he hands me the book and as I begin flipping through the pages I know that he is. "And what does he write about?" I demand, scanning the pages. "Does he apologize for abandoning me? For leaving my mother to die in Leeuwarden?"

Edouard moves toward the door. "I'm sorry. I wanted you to hear about this from me, not read about it in the papers. I believe your friend 'Bowtie' is penning something about it."

As soon as he closes the door I start reading. *The Life of Mata Hari: A Biography of My Daughter and My Grievances Against Her Former Husband.* Page after page details my father's flair for business, his former collection of art, his overall greatness that inevitably produced a person like me. In every chapter my father is the hero. I am a caricature and Rudolph is unrecognizable. My brothers are barely mentioned. And in my father's version of our life, my mother never existed.

The next morning Bowtie finds me in the Ritz taking my coffee in a shady little nook far removed from everyone else. The man has the homing abilities of a pigeon. He makes for my table and I wish to God he would make a right turn and perch with someone else. But I know why he's here. I might as well get it over with.

"Mata Hari!" His sandy hair is slicked back beneath his fedora. There's no *Press* card tucked inside the band today. He takes a seat and snaps for the waiter.

"Good morning," I tell him. I hope it's obvious from my voice that I don't mean it.

"It's always a good morning, Mata Hari. If you're walking and breathing, it's good." The waiter arrives and he orders a coffee. "Another?" he asks me.

"No."

"You just opened a new show. No rehearsals today?"

"Not until next week."

He nods. Then the coffee arrives and he's all business. "So." He takes a sip. "Is it true? Everything your father wrote about you?"

I don't have it in me to play the fool. "Of course not. It's trash."

"Doesn't matter, though, does it? Thousands of people will read his book. They'll read it and they'll be shocked." He straightens his bow tie; today it's deep magenta. "Is there anything you'd like to tell them? I'm offering you the chance."

There is tenderness in his voice. He's waiting for me to speak, his boyish face tilted to the side. He's exceedingly good-looking. I'm sure he has his pick of women wherever he goes. Or perhaps men. "Yes, there's something I'd like to say."

He takes a pen from behind his ear and sits forward, ready to write.

"Tell them that my father is—"

"Delusional?" he offers. "That you were born in India, not Caminghastate?"

"Yes."

"And what about your husband? Is any of that true?"

"I'd rather not speak about it."

"But you do have a daughter?"

"I can't talk—" My voice breaks. If Rudolph reads my father's horrible book, what will he do to Non? Will he take his rage out on her? Tears trail down my cheeks and I feel myself shaking. Bowtie offers me his handkerchief. I press it against my eyes. "Please," I say. "She's only a little girl. If my ex-husband reads this book—"

"Are you afraid of him?"

"Yes."

He shuts his notepad immediately. "Thank you," he says. He stands, leaving his coffee unfinished.

The next day in *Le Figaro* I am the headline again: BETRAYED: JEALOUS AND DELUSIONAL FATHER WRITES FALSE BIOGRAPHY OF THE FAMOUS MATA HARI.

I am so grateful to Bowtie I could kiss him.

If only Rudolph reads this article and not my father's book.

"An orchid among buttercups."

His voice is just as I remember it. I turn from my dressing table and there he is. After pruning the garden of my life, up pops a weed.

"M'greet," my father says. "My God, *look* at you!"

He rushes to me, clasping me in his arms, holding me as if we've been apart for too long. He is such a convincing performer I find myself thinking, *Has he finally come to apologize?*

Then he steps back and makes an imaginary toast. "To your success, Margaretha." He leans forward, hat in his hand. It is expensive, a Wolthausen. I can smell alcohol on him. There is a knock on the door.

"Come in," I call automatically, my eyes fixed on the man who deserted me.

"M'greet, I—"

It's Edouard. Thank God.

My father bounds over to him, extending his hand. "Adam Zelle," he says. "Margaretha's father. You must be her director. My M'greet, the star. Did she tell you she was born in Caminghastate?"

"*Papa*," I whisper.

"The world deserves to know! That's why I've written a book about you."

I could kill him.

My father looks between me and Edouard, sensing tension. "Don't you think I deserve a little of the success I helped you achieve?" he asks, belligerence creeping into his voice. He makes his way over to a table and picks through some crackers and cheese.

I've had enough. I don't remember my wedding ceremony beyond recalling that it was short, hot, and full of people I didn't know. But I do remember the banquet we held afterward, at the Café Americain. My father and a dozen of his friends were there, all men from the bottle factory dressed in suits that had fit them better twenty years earlier. It didn't surprise me that he would miss the ceremony and bring his own guests for the food, but I was ashamed that Rudolph's family had to witness it. I saw myself through their eyes, a harlot in yellow, a girl who answers ads in newspapers. They didn't know the beautiful house my family once owned, the servants we'd hired, the fountains that had trickled musically on our lawns. They didn't know the man my father once was. They only saw poverty masquerading as wealth, marrying into it, and I couldn't blame them for hating me.

I stand swiftly. "Edouard, please. Get him out of here."

I hear them on the stairs, in the street—my father, my knight in shining armor, reduced now to a little man making a scene.

The next night the owner of the Odéon is in the doorway of my dressing room, his mouth tight. "You will encore."

"I will not!" I fling my brush across the room, watch it smack into the wall with a satisfying thud. "I encored *twice* yesterday and *three times* the day before. I'm done tonight. I'm done for every other night. No more encores." I grab my cloak and slam the door behind me. In the cold December street, I can still hear the crowd in the theater, chanting *Mata Hari! Mata Hari!*

I search the busy streets for a cab. The night is a swirl of red and gold lights, a child's dream of Christmas trees and carolers. And what have I spent it doing? Dancing naked for men who lie to their wives about where they're going. Inside the shops, the cheerful lights remind me of the way my family decorated our house; of how, on the Feast of Sinterklaas, my brothers would jump on my bed before dawn to wake me so we could creep down the stairs together and spy on the presents that were waiting for us. How different my life was before my mother died and I was sent to the Haanstra School for Girls.

The holiday I spent at that school was difficult. We girls gathered together under the mistletoe at the end of November to draw names for a gift exchange to celebrate the Feast of Sinterklaas. No one wanted to pick Hendrika Ostrander's name.

"No one wants her," Naatje whispered.

Adda shook her head. "Last year, someone bought her a comb."

When Mrs. Van Tassel held the red hat in front of me, I fished out a name: Hendrika Ostrander.

We exchanged gifts in the drawing room. From Georgiana I received a thick scarf. Adda was given an exquisite silver bangle, with tiny etchings and a clasp. Naatje's present was a leather purse made in Italy. All the girls were rapt as Hendrika opened her gift from me. There was the sharp intake of breath when the girl who was Mrs. Van Tassel's designated toilet cleaner held up a rabbit's fur bonnet for everyone to see. It had cost me two weeks' wages.

Hendrika's eyes were red. "Thank you," she whispered to me and I nodded back.

Everyone deserved a little beauty in their life, I thought. Even Hendrika.

A black taxi pulls up next to the curb. Edouard is spending the evening with his mother; she is hosting a Christmas party. I want that. To have a mother who expects me every Christmas. Instead of a lying father.

"Where to, mademois—Mata Hari!"

I look out at the carolers. Last night Edouard invited me to his mother's party. I told him no. Now I change my mind. "Madame Clunet's," I tell him. "On la Rue Jacob." An hour's drive.

I wrap my fingers around the silver knocker and bang twice. The house is exactly as I imagined it, with cozy lace curtains and potted flowers.

The door swings open and there is Edouard: a drink in one hand, a cigar in the other. There is an expectant hush behind him, as if he were in the middle of a joke and I interrupted the punch line. It's an uncomfortable feeling.

"M'greet!" Edouard steps back. "You came." His smile is genuine. "I'm glad." The party turns to look at me, a woman arriving alone in a black dress and a mink stole. They are a refined group: ladies wearing ancestral pearls and men that smell of expensive business deals. Edouard picks up a spoon and taps his glass. "I would like to introduce a guest."

I feel my cheeks warm. "Edouard, please."

He clears his throat. "May I now have the pleasure of announcing Mademoiselle M'greet MacLeod."

I feel the color drain from my face. It's been a long time since I've heard this name.

"She is my client and a most talented dancer."

I am frightened to look up; will they recognize me like the taxi driver did? When I do, all their faces are still welcoming. No one at this party reads stories about Mata Hari. But they trust Edouard's judgment, and I am ushered in warmly.

They crowd around me, Edouard's grandpere in his black silk jacket, and his grandmere, with her strong perfume. They want to hear about Edouard as a businessman, they want to tell me stories from his childhood, and how Aunt Adorlee met Uncle Geoffrey on the dance floor to the song "L'Amour Venge." It is the most wonderful evening I've spent since I was a young girl and had a family. When it's time to go home, Edouard walks me out to his car. He smells like pine needles and brandy.

"I know why you came," he says as he opens the car door. "You were lonely."

I am mortified; hanging the embarrassing truth out like a girl's private laundry. "I wasn't!" I lie.

"Yes, you were." He is smiling. "I also know you didn't encore. The Odéon called before you arrived." He hesitates. "They fired you."

I don't believe it. "*Fired me?* He can't do that. Encoring isn't in the contract." I feel myself becoming enraged. I need that money for my daughter. "Edouard. I want that money. The full amount."

"I don't—"

"I will never dance for the Odéon again!"

"All right."

"And I want you to sue him for breach of contract."

That night, alone and furious in my apartment, I allow myself to remember Rudolph. I conjure him sitting at the table waiting for me.

"You're home so early," I said. "I—"

"Where have you been?"

"I visited a temple with Sofie." I hurried my words.

His face went red. "Goddamn it!" He pulled his arm back and hit me. "I told you to stay in this house!" I backed up toward the stairs. He grabbed my hair, jerking my head toward his. "You think you can defy me?" He twisted my arm behind my back and shoved me into the wall, crushing me with his weight. "Do you think I don't see how you look at other men, you little *hoer*?" He pushed me up the stairs and into the bedroom, throwing me on the floor.

The next thirty days stretched impossibly long.

When the blood didn't come, I had to acknowledge the horrible reality.

I was carrying Rudolph's child.

Chapter 12

I SHOULD HAVE
HEEDED THE DANGER

1905

*W*hen I see him across the lobby of the Plaza Athénée, I'm sure I'm mistaken. I stop and stare. He is sitting across from a woman I recognize. She is one of my dancers from my time at the Odéon. Audrey? Annique? Whatever her name, she is laughing, tossing back her head, touching invisible pearls at her neck. Across from her, hanging on every word, is Bowtie. His fedora with its *Press* card is in his lap. His notepad is out and he's writing furiously. Before I can stop myself I cross the lobby. The sharp click of my heels makes several people turn.

"Mata Hari!" Bowtie stands. A deep flush creeps along his cheeks. He hasn't interviewed me in months.

"What a surprise to see you here," I say drily.

The blonde smiles at me from her chair. It is the smile that women reserve only for their competition.

"Yes. Well, Annique," he nods toward the pretty blonde, "is opening her own show at the Odéon this week."

The Odéon!

Annique nods. "Nice to see you, Mata Hari."

There is nothing nice about it. Bowtie shifts his eyes from me to her and I can see the wheels spinning in his head. "Ladies, this is such a lucky meeting," he says. "Perhaps you'd care to tell *Le Figaro* your plans, Mata Hari? Will you be in attendance?"

"What is being performed?" I ask, as my entire body goes hot.

"*Cleopatra*," Annique says, without the barest hint of shame.

Bowtie is absolutely beside himself with glee. "Didn't you play Cleopatra in Madrid?" he asks, with false surprise. "The Odéon has two Cleopatras meeting by chance at the Plaza Athénée. Extraordinary. Two Cleopatras in one room!"

"My act is quite different from hers," Annique says. "In mine, all the dancers perform nude. We don't use veils. It is very modern."

They're both watching me. I think I'm going to be sick. Annique stole my act and now the Odéon is hiring her. I have a crushing feeling in my chest; I haven't had a new contract in months. Edouard took the owner of the Odéon to court and won, but that money isn't enough to keep his men working to rescue Non. I've paid for three scouting missions so far—each one more disappointing than the last. They can never get close to her. Whenever Non is not with Rudolph she's at school, and when she's at school a nanny sits outside waiting for her. The woman never misses a day, never leaves her post.

I turn on my heel and leave Bowtie with Annique. Then I take the long way home. Children are racing paper boats in the Seine. It's a beautiful day but all I see are the numbers dancing in my head. Ten thousand: what it will cost to bribe Rudolph's nanny; Edouard has told me this. Six thousand: the amount I'll need to pay for another reconnaissance mission, and there will need to be more, possibly many. Six: the number of weeks I haven't worked. Ten: the number of days since I last saw Edouard. Two: the number of men this last week who bought me something worth pawning. One: the only child

I have left. And she's waiting for me. Edouard says his men tell him she looks happy. She appears healthy and well cared for. She has friends in school and jokes with her nanny. Is it true? Or are they telling me lies to make the waiting easier?

When I get home, Edouard phones to tell me that La Madeline wants my *Cleopatra*.

"Charge them an outrageous sum," I tell him, feeling vindictive. They rejected me when I first arrived in Paris.

"I already have."

"Then double it."

I'm being crushed by the circle of reporters surrounding me. There are so many cameras and notepads that I couldn't find Bowtie in the crowd if I wanted to. When the bulbs finally stop flashing, I do see him. He thrusts a paper under my nose.

PARIS SHOWDOWN:
IN DUELING CLEOPATRAS MATA HARI CONQUERS

"Not bad." I keep walking, letting my white fur trail behind me. It's an older coat but no one would know it. And suddenly I feel I can conquer Annique and the world. I wait while my chauffeur opens the car door. Before he can close it, Bowtie is there. "Mata Hari, will you be around for—"

"For what? For something Annique isn't available for?"

"Hold on, now." He puts his hands up, as if I'm pointing a gun at him. "You know the ropes; this is business. Who knows that better than you? The 'Showdown' piece sold more copies for *Le Figaro* than every other article I've written this month combined. Meet me tomorrow," he pleads. "You're good for my career."

He's a pretty talker, but the truth is that he's good for mine, too. I make him wait several moments before answering. "Same lobby. Ten o'clock."

He tips his hat to me and the chauffeur closes my door.

I arrive in the lobby of the Plaza Athénée at ten minutes to ten.

Last night I had a terrible dream. I was standing on stage and no one was in the audience. I kept waiting and waiting, but no one came. The horror of the dream isn't how real it felt but that someday it will be true. How many years do I have left? Five? Three? There are younger girls duplicating my roles right now. There are no more veils to drop. How will I afford to bring Non home? How will I take care of myself?

"Mata Hari?"

"Yes?" I look up and realize that a balding man in an expensive suit wearing a striking gold watch is standing before me.

"Felix Rousseau," he says.

"It's a pleasure to make your acquaintance, Felix."

"I want to tell you how much I enjoy your shows. I've been to one in Madrid and I was there last night at La Madeline. I wish I had seen you in Berlin."

"You're a traveler, then?"

"For work. I'm a banker." A very wealthy banker, his smile adds.

I learn he has a château at Esvres. Fifteen butlers, seventeen maids, a stable full of horses. "He collects everything," I tell Edouard the next day when I see him for lunch at Maxim's. "Suits of armor, coins, musical instruments, cars."

"Women?" Edouard asks, and he actually looks jealous.

"He did say he is unhappy with his wife."

Edouard's lips thin. "So he's an original liar, too."

* * *

The next weekend Rousseau invites me to Esvres. "Give her whatever she wants," he tells the servants. And they do. There is coffee waiting for me after my morning ride, in the afternoon a dozen new books are arranged in the parlor, and in the evening we dine at the Plaza Athénée, my new favorite place.

"Mata Hari, I'd like you to meet a good friend of mine. An artist by the name of Pablo Picasso."

He's a little man in an oversize coat. I extend my arm and he kisses my hand briefly. "I've seen one of your shows," he says. "You are wonderful. Rousseau does nothing but talk about you."

"Oh, that's a lovely exaggeration."

He smiles. "Perhaps someday you will sit for a painting."

He must be very talented if Rousseau is interested in him. I am about to agree when Rousseau speaks. "Most unfortunately Mata Hari is very busy," he lies.

Both men look toward me.

"My schedule is full," I say, and I see Rousseau's shoulders relax. But perhaps he is too relaxed. "However, it is very flexible, like I am."

Later that evening Rousseau buys me a ring worth a thousand francs, and I recognize how easily he can be led. When he takes me to the races at Longchamp the following day, I search out Pablo. We talk and I laugh at everything he says as if he's the most charming man in Paris. It doesn't take very long: Pablo is in the middle of a story about Spain.

"Mata Hari," Rousseau interrupts.

I look at him and mouth *shhhh*. I turn back to Pablo.

"Mata Hari, it's time we leave."

"So soon? But Pablo—"

"Yes."

I take his arm and follow him out. Rousseau is silent. I wonder if I overplayed my hand.

In the car, he sits very still for several minutes without looking at me or saying a word. I begin to think of ways to placate him when he says, "I can get your daughter back."

I am stunned. "What do you mean?"

"I've been thinking about what you told me since the first day we met. I believe I have the means to help you," he says. "Nothing is more important to you, is it?"

"No." Now I feel guilty for flirting with Pablo. "My lawyer is already—"

"Edouard Clunet?"

I'm surprised he knows the name.

"I've dealt with him before. We don't need his help."

"But he's already—"

"Mata Hari, I know people."

I study him through sudden tears. He is earnest.

"Let me handle this." He holds out his hands. "Stay with me," he says.

I take his hands. And I do.

I live with Rousseau in his château for four weeks. There are so many promises he makes. Trips we'll take, gifts he'll buy, places we'll dine—and of course, most importantly, the rescue of Non. But by the end of the month, for all of the fancy dining, trinkets, and shows, he has done nothing to bring me my daughter. I take out my bags and start packing my things.

"Where are you going?" Rousseau actually sounds shocked. He is in the doorway, watching me fold clothes.

I don't want to tell him the truth so I say, "You know I can't stay in the country forever." I fold some silk nighties into my case. "I have to return to Paris. I have to dance. I must earn my living." If only I had a contract.

Rousseau is at a loss. A coin doesn't sell its owner. "Can't you stay?"

"You will find other women to entertain you," I tell him.

"Not like you!" He crosses the room and holds me with surprising strength. "I'll take care of you," he swears. "I *promise*."

My attempt to leave makes him more generous. I write to Edouard and ask about his progress with Non. I end with a postscript. "PS: Maybe this is love?"

Edouard writes back. The status of Non's custody remains the same. He ends with his own postscript: "For whom? You or the old man?"

"I have a surprise for you," Rousseau says, and the next day we go for a ride. His chauffeur turns left on Rue Windsor, one of the most expensive avenues in the fashionable suburb of Neuilly. The car stops in front of a glittering white villa with wide, arching windows and sweeping vistas. Rousseau turns to me. "The Villa Rémy." He hands me an envelope. "My surprise. It's yours." Inside the envelope is the deed. "All I ask is to be welcome to visit once in a while."

I am crying. "Why did you do this? Why?"

"Because I can."

I usher Edouard inside. The stained glass over the door reads *Sois le bienvenu*.

"Isn't it beautiful?"

I watch his eyes as they appraise the villa. *My* villa. Not an apartment belonging to someone else. "There are six bedrooms," I say. "Plus a pool and a garden and a stable with horses." I show him everything: my boxes of jewels, my closets filled with clothes. But I save the best for last. A room meant for Non. I've had the walls painted pink.

"Your banker friend must have a lot of money." Other men he has no trouble calling lovers. But Rousseau is "my banker friend."

"Imagine my daughter living here," I say. I will do for Non exactly what I dreamed my father would do for me.

Edouard takes a seat on the child-size bed. He looks at the dolls and frowns. "I know this is taking a long time," he says.

"Yes, but I have something to tell you." I am nervous.

"You aren't pregnant?" he asks.

"Of course not!"

He looks relieved.

"I told Rousseau about Non. I told him the first day we met."

"M'greet—"

"He's hired someone to get her."

"*What?*"

His expression makes me nervous. I rush the rest of my news. "Rousseau hired a woman named Anna. She speaks Dutch. She was born in the same town that I was. She knows what to do. She's going to find Non and bring her to Paris."

"Who is she? Do you trust her? M'greet, my men consistently report—"

"What? Don't you trust Rousseau?"

"Why should I trust him? I don't even know him."

"You know me and *I* know Rousseau—he interrogates everyone thoroughly. He hired Anna, so she is qualified. She's already in Amsterdam. Non will be here tomorrow!"

Edouard looks positively ill. "M'greet. My men are meticulous. They've been working for—"

"Months. And months and months! I can't wait any longer,

Edouard. Anna will arrive at my daughter's school early for dismissal and say she is Rudolph's new servant. She will produce a locket with my picture inside so Non won't be afraid. The two of them will go directly to the train station."

He watches me with a strange expression in his eyes.

"Non will be here tomorrow, Edouard. Be happy for me."

It is the Ides of March. An unlucky day for Caesar, but my day of triumph. In three hours, Anna will return to France with Non.

Edouard arrives at two o'clock. Together, in the salon, we wait.

I am so excited, I feel brave enough to talk about the past. I say to Edouard, "In Java, Rudolph stopped forcing me to stay in the house after I became a mother. He decided that with a child I was safe and undesirable. Norman and I—my son and I—we visited all of the ancient shrines to gods my people don't have names for. I took him to see Kraton, the two-hundred-year-old palace, and Tamansari, a water castle. Those were my favorite days. We would climb the stone steps and be the only people in the world. We'd be hypnotized by mango valleys newly washed with rain, listen to the chanting of monks. I told Norman about Buddhism and Hinduism. About why Brahma has four heads and Ganesh is an elephant. I began earnestly learning Malay. By that summer I was able to speak it."

"What happened to Norman?" Edouard asks gently.

I wave him off. I never allow myself to visit that dark corner of my memory.

When the clock strikes four o'clock, I begin pouring wine. "You don't think something's happened?" I ask. "Should we call the station? The train may be delayed."

He calls the station. No trains are delayed. I stare out the window as darkness begins falling. I had wanted so badly for her first sight of the villa to be in daylight. "Something has gone wrong."

"Perhaps . . ." He tries to think of a positive scenario.

"What?" My voice sounds foreign in my ears.

"I don't know."

At eight, when Anna arrives alone, Edouard holds me close to him as I cry. "I'm sorry, ma'am," Anna whispers. "I'm so very sorry—"

"What happened?" Edouard demands.

"Her father was there. He arrived moments after I had taken her by the hand. He began shouting for the police."

"No!" I scream. "He's going to kill her!"

"You don't know that."

"I do! I do know that! You wanted to know what happened to Norman? It was all Rudolph's fault!"

Edouard guides me to a chair. Anna sits on the edge of the couch and I tell them the whole ugly story. I tell them that when Non was a baby and Norman was three, Rudolph was made commander of a garrison in Melan. We had two weeks to pack all our belongings and move from our home. I hoped things would be different now that Rudolph had a high-status position; he would be required to entertain society, so I wouldn't be so isolated. In Melan, I became Lady MacLeod. Ours was the biggest house with the widest lawn and a marble fountain. Our garden parties saw more than two hundred people and soon I was so busy hosting that Rudolph hired a nurse to care for the children, a Javanese woman named Fairuza.

I hired Mahadevi and I watched her dance at my parties. I wanted to be her, to feel that free—like a child again in my father's hat shop, where anything was possible. Rudolph would never allow me to dance in public. But she agreed to teach me in private, to show me how to make magic with my hips and hands. She watched me practice with longing. The way Rudolph never watched me.

"Close your eyes," she instructed and I did as she told me.

We danced together wearing indigo silks, our bare feet flat on her polished floor. We danced until we were both dizzy, until my body felt as supple as the silk. She told me that you are what you believe yourself to be. She was able to look at a man and say, "He wants me for a week. No more, no less."

"If I'd had that skill," I tell them, "my heart would never have been broken. When she invited me to dance in public, I said yes."

Edouard leans forward. "So you performed—"

"Yes. I danced with Mahadevi at one of the parties I hosted. I dressed in a scarlet sarong I bought at the pasar. I was exotic. An orchid among buttercups. Three hundred people dressed in chiffon and gold sat in our garden: my husband's colleagues, his subordinates, their wives."

I danced with Mahadevi; primitive and wild. When we were finished, Mahadevi kissed me on the lips, and our bodies melted together in the warm island moonlight to the sound of applause.

"Your husband must have been shocked," Anna says.

"He was enraged." He seethed as I mingled with our guests. And when we were alone, he warned me, "You will never disgrace me like that again!" I said the worst thing I could think of in Malay. "Is that right?" he asked, reaching into a drawer. What was he going to do? I heard the click of his gun just as I heard the creak of a door from upstairs.

"Norman was on the landing," I tell them.

Edouard looks horrified.

"'Go to bed!' I said. 'Go to bed, Norman!' I heard little feet scamper down the hall and the click of a door. Rudolph whipped me across the face and afterward, all I could recall was his heavy weight on top of me and the smell of alcohol on his breath. I went to Mahadevi the next day, a veil over my face to hide my blackened eye and bruised cheek. 'Give me something that will keep him away from me,' I begged. She gave me cajeput oil. 'Smear this between your legs and he will never bother you again.' The next time he tried to take me his prick was covered with small red blotches. I told him, 'My body has turned against you.'"

Tears begin leaking from the corners of my eyes, remembering what happened next. Edouard reaches out and takes my hand. I try to catch my breath.

"It was the middle of the night," I tell them. "I went to Norman's crib. He was sleeping. I caressed his cheek. He was three years old. I looked at Non, all curled up and warm. I slipped one finger into her palm. Her little hand closed around it. I shut my eyes and sang softly, a nursery rhyme my mother sang to me when I was a child. Then I heard the screams. They were Fairuza's."

Edouard and Anna glance at each other.

"She was in the kitchen with Rudolph. He . . . my husband was violating her. The household came awake. I could hear doors opening along the corridors. I grabbed Rudolph's arm and pulled him off of her. I steeled myself, waiting for him to hit me. But he was too drunk. He collapsed on the floor. The servants stepped around him and waited to see what Fairuza would do. There was blood on her legs, bruises on her arms. She was hysterical."

"What did she do?"

"Nothing. We put her to bed in her room. We left him on the floor. The next morning Rudolph awoke and he found himself lying half-naked exactly where he fell. It was ten in the morning and already hot. He was late for work. I expected a terrible fight. But there was nothing. I crept downstairs after he was gone and wondered where Fairuza was; had she gotten up early and gone home to her family, or to the police?

"I had no idea who was in my own house.

"'Is she still here?' I asked Laksari.

"Laksari brought me into the parlor. Her voice was low. 'She is devastated, ma'am.' She spoke in Malay. 'She will not go to the police. It is bad luck for a woman to say she has been . . . she will leave the house tonight. After she has packed and said goodbye to the children.'

"'I should see her,' I said. 'I should pay her.'

"'She says she doesn't want to see anyone.'

"I should have heeded the danger in Laksari's words, but I was blinded by guilt. I spent the day worried about what would happen to Fairuza and what I would tell Norman about her absence. When Rudolph came home, Fairuza was still in the house. I found him reading. 'You raped a woman last night,' I said.

"'She's a servant.' He straightened the paper and raised it in front of his face. 'Let her disappear and find another house.'

"'She was a good nurse for the children! She's a human being.'

"'She's a goddamned native. Shut up for your own good.'

"I went into the kitchen. It was dark outside. The children were in bed. Laksari was bent over a bowl of rice and chicken. She stood when she saw me.

"'Please, sit down. Finish eating.' I pulled up a chair next to her. I was thinking my husband deserved to die. We sat for several minutes in the kitchen, and then my children started screaming. *My children.* The entire house awakened for the second night in a row.

"Laksari and I exchanged glances, and there was something in her eyes, something that still haunts me. We rushed up the stairs. Inside the nursery my children lay in their beds, writhing, their faces contorted, their bodies racked with convulsions. They were poisoned. No one thought to look for Fairuza. But by then she was gone.

"I held my children in my lap, praying for a miracle—if only he would let Non and Norman live. 'Please,' I whispered again and again. 'Please, God. Please.' My voice sounded feral, like a wild animal's. I rocked back and forth. Black vomit covered my nightgown. Non was still screaming but Norman's eyes were rolled back into his head. 'Norman. You'll be fine. Norman. Please.' I felt panic as Norman convulsed in my arms. 'Don't die! Norman, please don't die!' And then his three-year-old body stopped shaking. It went still. I held him in front of me and his face was pale. Non survived. But Norman was gone. Our first, our little boy. I hadn't spent enough time with him. Rudolph killed Norman. He raped our nanny so she killed our baby."

Edouard covers his mouth. Anna's eyes are red. It's a terrible story.

"I spent three months in bed. Then I got dressed and went outside to watch Non play. I sat on the swing and went back and forth, watching my daughter without seeing her at all. The house was haunted. Norman was everywhere. So now you know the kind of man my daughter is with. And he is angry."

Edouard has gone very still. I have to look close to see that he's even breathing. "We are going to get her away from that man," he says. "I have to leave now. I must make some calls."

"How? How are we going to get her now that Rudolph knows I want her?"

"I don't know." He rises. "I don't know."

Part 2

FECUNDITY

LINING UP OF THE ONE HUNDRED AND TWENTY-
FOUR AUSTRIAN ARCHDUKES AND ARCHDUCH-
ESSES FOR THE FIGHT OVER THE SUCCESSION HAS
BEGUN—BELIEF THAT THE TROUBLE, WHICH WILL
COME WITH THE DEATH OF THE KAISER FRANZ
JOSEF, IS CLOSE AT HAND—ONLY MUTUAL RESPECT
FOR THE AGING MONARCH KEEPS THE BITTER
COMBATANTS APART.

By Bernard Aston.

Special Correspondent.

Vienna, Oct. 1.

Secret strife rends the numerous Hapsburg clans. Only respect for the venerable Kaiser Franz Josef keeps it from open warfare. For twelve years past, but particularly since 1908, when Archduke Franz Ferdinand practically took command of the Empire, the one hundred and twenty-four archdukes and archduchesses have been divided sharply into two camps which hardly ever speak and seldom even meet one another. Of the seventy odd out of the one hundred and twenty-four who are old enough to have opinions, about twenty stand in with Archduke Franz Ferdinand: while about fifty are banded together to resist to the death the heir, his pretensions, and his morganatic wife. Members of the opposing groups no longer entertain one another, or even pay formal visits; they are at present engaged in severing their common property interest, and so universal is the feud that even the army is divided in mind as to what will be its duty when the great crash comes.

"The great crash" is involved in the decision for or against Franz Ferdinand, which is inevitable when Kaiser Franz Josef dies. It is a European issue. For with the Austrian Slavs gravitating to Russia, and the Austrian Germans gravitating to Germany, a civil war in Austria almost certainly means a general war in Europe. And at most within a few years, but possibly within a few months, Europe will be faced with this risk.

Chapter 13

WHAT'S DONE IS DONE

1913

*M*y opening of *Tristan and Isolde* in Berlin is stupendous. Every seat at the Deutsches Theater is filled. I should be happy, delirious even. I am thirty-seven years old today and my name is still flashing in lights. But it is a difficult anniversary for me. I am Aunt Marie's age when I took her husband; I am my mother's age when she died. My own daughter is no longer a little girl.

Edouard invites me to celebrate my birthday in an exquisite restaurant on the Kaiserdamm. I want to decline. After all, what am I celebrating? But Edouard is persistent.

"You glow," he says when I slip into the padded leather chair across from him.

I have been drinking since the final curtain. "That's what Evert used to say," I tell him, raising my glass and then finishing it. "He used to write poetry for me," I say, recalling Evert's voice, his eyes. I order another bottle and pour myself more wine. "He used to call me beautiful. Not Dutch beautiful, *exotically* beautiful," I clarify.

"Who is Evert?"

How many years have I known Edouard, and I've still never told him this story? "Someone I thought I knew," I say. "I met him after

I left the Walrus's school. I was living with my father's sister, Aunt Marie."

Edouard finishes his glass. "You told me about her years ago. Are you saying she wasn't too poor to take you in when you were a child?"

"Marie wasn't wealthy, but she wasn't impoverished either—my mother's sisters were misinformed. When I was expelled, Aunt Marie welcomed me into her home."

"After you left the Haanstra School?"

"Yes. I had no one else to turn to, no place to live. So I took a chance and went to The Hague. I had very little money. I deposited myself on her doorstep. If she had turned me away—"

"Did she contact your father?"

"No. We didn't speak of my father. She was an unusual woman. When I arrived at her door, the first thing she did was apologize to me. She realized who I was immediately and said she was so very sorry for missing my mother's funeral. She was lame in one leg, travel was difficult for her. She invited me to live in her home without any hesitation—I didn't tell her I had been expelled from the school and she never asked. The first evening I spent with her she took me to her church to light a candle for my mother."

"She was devout?"

"Very." I stare into my wineglass. "That's how I took advantage of her. After living with so many other girls my age I was bored at Aunt Marie's. There was nothing to read in her house except the Bible. And I had almost nothing to do except a few household chores. I had too much time to think. I became restless. The best part of my day was running errands. We were in a port city. When I went to town, I was unsupervised. I would linger on the boardwalk and watch navy boys who had just arrived. They looked so handsome in their uniforms."

Edouard says, "Some things never change."

He's right. "I desperately wanted to meet one of them. I wanted to dance with a boy in uniform at the Grand Hotel. It was a mythical place to me: all the shopkeepers' daughters gossiped about dances at the Grand. I would overhear them and feel such longing. I knew Aunt Marie would never let me attend an event as scandalous as a dance, so I asked her if she would take me to a particular church I had heard of in Scheveningen, knowing she couldn't and that she'd tell me to visit it on my own."

I can see my aunt now, her gray hair pulled back into a small, tight bun, her modest black dresses, her thin lips. "I'd like to visit the old church in Scheveningen," I told her. "I've heard there are ancient relics there. Do you think you could take me?"

"Oh, M'greet, I've visited many times!" she said, surprised and delighted at my interest in holy things. "It's such a struggle for me to take the tram. Why don't you go? The journey's so picturesque. It's an exquisite church."

"So I took the tram to Scheveningen the next day," I tell Edouard. "Ten minutes after I boarded I disembarked at Bains and walked along the beach until I arrived at the Grand. It was larger and more glamorous than any building I'd seen in my life, and I was dazzled by it. I stood in front of the hotel, hypnotized by its grandeur. Standing nearby were two sailors. Their uniforms were white against the sand."

"Evert?" says Edouard.

"Evert and his friend Zeeman." I remember it as if it were yesterday, not twenty years ago. The way they were laughing, full of their own adventures. I walked straight up to them without a moment's hesitation and introduced myself. I asked them where they were stationed.

"Java." Evert shaded his eyes so he could see me better. "Been there two years."

I learned of the Dutch East India Company's trading posts in school, and I knew that the government assumed control of Java after it ceased to exist. But I had never given much thought to the islands of the East Indies until Evert and Zeeman told me their stories—about Java's pristine beaches and temples as old as the ruins in Egypt. I was impressed to hear of their nights camped out under the stars and their days spent cutting their way through jungles. Zeeman read my emotions on my face. He said, "Don't let Evert's stories fool you. He may sleep on the ground with the rest of us in Java, but he comes from a very respectable family."

"I was born in Caminghastate," I said. "My father was a baron."

Zeeman narrowed his eyes as if he didn't believe me, but he was short and unattractive and I didn't care. Whereas Evert's gaze made me giddy. He was tall and blond and possessed what the Dutch call *Beïnvloeden*. Power, influence. "You glow," he told me, and I drank in his compliments, becoming intoxicated.

"I went to his hotel room," I tell Edouard. "I thought I'd never have to fear for my future again. The next evening, I lied to my aunt and said I was having dinner with the daughter of a shopkeeper, that I had found a friend. I took the tram and met Evert at the Grand. The hotel had a dance floor like a wide-open sea. We danced and I imagined I was Mrs. Margaretha Pallandt." I feel my cheeks warming, remembering how foolish I was. "Every Friday I lied to my aunt and went to meet Evert at the Grand."

Edouard orders us another bottle of wine.

"I will be with you forever," Evert promised me. He was so gracious and so eloquent: our evenings together were precisely as I imagined true love would be. Music from the dance floor drifting out onto the terrace. Stars like diamonds overhead. "In Java we'll have a house by the water," he whispered. "Then we'll start a family."

I tell Edouard about Evert Pallandt's plans. "He wanted a little girl and two little boys. He wanted to reproduce his own family, and he had grown up with two sisters."

"So what happened to this young prince?"

I finish my glass and pour myself another. How many glasses have I had? "Have I already told you that he was on leave? He was, and I waited for him to ask me to join him when he returned to duty."

"To Java?"

I nod. "To Java. I had created our life together in my mind. I had never been outside of The Netherlands but Java was as real to me then as you are right now. Eight days before his ship was to sail, Evert appeared at my aunt's house. It was a Monday. Aunt Marie was taken aback by my handsome visitor."

I remember how I rushed down the hall. "Evert!" I shook his hand as though we were old friends. "Aunt Marie," I said, "this is Evert Pallandt, the brother of one of the girls I used to teach with. What a wonderful surprise!" Of course, she believed my lie. She had faith in me.

"Everyone believed whatever I told them," I tell Edouard.

He doesn't look surprised. Neither did Evert. He introduced himself to my aunt and then said, "I have news for M'greet from my sister, who's fallen ill. May I take her for a walk to deliver the message? I will not keep her for long."

My aunt cast a nervous glance at her husband, as if he might object. He didn't. "I'm so sorry. Well, I don't see why not."

"I didn't realize your aunt was married," Edouard interrupts. "You didn't mention that."

"Yes. She was married. To a man named Taconis. They were a strange couple."

He was not at all religious. I couldn't imagine what had brought them together until my aunt confided in me that she wasn't born a cripple; she was once young and carefree.

"When they were married they were a good match, I suppose; her leg was crushed near the docks where Taconis worked. She was bringing him his lunch, when a cable snapped. That ill-fated day made her pious; it caused him to retreat into guilt."

"A sad story. Though now I have a more accurate vision of your circumstances. You were living with your aunt *and* her husband. What happened when Evert took you outside? Did your uncle reconsider giving you permission to walk alone with a young man?"

I recall the scene. How I'd teased Evert. "Are you nervous?" I'd asked. I was so confident in him.

"Nervous? No." He shoved his hands in his pockets. "I want to say," we paused under the shade of a maple, "that I love you, M'greet." He pulled his hand out of his pocket and placed something round and solid in my palm.

My heart beat so fast I could hear it in my ears. I closed my eyes, painting the moment behind my eyelids so I could see it always, even when I was asleep. Then I opened them and looked at what I was holding.

It was a locket containing a photo of the two of us.

"I don't understand," I whispered.

"It's a token," he said, "for when we're apart." He paused. "I told my parents about you." He wouldn't meet my eyes. "If I take you with me to Java, they'll disown me."

It's been twenty years and the memory still brings me to tears. I swirl the wine in my glass so I don't have to look at Edouard, who says quietly, "The boy was a fool."

I meet his eyes. "When he gave me that locket, I remembered something my mother told me one afternoon while we were sitting in the garden together. 'There are the girls you marry and there are the girls you enjoy but never take home.' I had given myself to Evert because I thought I was the girl he would marry. But I was wrong. I

was the other girl—the one no one wanted to take home." I dab my
eyes with my napkin.

"What did you say to him? You must have been deeply shocked
at the turn of events."

"I said nothing. I threw the locket in his face. Then I ran back
to Aunt Marie's house. I expected him to chase after me. When he
didn't, I cried for days. After a week passed I was *still* hoping he'd
change his mind. That he'd come back for me. That he would propose." I shake my head at my foolishness, my naivety.

"You were young," Edouard says. "You were gullible. You were
hoping he'd do what your father hadn't."

"Yes. Come back and rescue me." I hadn't learned anything. "The
date he was due to leave The Hague for Java came and went. I never
saw him again. But I loved him."

"You *think* you loved him," Edouard counters.

I cover my eyes. "I've never told anyone this story," I say.

"I'm honored you shared it with me."

We head down nearly deserted streets to my apartment and stumble
drunkenly across the doorway. "I think it's time I kissed you," Edouard
says. And I let him. I let him raise my chin and kiss my lips. Then I
let him kiss my arms, my neck, my breasts. And take me into the bedroom and make love to me, as if we've been apart for a hundred years.

In the morning, he finds me in the kitchen, already dressed. He is
wearing a half grin. He comes behind me, wraps his arms around my
waist. When he turns me around to kiss me, I can't meet his eyes.

"Oh, God, don't tell me you think it was a mistake," he jokes.

I don't say anything. My eyes grow hot with tears.

"Jesus Christ!" he says, stunned. He stares at me for a long moment. Then he kicks the counter. "I'm not one of your playthings! You want me and that makes you scared. You think I don't know you after all this time, Margaretha MacLeod?" He summons my old name, a judge pronouncing a verdict.

"Don't ever call me that again!" I say, appalled. "My name is Mata Hari. I'm not the person you think I am. You don't know me at all, Edouard Clunet!"

"Is that so? I don't know you at all? Tell me this—were those another girl's memories you shared with me last night?"

I am sickened with myself. "If you want to know me, call on my aunt Marie in The Hague."

"What are you talking about? Why would I do such a thing?"

"I didn't tell you everything last evening, Edouard. You don't know the true M'greet."

"Then tell me. Who is the true M'greet?"

We look across the counter at each other. All right. He wants to know what I really am? "After Evert left for Java, I took Taconis to the Grand."

"Aunt Marie's husband," he says quietly.

"Yes." He worked on the docks and was rugged, handsome. I led him onto the dance floor and he put his hand around my waist. I rested my head on his shoulder. "I wanted Evert to mean nothing to me. I wanted to extinguish him with new memories." A different face, the same room. I wrapped my shawl around Taconis's neck. I tugged on the silk and pulled him toward me. He bent forward to kiss my lips and I let him. We took a room at the Grand and I replaced Evert's memories there, too. Then we went back home for Aunt Marie's dinner.

"You were very young, M'greet—"

"I was old enough," I interrupt Edouard. "I knew *exactly* what I was doing."

Aunt Marie watched Taconis and me laughing together over stories in the newspaper, or telling each other jokes, and she would smile like a mother who is watching children she no longer understands. And this continued for months.

"On Aunt Marie's birthday, Taconis gave her a present. He'd secretly gifted me many pretty things, but he gave her a dowdy dressing gown and I was jealous. She whispered something in his ear that made him blush. As soon as we were alone, I wanted to know what she'd said."

I can still see the coldness in Taconis's eyes after I asked. "Be careful, M'greet," Taconis had warned me.

A rush of heat flowed into my face. "Why? Are you careful of my feelings?"

He caught my arm and held it tightly. "Don't think that telling her is going to assuage a guilty conscience. What's done is done. Don't hurt her more."

I found Aunt Marie in the parlor, knitting. I wanted to get out of the house, so I claimed I was going to church. To my surprise, she put down her needles and said she'd join me. I was trapped. We put on our coats and walked together to St. James in silence. We crossed the threshold of the church and side by side we entered the first pew and knelt together. For a fleeting moment I caught her watching me with an odd expression. Then she said, "It's never too late for redemption," and she started to pray.

St. James was chilly; I hugged the coat that Taconis had given me closer around myself. I watched Aunt Marie's lips move silently and I speculated on what she was praying for. I looked up at the crucifix, the gold and silver Christ.

"I want you out of my house."

For a moment, I thought he was talking to me.

"I want you to leave."

I turned, staring at her in shock. "Aunt Marie?"

"*Aunt?*" Her voice was high and bitter. "Is that what I am in my house?"

I hesitated, unsure what to call her. "Marie—"

"I treated you like a *daughter*. I allowed you into my house even after you disgraced yourself at that school." She shook her head. "I should have known, but I trusted in God." She laughed, a sound harsh and tainted. "God works only minor miracles today." She clicked her purse open, took out some money. "Pack your belongings when we return. I'll expect you'll be needing several suitcases to hoard all of the gifts my husband has bestowed on you. If he asks why you're leaving us, you'll do the first decent thing you've ever done and tell him you have relatives elsewhere who want you."

The next morning Taconis left at six for the docks. He suspected nothing and I told him nothing.

"By six that night I was gone," I tell Edouard. "My aunt cried while the coach drove me away. I saw her tearstained face through the curtains." And I felt the coins she had pressed into my hand. I could taste them in my mouth. "That's the kind of person I am. You deserve better."

"M'greet—"

"Don't say it!"

He leaves my apartment without another word.

Instead of dining with Edouard that evening I arrange to meet with Bowtie at the Grand Hotel Bellevue in Potsdamer Platz. He is in Berlin hoping to interview an actress, Henny Porten. After he rings, I dress in my most cheerful spring gown, white heels, and a white cashmere coat. When I arrive, he's standing in the garden behind the café. I'm prepared to accept his flattery and compliments, but he barely greets me.

"Hard day?" I ask, taken aback.

He hands me a newspaper clipping without a word. April 19, 1913:

MOTOR-CAR IN THE SEINE.
MME. ISADORA DUNCAN'S TWO CHILDREN DROWNED

I glance up, flustered, and he motions for me to read on.

> Yesterday, a little after three o'clock, the car carrying Isadora Duncan's nurse and her two children plunged into the river. Passersby tried to dive into the water but the car was beyond anybody's reach. On hearing the news, Isadora Duncan fainted. The children's chauffeur has been arrested for culpable homicide.

"This is horrible," I whisper. "Why are you showing me this?"

"I know you failed to get your daughter back," he says to me, and I feel the sentence like a blow. "I'm a reporter. It's my job to know these things. What I'm trying to say is, you still have hope—"

"I thought," I say, cutting him off, "that you wanted some gossip." I am fighting to keep my composure. "Ask me about *Tristan and Isolde*."

"Pay attention, Mata Hari. Isadora's children are *gone*. They are dead. Your daughter is still *alive*. If she's alive, there's still hope." He takes the clipping back and tucks it into his vest pocket. "We've known each other now for how many years?"

I can't be bothered with this. I don't know. Seven years? Eight? What does he know about my daughter and hope? I have done my best to let Non go. I have stretched my imagination to the limits fashioning a life for her in which she is happy living with her father.

A day after Anna's botched rescue attempt, a telegram arrived at Edouard's office. It said: *Your daughter is dead to you. Do not try again.* Still, I begged Edouard to send his men back, to arrange another attempt. I was nearly out of my mind with grief. I spent days drinking; I went to the south of France and visited every dance club on the Riviera. I took in the sights without seeing them, drank and danced all night, and then repeated it all the next day. Eventually, I accepted the truth. I had put Non in danger. The only way for me to keep my little girl safe was to leave her alone.

"I don't believe I know you at all," I say coldly. Then I go inside the hotel and straight to the bar. I order myself a gin and tonic.

The next morning, it's the first drink I have when I wake.

Chapter 14

A GOOD DEAL OF
MONEY TO BE MADE

$\mathcal{F}$or weeks and weeks I drink to excess, shop to excess, and rehearse until my dancers fall asleep on their feet. I do this until one day I'm so sick of my life I decide to stay in bed and never leave. I draw the curtains and lock the front door. I unplug the phone and turn off the lights. I stay like this for three days. On the third night I dream of the cavalry officer I spent time with during my first visit to Berlin: Alfred Kiepert.

When I awaken, I am curious: Is he still married? Is he still tall and handsome in his military uniform? Is he still enthralled with me?

I rise and dress. Beyond my desire to see Alfred blooms an awareness that the manager at the Deutsches must be frantic and wondering where I've been. Soon they'll be beating down my door. Then they'll send Edouard. Even though I miss him desperately, I don't want to see him. Not yet. We haven't spoken in a month.

I put on my favorite red gown and a black hat with a short veil that I bought in Paris. The dress feels snug: a consequence of indulging in alcohol. I put on one of the many bracelets that Alfred gifted to me—a gold dragon with beautiful ruby eyes. Then I go to the lobby and ask the concierge to look up his address.

He's still married, handsome, and wonderful.

"You don't ever change, do you, Mata Hari?"

I lay my cheek on his naked chest, wanting to believe that his compliment is true.

"What is it like not to have a care in the world?" he asks. "No demanding husband, no needy children?"

I laugh as if he's said something funny. But for a moment I find it difficult to speak. If I was honest, I'd tell him, "I have too many cares. That's why I'm with you." Instead, I make some silly remark about never being tethered down.

Later though, I can't shake off his question. I go back to my apartment and sit on my small balcony, watching the people go by. Men hurrying to the office. Women pushing prams with other women, laughing over something their babies did at home. So that's how I appear to all of these men. As a lighthearted diversion without any worries at all. A pretty dancing girl with a smile permanently etched on her face like one of the *apsaras* carved into the temples. I think of all the people in my life who know the truth, but all of them are gone. Even Edouard.

Six months somehow disappear and Edouard and I remain strangers. I know that he is still in Berlin, living in an apartment on Unter den Linden, because I see him one morning while I'm shopping for fruits and vegetables at the Bäckerei.

I catch his eye. He nods.

But we don't speak to each other.

The following Sunday as I am strolling with Alfred I spy Edouard window shopping with a woman. He doesn't see me and I watch them until they are out of sight. For days I can't get their image out of my head. How she gazed up at him with her big blue eyes, how his arm touched the pearl buttons on her waist as he gently steered her from shop to shop. I was the one who told him to leave, but my heart aches when Kiepert presents me with a pendant shaped like a dragon, because I realize I want to feel Edouard's arm on my waist, and instead I only feel gold, heavy around my neck.

I invite a German general named von Schilling into my dressing room after one of my shows. He is tall, strong, with a rigid jaw, graying blond hair, and sharp blue eyes. We drink together at the Hotel Fürstenhof and then go to his apartment, a five-bedroom suite in cream and gold. He has no pictures of any children, no wife. He professes to be an extremely practical man: children are too expensive, brass buttons are not cost effective in the military, war is good for the economy. But when he takes me to his bed a second time and gifts me diamond earrings for entertaining him, I understand how practical he is in actual fact.

We see each other for several weeks and I amass an impressive collection of jewelry: two bracelets, an anklet, a necklace, an emerald brooch. My conquest makes me feel giddy. I decide to telegram both Givenchy and Guimet to boast of my success in Berlin. Givenchy writes back at once, inviting me to an important soiree in Paris.

You have no idea how bored I am without you. All of Paris is black and gray for me now. Why don't you return and the two of us will attend the Marcell soiree? Think of the entrance we'd make! Maybe you're angry that I was photographed taking Edith Lane to the Rothschilds' château last week? Don't be, ma chérie. You know very well that your

Givenchy can't go anywhere alone. Come back and all of Paris will talk about us again. Then we can go south. Think of all the fun we'd have on the Riviera. Your Givenchy in a bathing costume. My exotic dancer in—well, preferably nothing at all.

I imagine myself with him. Perhaps I should catch a train, only for the weekend. But I have plans with Kiepert that I don't want to break. The Rothschilds and the Riviera will have to wait. I fold the letter into my collection. Guimet is more reserved. His brief response comes by telegram a week later. Givenchy, at least, is still mine.

"Come," Kiepert says. We are in my apartment, the bedsheets twisted around us like vines. He wants me to accompany him to Silesia where we are invited to watch the German army practice their maneuvers. It's tempting to join him. Especially when he drapes himself across the bed and watches me with his deep blue eyes. But I can't leave Berlin; Edouard may want to reconcile.

"I'm sorry," I say. "But you know I can't."

"If that lawyer needs to find you, he can send a telegram."

I look away and Kiepert goes alone. When he returns, a German reporter discovers him visiting my apartment. Berlin's leading paper runs a photo of us linked arm in arm. Underneath, the caption: SCANDAL! MATA HARI LURES GERMAN OFFICER FROM WIFE. The next day, another paper picks it up. By the end of the week we are everywhere. "The temptress Mata Hari and her innocent victim." Berlin was in love with me; now women hiss at me in the streets. I tell Kiepert that it is time for us to part.

"I rely on the papers to draw in audiences. If they focus on you—"

"I don't care what these papers print!" Kiepert rages.

He's so passionate that I can't make him see reason. It's as if he is on fire and using all of the oxygen in my apartment. I want him to leave, and I claim I must go to attend rehearsal. He says he will wait for me. Exasperated, I pretend to head to the theater and instead take a walk. It's winter and the streets are too cold. I spot a little shop selling stationery and confections. I go inside to browse and warm up. The items for sale are exquisite. I pick out a frosted pink card decorated with hearts and, unbidden, an image of Non comes to me. I wonder if she's an orchid among buttercups now? She's a young woman. When she was a child, Edouard's men reported that she had my dark hair and features; they said no one would fail to recognize her as mine.

I return to my apartment and Kiepert—thankfully—is gone.

I take out the pink card I purchased and write my lost daughter a letter that I know I'll never send. I tell her what I've been doing in Berlin these past six months without Edouard's guidance. I confide in her about Kiepert and von Schilling. Then I say what is truly important: I apologize for failing to save her. "If I had known what a disaster Anna's attempt would create and the danger it would put you in, I never would have undertaken it. One false move destroyed our future together. I have never forgiven Rousseau for hiring Anna and I never will. Never." I underline the last word. "He and I are no longer on speaking terms. How can I look at him when all he reminds me of is the way I failed you?"

We walk along the Ratsplatz beneath a vault of stars and I slip my hand inside my white muff. Von Schilling has taken me to Freiberg's Christmas Market. I am charmed by the dozens of stalls selling brightly colored toys, roasted almonds, and wooden trains. Everywhere, there are children laughing. Von Schilling doesn't notice; all he talks about is war.

"We don't want to be like the French, going into battle in red and blue."

I try to turn our conversation to something more pleasant as we walk arm in arm—the elaborate facades of the renaissance buildings, I say, are delightful—but von Schilling continues describing the importance of green uniforms over red. Music from the carousel dances into the night, German songs I've never heard before. The air is crisp and the Christmas stalls are decorated with fairy lights, selling bags of chocolate nuts and gingerbread cookies. *Edouard would love this,* I think. Out of habit and hope I glance around, but he isn't here. I notice straw shoes, hundreds of them, lined up on long tables and selling briskly.

"What are all those shoes for?" I ask.

"The *Pantoffeln?* Children find presents in them on Nikolaustag."

"In The Netherlands we put out *klompen*: wooden shoes."

"The Netherlands?"

I hesitate; that was careless. "Yes. My family—we settled there. After India."

The general nods and I focus on the Black Forest pines decorated with lights. I look at cinnamon cookies on red platters, spiced biscuits in the shape of snowmen. I ask von Schilling the names of everything: *Zimsterne, Spekulativs, Stube.*

"How many languages do you speak?" he asks me.

"If my Spanish was better, six."

"That's impressive, especially for a woman. You would enjoy meeting Elsbeth Schragmuller. She has a doctorate in political science. She's also a very unusual woman. She could develop your talents. There's a good deal of money to be made at this juncture in time. I will introduce you."

In the twinkling lights, our breaths are a pair of ghosts haunting the space between us. I let him slip his hand into my muff and I ask for some *Spekulativs.*

* * *

It's been eight months since I've last spoken to Edouard. I cancel my performances—I have no desire to dance. Still, he doesn't appear. I wait for him to bang down my door or at least phone and demand to know what I'm doing. I plan how I'll tell him that there's more money to be made in being a mistress than in dancing, but he doesn't materialize, doesn't even call. I consider sending him a telegram, something cryptic, forcing him to come to me. But what if it doesn't work? What if he's only interested in Pearl Buttons now? Immediately, I pick up the phone and dial. It rings several times before I'm put through.

"Von Schilling."

Six months after our stroll through the Ratsplatz, the general holds up a newspaper at the breakfast table. He reads the headline out loud. "Archduke Franz Ferdinand, heir to the Austro-Hungarian throne, assassinated in Sarajevo." There's a new light in his eyes. He is excited about this. "The Austro-Hungarians will blame the Serbs," he predicts.

"How terrible." I recall the archduke's marriage and the outrage it caused—the heir to the Hapsburg throne marrying a lady-in-waiting! It wasn't as if she had no royal blood at all, but all of Europe was consumed by the scandal. I calculate the dates; their marriage lasted fourteen years. How sad to think of it ending in such tragedy. "Who do you think will raise their children, now that they're gone?" I muse.

The general stares at me. "What does it matter?" He folds the newspaper and rises from the table. "There's going to be war, Mata Hari. Focus on what is important."

After this, he is relentless in mentioning Elsbeth Schragmuller. To appease him, I agree to go to the Palasthotel to meet with her. I dress in red, from my long silk skirt to my wide-brimmed hat. Schragmuller is a short woman; when she recognizes me, she marches across the lobby, and despite her green skirt and simple blouse, she moves like a man, stomping across the marble floor without any grace whatsoever. I feel embarrassed for her and suggest we walk outside, where there will be fewer spectators.

"You are a dancer," she says.

"Yes. Eastern dance."

"I've always wanted to visit Java," she discloses, holding my gaze.

Java, not India. I understand by her tone that Elsbeth Schragmuller is telling me she knows my story is false and I put myself on guard. "Is that so? Why?"

"I'm fascinated by Hinduism," she says. "Such an extraordinary religion. Are you Hindu?" she asks.

Do I believe that life is a cycle of birth, death, and rebirth, governed by Karma? "I don't know," I say, unwilling to share myself with her. I do believe in Karma. It's a Sanskrit word that literally means action. Every action will have an equal reaction. It can happen immediately or at some time in the future. Good actions will create good reactions. Bad actions will bring bad consequences.

"You've worn the mask for so long you're not sure anymore." Without giving me a chance to respond, she offers, "I'd like to visit Prambanan. Though I doubt I will." She glances up at me. "The world is changing, Mata Hari."

"How so?" I decide I will let her do the majority of the talking.

"Look around." She indicates the men and women leisurely strolling in the gardens. "Are any of these people preparing for the future? Or are they taking a pleasant stroll through life, spending what they earn, living for today, worrying nothing for tomorrow?"

I look at her. "What should they be doing, in your opinion?"

"Peace never lasts, Margaretha."

Her use of my real name startles me.

"Anyone who reads history knows this. Yet these people act as if the good times are going to last forever. They should be reading. Talking about things that matter."

I'm curious. "How do you know they aren't? This is only one activity in their day."

"Look." She gestures to a group of men sitting on a bench, talking excitedly. A newspaper is spread out over the lap of the man in the middle. "Horse races," she says, and I hear the disgust in her voice, the disdain.

"But you're preparing," I say cautiously. She has been talking to me about guns, planes, and ships.

"Of course."

We walk and talk together for some time, although what von Schilling imagines she can teach me I cannot conceive. She enjoys talking about books—especially *The Riddle of the Sands*. But in the main she talks about this phantom war, while I would rather discuss just about anything else. When I relay her preferred topic to von Schilling, he scolds me.

"What else is more pressing? Mata Hari, when Austria-Hungary declares war on Serbia, Russia will come to Serbia's aid. Then Germany, as an ally of Austria, must declare war on Russia."

How can the actions of one crazy man be so significant? I am sure he is mistaken, but von Schilling misinterprets my silence.

"I understand. The implications are sobering. This hasn't been made public yet. Tomorrow." He reaches out and pulls me to his chest. "We have until tomorrow to enjoy ourselves."

He takes me into his bedroom. A chilled bottle of wine is waiting. We drink and he toasts to the future of Germany.

*   *   *

The next morning the news is released as promised. Austria-Hungary will have Germany's help if war is declared. Von Schilling looks alive in a way I've never seen before. But he is gone from morning until night. I call Alfred, deciding that I will risk women hissing at me, yet I don't hear back from him. After a week, a phone call explains why. His family is offering me three hundred thousand marks never to call on him again. The choice is so simple I don't even think twice. The next evening I take a train to the Potsdamer Platz, and at the Grand Hotel Bellevue, I take tea with the Kiepert family attorney.

We sit across from each other in the pastel-colored room with its pretty lace curtains and finely dressed women. I can hear mothers gently scolding their children and women talking to each other about sewing. A grandmother is bouncing a baby girl on her lap.

"The money?" I say.

The old man pushes a fat envelope across the table at me. I tuck it into my purse. "I'm delighted we could come to such a satisfactory arrangement."

"My clients are far less delighted," he says, but his voice isn't stern. He's staring at me, trying to divine the secret of my power over Alfred.

"I'm sorry to hear that. But they can rest assured they will never see me again."

"How will you do it?" he asks. "Force their boy to leave you alone?"

"I'll let him see me with someone else."

"He might not be deterred."

"Don't tell me," I lean forward and whisper in his ear, "that you wouldn't stop chasing a woman on the arm of a crown prince?"

The attorney is impressed. "Is that true?"

I shrug—it could be.

Back at my own apartment, Irving Berlin is playing. I pour myself a drink and count out three hundred thousand marks.

I answer a knock on my door, and it's Edouard. He doesn't say a word as he moves past me and looks through my window at the people singing in the streets, and the military officers hanging posters urging men to join the army. "We need to leave Berlin and go back to France. Pack your things."

Even though I have longed to see him, I am surprised at how angry I feel. How many months has he ignored me? "Don't be ridiculous. I plan to perform—"

"The theaters are going to be closed, M'greet. There is going to be a *war*. Do you understand? Dangerous things are happening—"

"Do what you like. I'm not leaving Berlin."

"*Jesus*. You don't know what you're saying, Margaretha."

"Mata Hari," I correct him. I look out the window. "It doesn't matter where we go, Edouard. Germany or France—everyone will be at war. That's what General von Schilling says." I'm exaggerating. He hasn't said a word about France going to war. The idea is preposterous and I wait for him to contradict me.

Instead, his eyes meet mine. "This is serious. We have to go. I'm leaving as soon as possible."

I don't want Edouard to leave me alone in Berlin. I look out the window and gesture to the streets below. "It will only last a few weeks."

"Are you coming with me or no? This isn't the time for nursing feelings."

"No. I'm staying in Berlin."

He walks out, slamming the door behind him.

*   *   *

During the days, I hear cheering from the streets. I see women waving red and black flags. The men in their starched uniforms look young and excited. The general arrives to collect me and we are escorted into a long, black convertible. The car rolls along the street and the people begin chanting the general's name, blowing kisses to him and even to me. Kiepert has been forgotten. Berlin loves me again. I wave back, caught up in the euphoria. There is elation in the air, as if spring has descended and everyone is in love.

In August, Germany declares war on Russia and France. The news comes to us over the radio in the general's apartment. For a moment I feel as if I can't breathe. I think of Edouard hearing the news in Paris. I think of Non and wonder if she'll be safe in Amsterdam. Russia *and* France. The Germans want to battle them both. I express my horror to the general, who's so still behind his newspaper that at first I believe he isn't listening.

"Yes, a two-front war," he says simply. He lowers the paper. "That's been von Schlieffen's plan all along."

Alfred von Schlieffen, the chief of staff of the German army.

"A man named Günther Burstyn, an engineer, makes this possible." The way the general says this drowns out the sound of everything else around us, even the somber-voiced man on the radio. "He's invented an armored vehicle with a powerful gun. It will change war."

"How can a vehicle do that, change war?" It sounds preposterous.

"They're calling it a tank."

He pours me more coffee, but I'm not warmed by it. "A tank?"

"It can destroy anything in its path. Imagine that."

He's smiling and I'm glad he doesn't have a wife or children.

*   *   *

"What do you mean there isn't bread? There was bread last week."

This is the fifth shop we've come to this morning, and in each one the story is the same. An abundance of nothing.

"I want an explanation," von Schilling tells the baker after the man informs us there is no bread.

The man shrugs. "I'm sorry, general. The farmers are on strike."

"And how long is this situation"—he means the bread—"going to last?"

"As long as the strike does, general."

Outside, von Schilling is red in the face. I've never seen him truly angry. I wonder what he'll do. "Do you know how many strikes there have been in the last year?"

I don't bother to guess because I know he'll tell me.

"A hundred. Farmers, drivers, butchers—everyone thinks they have rights! Tell me, what rights do men think they have in war?"

I realize that I like him less and less each day. Maybe it's the war. Or maybe this is who he's been all along.

"We're going to the Hotel Adlon," he says.

In the chandeliered dining room of Adlon, of course, there's bread, and a great many other things as well. We're seated at the best table, and while women go from shop to shop outside, looking for meat and bread and milk, all around us are the merry sounds of wealthy people eating. Nothing is in short supply here. The men are wearing only the finest coats. The women's shoulders are trimmed in fur. I'm underdressed for the occasion, but what does it matter? If there are food shortages in Berlin, on the same morning the kaiser has firmly declared God to be on the side of the Germans, then what's happening in The Netherlands? Does Non have enough to eat? Is Rudolph providing for her?

"You're distant," the general says.

I don't disagree. I don't smile prettily or try to change the subject. "The shortages worry me."

"You'll never want for anything," he promises.

I want to believe him, but I can't. I don't.

"You know that I'll be leaving soon," he says.

"Yes." I've been expecting it.

"Then enjoy this meal. It may be our last together."

The general takes my hands in his and kisses them. "I want you to take care of yourself." He hands me a folded piece of paper and a check. I see the money first and he explains. "For your expenses while I'm gone."

For a hard man, he's been very, very generous to me. I glance at the paper and see Elsbeth Schragmuller's address.

"Those who train here will never be acknowledged," he says quietly. "But they will be paid great sums of money for their talents."

I tuck the piece of paper into my purse. What sort of spy does he believe I'd make? The entire world knows my name and recognizes my face! I ride with him to the train station in Friedrichstrasse, then stand on the platform and wave him farewell. He has assured me that this war will only last a month, but there are wives standing next to me with their children, weeping into their handkerchiefs.

A week passes, then another, and the theaters are shut down. Newspapers begin printing stories about spies. The kind of articles Bowtie specialized in are gone; there are no pretty photos of actresses and bracing shots of sports players. Everything is BEWARE OF YOUR NEIGHBOR and TWO MEN CAUGHT SPYING ON ARMY MANEUVERS IN BERLIN.

I notice a copy of the *Times of London*, and pick it up. ATROCITIES IN BELGIUM AND OUTRAGES ON WOMEN AND NON-COMBATANTS catches my eye. I read the article:

> The Press Bureau issued yesterday afternoon a translation of the second report of the Belgian Commission of Inquiry on the Violation of the Rights of Nations and of the Laws and Customs of War. The report, which was communicated by the Belgian Legation on September 11, is as follows:—

> Antwerp, August 31, 1914.
> To Monsieur Carton De Wiart,
> Minister of Justice.

> Sir,
> The Commission of Inquiry have the honour to make the following report on acts of which the town of Louvain, the neighbourhood, and the district of Malines have been the scene:—
> The German army entered Louvain on Wednesday, August 19, after having burnt down the villages through which it had passed.
> As soon as they had entered the town of Louvain the Germans requisitioned food and lodging for their troops. They went to all the banks of the town and took possession of the cash in hand. German soldiers burst open the doors of houses which had been abandoned by their inhabitants, pillaged them, and committed other excesses.

The German authorities took as hostages the Mayor of the City, Senator Van der Kelen, the Vice-Rector of the Catholic University, and the Senior Priest of the city, besides certain magistrates and aldermen. All the weapons possessed by the inhabitants, even fencing swords, had already been given up to the municipal authorities, and placed by them in the Church of Saint Pierre.

In a neighbouring village, Corbeck-Loo, on Wednesday, August 19, a young woman, aged 22, whose husband was with the army, and some of her relations were surprised by a band of German soldiers. The persons who were with her were locked up in a deserted house, while she herself was raped by five soldiers successively.

In the same village, on Thursday, August 20, German soldiers fetched from their house a young girl, about 16 years old, and her parents. They conducted them to a small deserted country house, and while some of them held back the father and mother, others entered the house, and, finding the cellar open, forced the girl to drink. They then brought her on to the lawn in front of the house, and raped her successively. Finally they stabbed her in the breast with their bayonets. When this young girl had been abandoned by them after these abominable deeds, she was brought back to her parents' house, and the following day, in view of the gravity of her condition, she received Extreme Unction from the parish priest, and was taken to the hospital of Louvain, as her life was despaired of.

I can't read any more. I put the paper down; it is a viper in my hand.

The German response is swift:

> As representatives of German Science and Art, we
> hereby protest to the civilized world against the lies and
> calumnies with which our enemies are endeavoring to
> stain the honor of Germany in her hard struggle for
> existence—in a struggle that has been forced on her.
>
> The iron mouth of events has proved the untruth of
> the fictitious German defeats; consequently misrepre-
> sentation and calumny are all the more eagerly at work.
> As heralds of truth we raise our voices against these.
>
> *It is not true* that Germany is guilty of having caused
> this war. Neither the people, the Government, nor the
> Kaiser wanted war. Germany did her utmost to prevent
> it; for this assertion the world has documental proof.
> Often enough during the twenty-six years of his reign
> has Wilhelm II shown himself to be the upholder of
> peace, and often enough has this fact been acknowledged
> by our opponents. Nay, even the Kaiser, whom they now
> dare to call an Attila, has been ridiculed by them for
> years, because of his steadfast endeavors to maintain
> universal peace. Not till a numerical superiority which
> has been lying in wait on the frontiers assailed us did the
> whole nation rise to a man.
>
> *It is not true* that we trespassed in neutral Belgium. It
> has been proved that France and England had resolved
> on such a trespass, and it has likewise been proved that
> Belgium had agreed to their doing so. It would have
> been suicide on our part not to have preempted this.
>
> *It is not true* that the life and property of a single Bel-
> gian citizen was injured by our soldiers without the bit-

terest self-defense having made it necessary; for again
and again, notwithstanding repeated threats, the citizens
lay in ambush, shooting at the troops out of the houses,
mutilating the wounded, and murdering in cold blood
the medical men while they were doing their Samaritan
work. There can be no baser abuse than the suppression
of these crimes with the view of letting the Germans
appear to be criminals, only for having justly punished
these assassins for their wicked deeds.

It is not true that our troops treated Louvain brutally.
Furious inhabitants having treacherously fallen upon
them in their quarters, our troops with aching hearts
were obliged to fire a part of the town as a punishment.
The greatest part of Louvain has been preserved. The
famous Town Hall stands quite intact; for at great self-
sacrifice our soldiers saved it from destruction by the
flames. Every German would of course greatly regret if
in the course of this terrible war any works of art should
already have been destroyed or be destroyed at some
future time, but inasmuch as in our great love for art we
cannot be surpassed by any other nation, in the same
degree we must decidedly refuse to buy a German defeat
at the cost of saving a work of art.

It is not true that our warfare pays no respect to international laws. It knows no indisciplined cruelty. But in
the east the earth is saturated with the blood of women
and children unmercifully butchered by the wild Russian troops, and in the west dumdum bullets mutilate the
breasts of our soldiers. Those who have allied themselves
with Russians and Serbians, and present such a shameful
scene to the world as that of inciting Mongolians and

negroes against the white race, have no right whatever
to call themselves upholders of civilization.

It is not true that the combat against our so-called
militarism is not a combat against our civilization, as our
enemies hypocritically pretend it is. Were it not for German militarism, German civilization would long since
have been extirpated. For its protection it arose in a land
which for centuries had been plagued by bands of rob-
bers as no other land had been. The German Army and
the German people are one and today this consciousness
fraternizes 70,000,000 Germans, all ranks, positions,
and parties being one.

We cannot wrest the poisonous weapon—the lie—out
of the hands of our enemies. All we can do is to proclaim
to all the world that our enemies are giving false witness
against us. You, who know us, who with us have protected the most holy possessions of man, we call to you:

Have faith in us! Believe, that we shall carry on this
war to the end as a civilized nation, to whom the legacy
of a Goethe, a Beethoven, and a Kant is just as sacred as
its own hearths and homes.

For this we pledge you our names and our honor.

I am amazed to see ninety-three signatures, including many men
I've met socially. There are artists, physicians, and Nobel Prize Lau-
reates. What is truth and what is propaganda?

Berlin is miserable. It is constant rain and watching miserable
women wandering the streets with their silent children. I have no
lovers. I miss Edouard. I no longer trust Germany. I don't know what

to believe when I read the papers. I want to go home. I phone the concierge and tell him to book the next train ticket to Paris.

"The next train to Paris departs in two weeks," he says.

"There are no tickets today at all?" I hear myself sounding desperate.

"Indeed, there are tickets to be had. For a price. Everyone wants to leave Berlin."

"I don't care about the price. Please buy me one."

He telephones back an hour later. "Is tomorrow acceptable, Fraulein Mata Hari?"

There are massive crowds at the station. Infants have been taken out of their prams and the buggies are being used to carry luggage and food. No one is standing still. Even the children look afraid. I push my way to the front and board the train. It seems as though there are no young men at all in Berlin, while the older gentlemen are buried in their newspapers. I read the headlines as I move along: HUGE CROWDS CHEER AT THEIR MAJESTIES' PALACE; "WAR WON'T LAST" TOP GENERAL SAYS. Is any of this true?

The war might not last, but as the train pulls out of the station and I look at Berlin, I see how it has already changed her. Streets once filled with people are practically empty. I see a boy kicking a can without any companions. With so many fathers at war, I've heard children are being sent to work to earn money. Food continues to be scarce.

We haven't been traveling for more than ten minutes before the train comes to a complete stop. Passengers exchange glances, concerned. Uniformed men enter the car and begin searching through our bags.

"Stand," I'm instructed. The iron in the soldier's voice makes me jump.

"How dare you speak to me in that—"

"Do it now!"

If von Schilling knew the way this underling was treating me, he'd have this boy discharged. I protest, but the other passengers have gone silent. Soldiers are rifling through several bags, and the one who ordered me to stand has opened my largest case, the one containing all of my furs.

"Are you planning to sell these to make a profit?" he demands.

"Don't be absurd! Surely you recognize me. I wear them—"

I have addressed him in German yet he replies, "Sit down!"

The other passengers remain mute as he gathers up all of my furs, worth at least ten thousand marks. Soldiers are stealing from other passengers as well. No one says a word. What can we do? Nothing. They take what they want and then are gone.

Chapter 15

I WANT TO BE HOME

I'm so angry my hands are actually shaking. I open my purse and take out von Schilling's note. "In case you run into difficulties," he had said. Along with Elsbeth Schragmuller's address there are two dozen names located in half a dozen countries. There is no one listed in Paris, but at the bottom, in von Schilling's perfect script, are the words "Consul Karl Cramer," and an address in Amsterdam. I decide to disembark in Amsterdam.

As soon as the train pulls into the Centraal, I locate my bags and tip a boy to carry them to the nearest cab. I'm still so filled with rage that we're already driving before I realize how full the city is. The Netherlands has refused to enter the war, and it's strange to see young men again. But it's not just the men that make the city seem busy. I stare out the window. It's not my imagination. There are lines outside of most of the shops.

"What's happening?" I ask. "Is today a holiday?"

The driver frowns. "What do you mean, ma'am?"

"Why are there so many people waiting in lines?" I say impatiently.

"The war," he replies, as if it should be obvious. "The boys who don't want to fight have come over. There are thousands of French and Germans here now, and all of them are wanting food and clothes. Where do they think it's going to come from with all these blockades?"

"Food is difficult, then?"

"If you don't mind my asking, where have you been?"

His question stings. "Away."

"People are starving here, ma'am."

I stare out the window. There are women huddled with their children inside blankets, standing on the roads with their hands out in front of them. *Where have I been?* In hotels, in men's suites, in restaurants where the crystal is still polished daily. I think about my furs and feel disgusted. How dare those men take anything from civilians in times like these. . . .

The driver turns down a narrow street and the car shakes over the cobbled road. I hold on to the seat in front of me. He stops in front of a plain gray building and I compare the address with the one in von Schilling's note. "This the place?" the driver asks.

"Yes. If you'll please wait—"

"That will be an extra charge."

"I understand." I go inside. It's an office. Busy-looking men, some in uniform and others in suits, rush about. The woman who greets me asks what my business is at the German Consulate. I try not to look surprised; this non-descript building is a consulate?

"I'm here to see Consul Karl Cramer. Immediately."

She frowns at me over her desk. "You wish to see the consul?"

"Yes. I do."

"What is your business?"

"I was sent to him by General von Schilling. He'll understand."

She hesitates, then stands and disappears through a doorway. A minute later she returns and asks me to follow her down the hall.

The interior of the building is as plain as the outside, as if they are trying to hide. We come to a wooden door and the woman knocks, even though the door is slightly ajar, and I can see a balding man sitting behind his desk. He calls for me to be shown in. When I enter, she shuts the door behind me.

Consul Cramer raises his brows. "Can I help you?"

"Yes." I take a seat in front of his desk. "My name is Mata Hari. Perhaps you've heard of me."

He puts down the papers in his hands. I have his full attention now. "The dancer?"

"Yes."

His eyes wander from my face to my body, imagining what I look like beneath my black dress. Perhaps he's been to one of my shows. If he has, he doesn't admit to it. "I was told von Schilling sent you," he says.

"Yes. He gave me a list of names where I might find help if I should need it. This morning, German soldiers barged onto my train in Berlin and stole my furs. They treated me like an animal."

"I'm very sorry to hear that."

"Thank you, but I want more than an apology. I want my property returned, and von Schilling believes you're the man to make that happen."

"How do you know the general?"

I lean toward him. "Didn't I mention that General von Schilling and I are very good friends, Karl?"

His eyes light up at the implication.

"Will you help me?" I ask.

He sighs. "Mata Hari, what you are—"

"I want what is mine."

"Perhaps we can discuss this over dinner. Shall I make reservations at Hotel Krasnapolsky?"

It's the best hotel in Amsterdam. But I sit back, refusing to be deterred. "I'm on my way to Paris. I want to be home."

"Paris is no place to call home right now, Mata Hari."

I'm not in the mood for a lecture. "Can you or can you not return my furs to me?"

"You claim they were confiscated in Berlin. Yet we are sitting in Amsterdam. The appropriate place to register a complaint would be in Berlin."

These Germans are infuriating! "Von Schilling said—"

"Yes." He holds up his hand. "I understand."

"They were taken from me by your men! *Stolen!*"

He doesn't look in the least bit surprised.

"If you can't return them, then I will accept compensation."

He has the gall to look amused. Then he says, "The consulate does not reimburse travelers for lost clothing. This applies in times of peace as well as war."

"This is outrageous. I have given so much to Berlin. So much! And in return I am robbed of thirty thousand marks." It's the first number that comes to my mind.

The consul rubs his temple with his fingers. Perhaps I'm not the first person to complain about this today. "Is that the market value of your confiscated property?"

"That is a low estimate. I never travel lightly."

"Perhaps, then, we can come to a compromise."

"I'm listening."

"I will give you a check. Twenty thousand marks."

I open my mouth to protest but he shakes his head.

"I am doing you a favor, fraulein. For von Schilling. I will inform my superiors that you have agreed to keep your ears and eyes open on behalf of Germany. They won't pay you for lost goods. Are we agreed?"

We are.

"Mata Hari," he says as I am gathering myself to leave. "I suggest that the next time you travel it not be by train." He pauses, organizes his thoughts. "I will arrange your passage on the next available ship to France. If you are amenable."

I can't believe what I'm hearing. "This type of thievery might happen again?"

He spreads his hands. "This is war, Mata Hari."

We watch each other. "Please book my passage," I say.

For three days in a row I wait outside of her school without seeing her. Is she ill? Has he moved her? Did something else happen? Girls walk down the steps of the schoolhouse arm in arm, chatting with each other, making plans. I search their smiling faces, and none of them look like Non. But on the fourth day, when I see a solemn dark-haired girl walking alone, I know that it's her. All of the other girls are carefree; there's a misery in this young girl's face that makes her look older than her years.

My heart beats too quickly. I could call to her, reveal myself. But what would I say? And where would I go to spirit her away? I'm still waiting for my own passage to France. I have no papers for my daughter. The old woman waiting for her across the street would scream for help. And then what? Would we run? Would Non want to leave with me?

A thousand scenarios pass through my head. In the end, I simply watch her while she walks away, committing every detail of my daughter to memory. The way her hair falls in dark curls down her back, her slender waist, her blue school uniform. I drink her in until she disappears from sight.

*   *   *

A newspaper has been delivered and waits outside my room at the hotel where I'm staying until I can sail for Paris. The lead story describes a French cavalry unit dressed in blue feathers, red caps, and newly polished brass buckles. As they rode their horses into battle they mocked the British soldiers they were meant to aid. "Cowards!" they yelled. "You English are not fighters. We will show you how it is done." Two hundred Frenchmen armed with lances charged into machine-gun fire. "Not one of them asked us what the Germans were fighting with," an English soldier is quoted. "And not one of them came back."

I think of von Schilling. He would say, "This is why Deutschland will prevail." And I feel a true jolt of fear. What if France doesn't prevail? What will happen to us? What will happen to The Netherlands?

I go downstairs and gather a copy of every newspaper in the lobby, then read them from front to back in my room. Milk shortages in Paris. Not enough petrol in the south of France. Then a small article buried deep in *Le Figaro* about a man from Normandy caught with invisible inks and working for the Germans. What if I could use invisible ink to communicate with Non? Where would I find such a thing? And how would she know how to decipher it?

I phone the consulate and learn my ship won't leave for Paris for one more week. I will spend every afternoon outside the yellow schoolhouse, secretly watching Non.

I am eager to leave Amsterdam for Paris. I will apologize to Edouard. I will tell him whatever he wants to hear. That he was right, that he's always been right, that it was foolish of me to insist on staying in Germany. Then I will ask him to renew his efforts to bring Non home to me, whatever the cost. I want him to come with us to New York. This is where we will finally find refuge. I'm certain of this after reading an article about the generosity of the Americans:

GIVES $18,000 CHECK TO HELP ARMENIANS

Stranger First Decided on $5,000 but Tale of Suffering Caused Him to Increase Amount.

A well-dressed but unassuming man walked modestly into the office of the American Committee for Armenian and Syrian Relief, 708 Fifth Avenue, Manhattan, the other day, and inquired for the secretary. He named a Middle West State as his home, and said he had been thinking about making a contribution on "Armenian Sunday," October 22, to help the Armenian refugees in Turkey, but had concluded, from what he had read in the newspapers, that money is badly needed now.

"I can give $5,000." He said, "but I would like to hear something about the facts."

The assistant secretary of the committee, Walter Mallory, summarized the situation in accordance with information which had been received in recent letters and cablegrams. One of the facts stated by Mr. Mallory is that there are about a million Armenian and Syrian Christian refugees in Turkey and Persia, largely women and children, nearly all of whom are destitute. Deported from their homes by Turkish soldiers, many thousands are suffering for lack of the bare necessities of life. Then he began to tell of sacrifices which contributors to the relief fund had made.

The visitor listened to the story of a minister in Ohio who had written that from a salary of $80 a month his wife and himself would contribute $40 a month for six months.

"Well," said the stranger, "if they can make a sacrifice like that I think I can give $10,000."

On the way to the office of Charles R. Crane, the treasurer, the donor was told of an old woman who wrote she had no money, but would give her old paisley shawl—an heirloom which had been in the family many years and had once been her mother's. He listened also to a letter from the mother of a little girl, 4 years old, who had earned 2 cents sweeping the sidewalk. She wanted to give 1 cent to the Belgian babies and the other to the starving Armenians.

"If other people are willing to give up things," commented the stranger, "I ought to be willing to do the same. I think that every one ought to help save this old Christian race. I believe I can give $15,000."

Before he entered the treasurer's office the stranger seemed to make some mental calculations and when he wrote out his check it read $18,000.00. "Under no circumstances is my name to be made public," said the stranger, so the treasurer, to keep faith, personally deposited the check in the bank.

When I board the *Zeelandia*, I am one of four hundred people. The other passengers walking the gangplank with me seem reserved. Before the war we all would have greeted each other warmly, maybe invited each other to drinks after dinner. But everyone is suspicious now: of traitors, of enemies, of anyone with more. I can sense the other passengers watching me warily. A woman by herself, no husband or even children in tow. What must I look like to them? A widow maybe. The war has certainly made enough of them.

On board, I keep to myself. No one trusts a woman alone. If I speak with a married man, it's because I'm interested in seducing him. If I chat with a woman, she will want to know about my children. No one is safe, so I sit in my room or on the hard metal chairs of the windy deck and read the papers. It's gloomy reading. How many soldiers have died in this ridiculous war? How many women and children have starved? I keep reading and reading, but there's never any answer.

When the ship sails into port, I'm the first one down the gangplank. I don't want to see the bittersweet reunions or the tears of the women returning, widowed, to their mothers' homes. At dockside, I hail a cab. A freezing bitter wind is blowing and I curse the German soldiers who seized my furs. As we drive down Rue Danton I am shocked: Paris has become a stranger to me. Planes fly overhead, making low, ominous sweeps. I look out the car window and the streets are desolate. The cafés and shops are empty. I see women gathered around papers nailed to posts. Some of them are doubled over, wailing.

"What are they reading?" I ask the driver.

"Names. Those who are crying have sons and husbands who aren't coming home."

He passes Boulevard Voltaire. I'm unnerved by the silence of the thoroughfare, by all of the white flowers hung over closed doors. We stop at the entrance to the Grand Hotel. I hand him a generous tip and he carts my remaining luggage, fifteen pieces, into a glittering foyer. Inside the hotel the war doesn't exist. I allow myself to imagine that Edouard is just around the corner, coming to tell me our rooms are ready. I act lighthearted as I check in and am given a suite on the second floor. But as I stand alone, gazing out over Paris, my heart aches. There's a radio in my room and I turn it on. It's all news of the war. I should eat, but I want to find Edouard.

I know I could call, but I want to hear his voice. I want to see his face.

I walk the three blocks from my hotel to his office. In the streets, I see the same patterns again and again on women's dresses. They've been made from sacks. Flour companies have taken to embroidering pretty patterns on their cotton bags so women can turn them into clothes when they are empty. I haven't purchased a new dress in months, but now I feel wealthy.

I reach Edouard's office and knock. His secretary answers.

"Mata Hari." She makes no move to let me inside. "I don't believe Monsieur Clunet will want to see you," she says.

"That is not your decision to make," I reply, affronted. I am ready to say more when she shocks me into silence.

"He is married, madam. He's a respectable man now and does not require your services anymore."

She shuts the door and for several moments I can't breathe. I press my back against the door to keep from sliding to the pavement. Married? It has to be the blonde from Berlin. Pearl Buttons. The thought of them together, living in a house, talking about the war over coffee at breakfast, makes me physically ill.

I return directly to the Grand Hotel. I order dinner in bed. I stay in my blue silk robe all the following day. When I hear the bellboy leaving newspapers outside my door, I don't rise to fetch them. I don't even turn on the radio for news. I don't care what's happening anymore. I stay in bed for days.

After a week, I feel the strength to get up and get dressed.

I go downstairs, to the ivory-colored foyer.

There is no war or heartache in the Grand. In one of the back rooms is a piano, a black Steinway. A young man is playing and immediately I'm reminded of Evert. The double-breasted uniform decorated with medals. His high cheekbones and blue sapphire eyes. "You're a beautiful pianist," I say.

"Thank you."

"Russian?" I ask.

"Is my French that bad?"

"No, I have a good ear." I motion for him to slide down the bench; then I sit next to him and pick up his tune. We play together.

"You are Mata Hari."

For some reason, I'm disappointed. "Yes."

"Vadime de Massloff," he introduces himself. "An army captain."

"What are you doing in Paris?"

"I have two weeks off before I return."

"I didn't realize holidays were allowed in the middle of a war," I say, flirting. We keep playing together, our fingers brushing on the ivory keys.

"Depends on how long you've been fighting." He sounds a thousand years old. I'm guessing he's twenty-three or twenty-four. Just a few years older than Norman would have been, if he had survived.

"Where did you learn to play?" he asks.

In Leeuwarden. "Around." I stop playing. "Would you like to take a walk with me?"

He nearly leaps out of his chair. I give him my arm and allow him to lead me along the Grand Boulevard, where we can admire the shops. No one has told the storefront decorators that a war is being fought.

"So is your family in Russia?" I ask.

"Yes. My family leads a hard life there."

Meaning they are poor. "Do they have a trade?"

"Yes. They are shop owners." I indicate a café and we go inside. "But the men in my family all serve their country. We are military men." He is proud.

We order coffee and sit across from each other. There are other men in the café, some injured and some probably on leave. What must it feel like to be granted leave from hell, knowing eventually you'll have to go back? To come to Café de la Paix while your comrades are flying missions over Berlin, being shot down, wounded, maimed. And then to return a week later and fly those same missions. It must be unbearable.

"What are you thinking about?" he asks.

I consider lying to him. "War. How uncertain life is."

"Let's not think about war, then," he says in the way that only young people can. "Let's go back to the hotel."

He smells like rainwater and musk. I lead him to my room and his strength becomes my new shelter in this world.

During the next two weeks we are inseparable. I learn about Vadime's family in northern Russia and I tell him about my childhood in Leeuwarden. He's surprised to learn I'm not from India.

"So all of those dances?"

"I learned them in Java," I confess.

It's still exotic to him. India, Java . . . both are entire worlds away from machine guns and trenches. We don't speak about war. In my suite in the Grand we don't open a single newspaper. Europe may be crumbling beneath our feet or sliding into the sea, but neither of us wants to know.

*　　*　　*

I dream of Evert, and in the dream he is sailing away. The signifi-
cance isn't lost on me: In two days Vadime will return to his unit.
I do not want to feel the pain of loss before it is necessary, but it's
almost impossible to ignore. I focus on enjoying the moments, but in
the dance hall, outside the café, in my suite—all I can think about is
vanishing time.

On our last day in Paris together, I wake early and dress while
Vadime's still in bed. Downstairs in the lounge I order a gin and
tonic.

"Excuse me, Mata Hari?" A waiter stops at my table. "The man
across the room has asked me to deliver this."

He hands me a card. It reads JEAN HALLURE, LIEUTENANT. I search
my memory. The Kursaal. He was the musician who had gotten so
drunk we'd had to cancel our rehearsal. A lifetime ago. That afternoon, Edouard and I went to the museum. I squeeze my eyes shut
against the memory. I don't want to think about that day. I don't want
to think about Edouard being married. I look at Lieutenant Hallure
and he tips his hat to me. The years have been good to him: He is
tan; his hair is still thick and dark. He also looks sober.

"Jean." I hold out my hand as he approaches my table.

"Mata Hari," he says, kissing it. "After all these years, what a surprise."

"A delightful one. Are you really a lieutenant? What brings you
to the Grand?"

"I am—discharged. My hearing is not so good anymore. What
are you doing in Paris?"

I tell the shortest version of my story. "I met a man," I say.

"Let me guess. An officer?"

Of course. "Vadime de Massloff. But his leave is up tomorrow."

"Where is he going?"

"Vittel."

"That's not bad. I'd call it a resort."

"Until they send him to the front," I counter. "I'm hoping to visit him."

"Has the government given you permission?"

I stare at him. Why would I need permission to visit a French town?

"There's an airbase in Vittel," he explains, glancing at my drink. "You can't drop in for a social call."

"He didn't tell me that." Do I have any contacts left in Paris? I have more in Berlin.

"I can ring the Secret Service and tell them Mata Hari is looking for a pass."

I think he is joking. But he takes out a pen from his vest pocket and writes down an address. Then he reaches over and tucks it into my brassiere, an intimacy that gives me chills.

"When the time comes." He winks. "Tell them Jean Hallure sent you."

Vadime takes off his scarf and wraps it around my neck, holding the ends down and pulling me toward him. "Will you think of me when I'm gone?"

"Of course." I feel my throat close. "And you'll be fine," I say, convincing myself.

"I want to come back to you." He stands at the door, ready to go. "I love you, Mata Hari. I've loved you since the first time I saw you performing Salome."

"You never told me that."

He shrugs, embarrassed. "There were men going back stage to see you. I knew I'd never be invited, so I didn't try."

"I'm sure I would have." My face warms and my eyes fill with tears. "Come back, Vadime."

"I will."

When he leaves, I don't retreat to my room. I haven't lost him. When the war is finished and the broken pieces of Europe slip back together, he'll return to me.

I fill my days with trips to museums and dinners with men who don't interest me. Ambassadors, police chiefs, military men of various ranks. I don't phone Edouard or Givenchy to tell them that I've returned to Paris. If they care about me, they will find me. I'm preparing to go out to dinner with a new acquaintance when the concierge stops me as I am leaving the Grand.

"Madam, if you would come back inside for a moment? A telegram has arrived."

The look on the concierge's face is grave and immediately I'm unsettled. I follow him across the lobby and he hands me a slip of paper. I take it with trembling hands. My eyes scan so quickly I can barely understand the contents. I see "Vadime" and "hospital in Vittel." I read it again, slower this time, and the world stops.

Vadime has been seriously injured. He may be blind.

Chapter 16

WELCOME TO THE FRENCH SECRET SERVICE

$\mathscr{I}$'m from The Netherlands, Commandant. We are neutral. My passport allows me to travel to any nation. How many of your people can do that?"

Commandant Ladoux studies me from across his desk. I have gone to the address Jean Hallure gave me, to the heart of the French Secret Service, and have offered to bring them information. Spain, Germany, Belgium, England—wherever they want me to go. All I am asking for is a million francs in return. Enough to get myself and Vadime out of France. I want to take him far from this horrible war to America, where it is safe. I want us to live in New York. We can start over in that city of magic.

The Commandant nods slowly and my heart leaps.

"For that sum, significant information must be produced. Information that will benefit France."

"I have a way with military men, Commandant. Whatever they tell me I will pass on to you."

"We would need you in Belgium."

"That's fine."

"And you understand what's required? To reach Belgium you

must travel through Amsterdam. To reach Amsterdam, you must pass through Spain. Intelligence from any of these countries—"

"I have relationships with men in every major city in Europe, monsieur." What do I care about the route I travel? "You read the papers, don't you?"

"Then welcome to the French Secret Service, Mata Hari."

I show my papers from Commandant Ladoux to the soldier at the Hôtel de Ville in Vittel. I smile at him so he thinks that I'm at ease, but the sounds of dying men from beyond the lobby are making me feel very uncomfortable. While the uniform continues to check over my papers, every few moments the doors swing open and men carry wounded soldiers in on stretchers. Some of them are covered in blood. Others are so pale I wonder if they're already dead. The entire hotel has been turned into an American military hospital with very few rooms still reserved for guests. There's nothing of the resort town Vadime wrote to me about. It's all military tents and army cars now.

"If you'll wait here," the soldier behind the desk says, "I'll find someone to escort you back."

I try to make myself comfortable in the lobby, but I don't know where to look and the sounds of men crying out for their mothers is heartbreaking. Is Vadime's voice among them? What will I find when they take me back there? My stomach begins to tie itself in knots.

I search the lobby for something to read—*anything*—and discover several old copies of the New York *Tribune*. I wonder who left them and why they're here. I read the date of the paper on top. August 31, 1914. I can't imagine why anyone would want to keep such old news. There's an article by Richard Harding Davis. I skim it, not wanting

to face anything more horrible than the wails around me, but my
hands grow cold as I read.

> *London, August 30*—I left Brussels on Thursday after-
> noon and have just arrived in London. For two hours on
> Thursday night I was in what for six hundred years has
> been the city of Louvain. The Germans were burning
> it, and to hide their work kept us locked in the railway
> carriages. But the story was written against the sky, was
> told to us by German soldiers incoherent with excesses;
> and we could read it in the faces of women and chil-
> dren being led to concentration camps and of citizens on
> their way to be shot.

On their way to be shot. Is this what would have happened to Vadime if he'd been captured? If the Germans are shooting civilians,
what are they doing to soldiers?

"Mata Hari?" someone calls, but I can't respond. I'm transfixed by
the story.

> In the darkness the gray uniforms filled the station
> with an army of ghosts. You distinguished men only
> when pipes hanging from their teeth glowed red or their
> bayonets flashed.
>
> Outside the station in the public square the people
> of Louvain passed in an unending procession, women
> bareheaded, weeping, men carrying the children asleep
> on their shoulders, all hemmed in by the shadowy army
> of gray wolves. Once they were halted, and among them
> marched a line of men. They well knew their fellow
> townsmen. These were on their way to be shot. And bet-

ter to point the moral an officer halted both processions and, climbing to a cart, explained why the men were going to die. He warned others not to bring down upon themselves a like vengeance.

As those being led to spend the night in the fields looked across to those marked for death they saw old friends, neighbors of long standing, men of their own household. The officer bellowing at them from the cart was illuminated by the headlights of an automobile. He looked like an actor held in a spotlight on a darkened stage. It was all like a scene upon the stage, so unreal, so inhuman, you felt that it could not be true, that the curtain of fire, purring and crackling and sending up hot sparks to meet the kind, calm stars, was only a painted backdrop; that the reports of rifles from the dark rooms came from blank cartridges, and that these trembling shopkeepers and peasants ringed in bayonets would not in a few minutes really die, but that they themselves and their homes would be restored to their wives and children. You felt it was only a nightmare, cruel and uncivilized. And then you remembered that the German Emperor has told us what it is. It is his Holy War.

Holy War.

"Mata Hari?"

I look up and realize that I'm crying. The author of the piece has such a way with words that for several minutes it was as if I was standing right there with him. I could see the German officers as he saw them. I could hear their boots crunch against the gravel as they moved in unison to destroy people's homes. I stand and wipe the tears from my eyes.

"We ask that our visitors remain composed," the man says. "If you don't feel you can see wounded men on their deathbeds without being overcome, I ask that you reconsider."

"No. I can do it."

He stares at me as if he's unsure. Then he nods and leads the way. The hotel carpets are stained with blood. I do not allow myself to wonder who bled their last here and what happened to them. Did they die here alone? Did their mothers come for them? Perhaps, like Vadime, this isn't even their country. The man takes me through a series of halls to a second lobby that has been transformed into a makeshift hospital room. Two dozen beds line the walls, and nurses in white uniforms rush from patient to patient. In the farthest corner of the room, I see him. It takes all of my reserve not to run.

We walk across the lobby and the men who are able sit up straighter in their beds to watch me. When we arrive at Vadime, he gapes at me, as if he thinks I am not real.

"Vadime! Oh my God, Vadime." I want to smother him with kisses. I want to wrap him in my arms. His one eye is covered by a thick black patch, but he's alive. I sit on the side of his bed and try my best not to be overcome. He takes my hands in his and squeezes tightly.

"Mata Hari, you came."

The soldier leaves us to our privacy and I allow several tears to spill onto Vadime's pillow. "Of course. What did you think?"

"So few of us here get visitors. I've heard it is almost impossible to get a pass. How—"

"I'm here." I put my finger to his lips. They're cracked and dry. "That's all that matters."

Now he is the one who is weeping.

We sit like this, holding each other's hands in silence, sobbing quietly, until he asks me where I've come from.

"Paris. It's not the same though. You wouldn't recognize her now."

"Nothing will be when this war is finished. All of Europe will be burning rubble."

"Let's go to America," I say.

Vadime tightens his grip. "Honestly?"

"Yes. New York. Look at these Americans." I keep my voice low. "There's no war on American soil. They aren't starving in the streets. Look how healthy they are."

"How? How can we get to New York?"

"I'll make all the arrangements," I promise him.

"When?"

As soon as I have the money, I think.

By the sixth of November I am in Madrid. I book a room at La Paz and recall Edouard in his silk evening gown, smoking cigars on the balcony of his room in this very hotel. I've made so many foolish mistakes in my life. But I will not be reckless or imprudent with Vadime.

I have saved every mark I received from Cramer. When Ladoux sends my payment, I will have enough money to support both of us in America. I will have enough capital to begin a new campaign to contact Non. I dare to dream that the three of us will be a family.

The leaves have started to turn on the trees, and I am pleased to learn that even this far south November still feels crisp. I worry about Vadime as I roam the streets of Madrid; I am so impatient to see him yet I must linger here for three weeks. That is when my papers will be ready, Commandant Ladoux will forward them to me, and I'll sail for Amsterdam. After that I should be only a short time in Belgium—it will not take me long to find a military man to charm secrets out of while we're in bed. I've promised Vadime I will be by his side at Christmas. A nurse has been reading the letters I've been writing to him and sending me his replies; the notes are not penned in his hand, but I recognize his voice, his words. He promises he will wait for me. But God, the time passes slowly! I want to board that ship to Amsterdam and be done with all of this business. I am finished with my life in Europe, of this I have never been more certain.

The room I've been given on board ship is tiny: a bed, two chairs, a wooden table.

But I don't complain because I'm not truly present on this vessel; my heart is in a military hospital in Vittel. When I am not in my room writing to Vadime, I walk the deck taking the fresh air and keeping to myself. I am propping up my feet in the cozy reading room and writing to Vadime when I overhear another passenger say the ship is making a brief stop in England. I add this to my letter.

"You." A British soldier is looking at me. "What is your name?"

As soon as the ship docked at Falmouth we passengers were instructed to gather at the muster station. Several uniformed men have boarded and demand to see our passports.

"You don't read the papers?" I say flirtatiously. I want to lighten the mood; the other passengers look grim.

"This is not the time to be flippant," he warns. "Tell me your name."

"My name is Mata Hari."

He looks me up and down, then motions for the other men to come over. They confer in whispers, then one of them says, "Clara Benedix, you will be coming with us."

I glance at the other passengers, wondering who Clara Benedix is and what she has done. Then I realize that he is addressing me.

"You are mistaken," I say. "My name is Mata Hari." The only Clara I've known was blonde and never had to worry over money. Her father rescued her from the Haanstra School for Girls after she agreed to marry the man he had chosen for her. "I am a dancer."

"And I'm the queen of England," he says. "You are coming with us."

I look around at the other passengers, waiting for them to confirm my identity. They know who I am. They must. Not one of them says a word. "You can't take me off of this ship," I say defiantly.

"We're not," the officer replies. "We're taking you to your cabin."

I sit on my bed while the soldiers search through my tiny cabin, tearing apart my luggage. One of the men leaves and returns with a woman. She has severe features and introduces herself as Janet Grant. She orders the men to leave.

"Thank you," I tell her, vastly relieved. "This is ludicrous—"

"Strip."

I think I've misheard. "I'm sorry, what did you say?"

"They tell me you claim to be Mata Hari. So this shouldn't be difficult for you—I said strip. That means remove your clothes. I am here to perform a body-cavity search."

I do as she says and her hands explore every part of me. Not even Rudolph was able to make me feel so violated. When she's finished, she turns her back to let me dress.

"Why bother?" I snap, but my voice is shaking. "Why are you doing this to me?"

"This is my job."

I have barely finished dressing when there's a knock at the door. Janet Grant opens it and I count six men in uniform.

"Miss Benedix," one of them says, "we ask that you come with us."

I am almost uncertain if I am awake or dreaming. "My name is Mata Hari and I—"

"We'll let Scotland Yard determine that."

Despite my protests, I'm removed from the ship. The other passengers watch as six men escort me away like a wily criminal capable of executing an ingenious escape. They take me to a car waiting beyond the dock.

"Where are you taking me?"

"London," one of the men says.

"I can't go there. I don't have the time to go there."

No one listens.

"Do you hear me? Is anyone listening? I have somewhere else to be! It is important—"

"Tell that to investigators at Scotland Yard."

The driver starts the car and when I see the railway station in the distance, I begin to panic. "You understand you're making a big mistake. No one in London is going to believe this. My photograph is in every newspaper!"

"Miss Benedix, it would be better for you if you simply stop talking."

"I'm not Miss Benedix!" I say, ice in my voice.

I'm taken directly to Scotland Yard. I feel both humiliated and enraged. If I live to be a hundred, I will never set foot in England again.

Everyone turns to look at me as I'm marched through the building. Is it possible that not a single person—at Scotland Yard of all places!—can recognize me? I can't fathom the odds. It is absurd. Who is so removed from day-to-day news that they can't instantly spot that I'm not Miss Clara Benedix—whoever she is. I acknowledge the onlookers, imagining that any moment this charade will end. It must. But then we pass into a windowless hall and I am led to a cell that contains nothing but a single bed and a chair.

"You can't leave me in here," I say, distraught. "I'm not Clara Benedix! For God's sake, go outside and pick up a newspaper!"

The men retreat without a single word.

I'm left without food or water, without a place to relieve myself. Hours pass. No one will believe this. I can't believe it myself. I sit on my chair and simmer with anger. *Clara,* I think with contempt. I already have negative memories associated with that name. At the Haanstra School, we were meant to "be useful" in the evenings—expected to sit in the parlor under the steel gaze of Van Tassel and knit or sew.

"Concentrate, Miss Zelle," Mrs. Van Tassel snaps at me.

"I'm sorry," I apologize. "I never learned how to knit."

"If that is true, your parents did a woeful job raising you. What kind of a girl doesn't learn how to knit?"

"I doubt Clara knows how to knit or sew," I counter, speaking without thinking, and all eyes shift to Clara, who is reading. She blushes to the roots of her long, blonde hair.

"Clara comes from a family with means," Mrs. Van Tassel clarifies. "She has no need to learn trivial things. You must be trained to knit and sew properly, Miss Zelle. A girl like you requires such skills to earn her way in the world."

Sitting in this uncomfortable cell, I wonder about Clara, my fellow inmate at the Haanstra School. She married an old man she didn't love. Is she as miserable as I am right now?

"I'm taking you to see Sir Basil Thomson in the Interrogation Room."

"I'm sorry," I say to the officer, so grateful to see another human being after so much time alone. "That name doesn't mean anything to me. Who is Sir Basil Thomson?"

The man stares at me. Then he says simply, "Interrogation Room."

*   *   *

Sir Basil Thomson is dressed in a suit and a long woolen scarf. His thin face is drawn. The door shuts behind me and he gestures to a seat. Like the cell, the Interrogation Room is gray and windowless. It is also colder.

"I told them, I'm not Miss Benedix," I say, taking the seat he has indicated.

"I'm told that you claim you are Mata Hari. Is that your true name?"

"Yes," I say, as the door opens and a man with a stenograph appears. I clarify my answer. "It's my stage name. My birth name is Margaretha Zelle."

The stenographer sits and Sir Basil instructs him to write, "The woman named Clara Benedix insists her name is Margaretha Zelle."

"I insist because I am!" I am tired and cold and hungry and this is infuriating. "My name is Margaretha Zelle! I was married once and my name changed to MacLeod. But now I go by Margaretha Zelle and my stage name is Mata Hari. This is easily verified. Why isn't anyone listening to me? I want to register a complaint. Who is in charge?" I desperately conjure von Schilling's list of names in my mind's eye. Is there anyone in England I can call?

"You are a German spy. Your name is Clara Benedix."

"That is ridiculous!"

But this is how it goes for hours. Lunch comes, then dinner, and Sir Thomson eats and I go hungry. He wants to know what I was doing in South America. I tell him I haven't been to South America. I inform him that any number of reputable people can identify me. But he won't look at an old newspaper or let me make a phone call. I have debated whether or not to give him Commandant Ladoux's name. Doing so will free me—but even though we are allies, giving up my association with the French Secret Service to a British authority may spoil my assignment in Belgium. And I don't want that; I need the money that France has promised me to start my new life in New York with Vadime.

I keep my relationship with the French Secret Service to myself, and Sir Thomson continues to interrogate me, persisting in calling me Miss Benedix. It's a nightmare. At last I shut my eyes and real tears leak out. "Please, *please* believe me. I am Mata Hari."

"Miss Benedix, I will believe you when you are honest with me." He stands and the stenographer rises with him.

"Where are you going?"

"Home." Sir Thomson reaches for his hat. "I will see you tomorrow." I'm taken back to my cell and the bars clang shut.

There's nothing to keep me warm for the night, not even a towel. A bucket was placed on the floor while I was being interrogated by Sir Thomson. Apparently, that's where I'm supposed to relieve myself. I collapse onto the bed and cry. Then I think about Vadime in his hospital bed in Vittel, waiting for me to return with the money that will take us away to New York from the wretchedness that is Europe.

I must survive this. Whatever happens, I must continue my mission and find my way to Belgium. I close my eyes and let myself dream about life in New York. We'll rent an apartment in one of the unbelievably tall buildings Guimet spoke about so long ago. My God, has it only been twelve years? It feels like a lifetime. I was so innocent then, so hopeful that everything would work out. I think of all the money that's come my way, passing through my fingers like sand. How many times did Edouard warn me? Save. Don't spend on foolish trinkets. No one needs three fur coats and diamond rings. I'm going to save everything from this Belgian mission. Not a single franc is going to be spent before we reach New York.

But first, I have to leave London.

Eggs, milk, two pieces of buttered toast. When it is brought to my cell, I eat every bite because I know I'll need my strength. Then I am taken to meet Sir Thomson in the same windowless room. As soon as I take my seat he says, "We have had confirmation of your identity, Miss Zelle. It seems we must offer you an apology."

I am relieved beyond description.

"But I'm afraid I still have questions for you to answer. Why are you traveling from Madrid to Amsterdam?"

"To see my daughter." The answer comes to me immediately.

"Are you referring to Jeanne Louise MacLeod? The girl hasn't seen you in more than a decade. Why the urge to see her now?"

I flinch. It is painful to hear the truth. "I miss her," I say.

"I don't believe you planned to visit Jeanne Louise MacLeod. So. Who sent you to Amsterdam, Miss Zelle?"

In the end, I tell him everything—or nearly everything. He sits across from me and listens while the stenographer writes. When I'm finished, he says, "I will send a telegram to Commandant Ladoux. If he confirms your employment, you are free to go."

A basket of fruit awaits my arrival at the Savoy, on a bed that smells of freshly picked lavender. Like the Grand in Paris, it's as if the war does not exist here. The first thing I do is run the bath, then sit in the water until my fingers become small pink prunes.

I dress in my favorite silk robe and take a packet of letters out of one of my returned trunks; the men at Scotland Yard have read them. That's fine. So now they've learned that I'm in love with Vadime. I wasn't foolish enough to write anything down that would be of concern to Commandant Ladoux. I find the letter I was writing when I was detained. I'll never be home by Christmas now. I take out a pen and complete it:

> *On February 3rd, meet me in the lobby of the Grand, my love. From there we will start a new life together. One without fear or loneliness or war. I'll be waiting for you with open arms.*

The next morning I give my letter to the concierge and return to my room to wait for Sir Thomson.

I wait all day, but he doesn't arrive.

The following evening, I am beginning to feel very uneasy. When Sir Thomson arrives at the Savoy and tells me that Commandant Ladoux has confirmed my employment, I am overwhelmed with relief.

"He has also given you instructions," he says. He hands me a telegram.

The paper says: RETURN TO MADRID. Three terse words.

"I suggest you leave London at the next opportunity," Sir Thomson says.

Does he think I'm a fool? I wait until Sir Thomson has departed before destroying the telegram. Of course I will leave London. My mission is to reach Belgium. And that is what I am going to do. I will prove to Commandant Ladoux that I am a trustworthy emissary for France.

Chapter 17

SENT IN CODE

$\mathscr{A}$ day passes. Then three. Finally, a week slips by and I am still at the Savoy. I send another telegram to Ladoux. "Without instructions for Madrid," I say. "Immediately advise."

By the second week I begin to worry about the silence, and soon my fear becomes a vise grip. Has Ladoux dismissed me? Or are the British detaining his telegrams? I can't tolerate more delay; I have already arranged a date to meet Vadime. He expects me to collect him at the Grand in Paris. I will not disappoint him.

I must have Ladoux's money by then.

If I don't complete this mission, there will be no money. My future depends on completing the task the French Secret Service has set for me.

Von Schilling gave me no names to call on in London, but there is a German military attaché, a Major Arnold Kalle, listed in Madrid. I decide on a course of action.

On the first of December I travel back to Madrid to begin my assignment for the French Secret Service.

"Mata Hari the dancer?" Major Kalle confirms, surprised by my phone call.

"Yes. I was given your name by a good friend of ours."

There is silence on the phone.

I continue, "General von Schilling said that if I found myself in Madrid I must call on Major Arnold Kalle. And here I am, in your beautiful city, not knowing a single soul."

"Perhaps we should have dinner, then," he suggests.

If Mrs. Van Tassel were here, I would gloat: My skills are far more valuable than knitting. My talent in bedding officers will gain me information that may help France win this dreadful war. Whatever Major Kalle divulges I will share with Ladoux. This is how France will remember me when I am living in New York.

We meet at Botín, with its warm paneled exterior and redbrick arches dating back to 1725. It's the oldest restaurant in the world, Kalle says. He has clear blue eyes and thick blond hair. "A traditional *horno de asar.*"

I glance under my eyelashes at him, playing the role of a girl infatuated. "What does that mean?"

"Roasted meat."

"I had hoped," I say and touch my hair, "the translation would be something romantic."

We dine and talk about the most trivial of things. The weather (good), the shops (so many closing), the food (I've never had its equal in Spain). Then he invites me back to his home. He slips his arm around my waist and within a few cobbled streets we reach his apartment. A few hours later, both of us are drunk. By midnight, we are lying together on his sheets. I brush my hand against his chest, an invitation to make love again, but he sighs and puts his forearm over his eyes.

"I'm too tired to move," he says. "It's a great deal of work arranging for German soldiers to be deployed in Morocco."

I prop myself up on one elbow and gaze at him sympathetically, willing him to continue speaking.

"A submarine is dropping them off." He lifts his arm briefly to look at me. "In the French zone."

My heart is racing—German troops being transported to French soil; I am horrified. Yet my expression remains neutral.

"You will not tell anybody, I hope?" He leans back. "It's all very confidential information."

"I understand." I keep stroking his chest, thinking of Ladoux. Surely this intelligence is equal to what I might have learned in Belgium? God only knows when Kalle's plan will be implemented. Perhaps I have just saved French lives.

He turns and takes me in his arms. "Then again, maybe I'm not so tired."

I don't wait for morning; as soon as I leave Kalle's apartment I rush to the French Embassy in Madrid and tell them that I have information for Commandant Ladoux.

"We can place a call—"

I immediately wave this offer away. "This is sensitive information, madam. A phone call would not be safe."

They arrange for a telegram to be sent in code. A man takes me to a private room and I tell him what I know, carefully, slowly. Then he makes me repeat it and copies it out by hand. He assures me the message will be sent at once.

"Thank you," he says when he's sure he's got it.

"When do you think we'll hear back? I'm expecting the commandant to send me further instructions," I explain.

"Where are you staying, madam?"

"La Paz."

"Then wait there, madam. I'm sure word will come."

On Christmas there is snow on the peaks of Peñalara. How this sight would delight Edouard! How pleased Vadime would be if he were here and able to see it with me! His nurse wrote to tell me that he is blind now, in one eye. The other is healing, if slowly. "It is healing," I wrote to him. "Rejoice in that. It could be so much worse." But there has been no joy in Vadime's latest letters. "All of my hope for the future rests with you," he says. "I am counting the days—is it still more than a month?—when we will be together again."

Together, not alone anymore.

I look around. While the world celebrates Christmas with their families, I sit by myself in a tiny café, reading a newspaper.

NAVY MEN BACK U.S. TO DUPLICATE FEAT

Declare American Submarines Could Cross Ocean as Did the *Deutschland*.

United States submarines can duplicate the *Deutschland*'s trans-Atlantic feat if the occasion arises, Navy experts asserted today.

A flotilla of K-class submarines last summer cruised 2,000 miles from Honolulu to San Francisco. They could have cruised for a week longer, according to navy men. They could have traveled as far as the *Deutschland* under the same conditions and at the same low speed maintained by the German super-submarine . . .

There is no one on the streets, so I'm shocked when a man comes inside and stands directly in front of my table, blocking my view of the mountain.

"Madam, my name is Pierre-Martin. I have a message for you. From a man who works with Ladoux."

Finally! I sit up and take my purse off an empty seat. "Please. Sit down. I have been awaiting his instructions."

He takes off his hat and sits. Without further introduction, he whispers, "I am to warn you to never go back to France."

"Is this a joke?" It is in extremely poor taste. "Who are you?" I demand.

He leans across the table. "This person believes that you should not go back. Do you understand?"

I shake my head. "I have no idea who would ask you to deliver such a message. Commandant Ladoux—"

"Ladoux believes you're a double agent." He looks at me critically. "A traitor."

"Never!" I say, shocked. "France is my *home*."

"If you return to France, you will be arrested on arrival. Arrested, tried for espionage, and executed." The messenger stands.

"Who sent you?" My mind races for a candidate and I come up empty. There is no one who knows that I am in Madrid except Ladoux.

He shakes his head. "Never return to Paris, Mata Hari." He puts on his hat, tips it to me, and walks away.

I go immediately to my hotel and phone the bellman. Because it's Christmas I must wait forty minutes before a taxi arrives to take me to the French Embassy.

The white halls inside the embassy are as barren as the streets. Even the woman who signs in visitors at the front desk is on holiday. I wait for ten minutes before walking down the hall on my own. A man in a uniform sees me and asks what my business is.

"I'm here with an urgent message for Commandant Ladoux."

"It is Christmas, madam."

"Yes, but war doesn't stop for Christmas."

He hesitates, as though debating the truth of this. "What is your urgent message?" he asks.

I glance behind me. "Not here," I say, though there's no one present to spy on us.

We go to an empty room and he shuts the door. I tell him what I know about the German submarine taking soldiers to French soil.

"And you're sure that this German, this Major Arnold Kalle, said—'French soil'?"

"His exact words were 'the French zone,'" I clarify.

"Am I the first person you've spoken to at this embassy?"

"No. I've been here before." He thinks I'm wasting his time. And on Christmas Day.

"A man promised he would send this very message to—"

He puffs out his cheeks, exasperated. "Then why are you here now, madam?"

"Because I don't believe the message was ever sent! Now I'm warned not to return to Paris. French lives are in danger, do you not understand?" I am agitated and can see that I am more than this man has bargained for on a day when he wants to be home, with his family. "I must get a message to him today," I insist, undeterred.

"Very well, madam. As you wish." He goes to a desk and grabs a pen and paper. "What is your message?"

"Tell Commandant Ladoux that Mata Hari is awaiting instructions in Madrid. Tell him that I have information about German submarines."

He writes this down, without showing me any sign of recognition.

I say, "I want to add something else."

He straightens. "Yes?"

"Tell him—no, *ask* him if it's true that I'm not welcome in Paris. There's no chance it can be true. But to be certain. Ask if I'm in danger."

"Exactly like that?"

"Yes. 'Am I in danger if I should return from Madrid?'"

He does as he's told. "Satisfied?"

"Yes."

I have an uneasy feeling in my stomach as he tucks the paper into his shirt pocket.

"When will you send it?"

"The moment you leave, madam."

I can't sleep on the way to Paris. I waited for a month in Madrid, yet heard no word from Commandant Ladoux. I've lost faith in the French Embassy. I don't believe they sent him any of my telegrams. Now I am worrying: What if Pierre-Martin is right? What if they arrest me when I leave the train station? They won't act toward me the way Scotland Yard did, I decide, because I'll tell them that I work for Ladoux immediately.

I check into the Élysée Palace under the name Marguerite Mac-dowd. Then I spend a sleepless night rereading Vadime's letters to me. In three hours we will be reunited. I have enough money for our plane tickets to America. The rest I will worry about later.

I dress in a simple blue skirt and blouse that make me look dowdy; then I tie my least favorite scarf around my head, covering my hair.

I go downstairs and find a taxi. I tell the driver to take me to the Grand.

Inside, I ask the concierge for the room number of Vadime de Massloff.

"Massloff." The man taps his pencil along the list. "No Massloff today, madam."

That can't be correct. Unless . . . something happened to him? He can't have changed his mind. I think of the letters he's sending faithfully. He calls me his only hope. His *star in a night filled with darkness.* "Please check again. He may have arrived yesterday."

He turns pages and scans them. "I'm sorry, we have no such guest, Mata Hari."

Hearing my name is jolting. I've taken such care: my simple dress, my plain scarf.

The concierge notes my reaction. "I would recognize you any-where, madam."

I close my eyes and will myself to think of a quick solution. I cannot leave Paris without Vadime. He is sick and almost blind. Who will take care of him? "Then may I ask you for a favor?"

The concierge nods. "Certainly."

I lean over his desk and write down the number of my suite at the Élysée Palace. Under it I slip a fifty franc note. "The moment Vadime de Massloff checks in, will you give this to him?"

He slips the fifty into his shirt pocket. "Of course."

That night the door of my suite swings open with a violent crash. Five men with rifles enter my hotel room. I am dreaming of the Walrus, of escaping his meaty hands. Now I scream, grab the covers, and pull them to my chest. I glance at the clock on the bedside. It's six a.m.

"What is the meaning of this?" I demand.

"Madam, I am Inspecteur Marcadier." He steps around my luggage.

I'm packed and ready to leave. There are sixteen bags in all. Plus one blue-green purse. Even as the inspecteur is speaking, I'm thinking that it isn't much, the things that belong to me in this life.

"These are inspecteurs Quentin, Priolet, Curnier, and Des Logères." The other men step forward.

"What are you doing here?" I demand. "This is outrageous! I am employed by Commandant Ladoux of the French Secret Service!"

"Mata Hari," Marcadier continues, as if I haven't spoken a word, "also known as M'greet MacLeod, also known as Margaretha Zelle, you are charged with espionage against the Republic of France."

They allow me to dress and while I'm given my coat Inspecteur Marcadier reads the *mandat d'arrêt*.

"How do you answer these charges?"

I repeat that I am in the employ of Commandant Ladoux. It has the same impact: They ignore me completely. They lead me down three flights of stairs to the lobby of the Élysée Palace. The hotel employees are huddled in a tight circle, whispering. Shame floods my face as they parade me to the door like a criminal. Outside, the streets are thick with mist and dreamlike. Maybe I'm still sleeping, I tell myself. Maybe none of this is true.

Part 3

DESTRUCTION

(By United Press)

Washington, March 1.—Germany, in planning unrestricted submarine warfare and counting its consequences, proposed an alliance with Mexico and Japan to make war on the United Sates, if this country should not remain neutral.

Japan, through Mexican mediation, was to be urged to abandon her allies and join in the attack on the United States.

Mexico, for her reward, was to receive general financial support from Germany, re-conquer Texas, New Mexico and Arizona—lost provinces—and share in the victorious peace terms Germany contemplated.

Details were left to German Minister von Eckhardt in Mexico City, who by instructions signed by German Foreign Minister Zimmerman, at Berlin, January 19, 1917, was directed to propose the alliance with Mexico to General Carranza and suggest that Mexico seek to bring Japan into the plot.

Sent Through Bernstorff.

These instructions were transmitted to von Eckhardt through Count von Bernstorff, former German ambassador here, now on his way home to Germany under a safe conduct obtained from his enemies by the country against which he was plotting war.

Germany pictured to Mexico, by broad intimation, England and the entente allies defeated; Germany and her allies triumphant and in world domination by the instrument of unrestricted warfare.

Text of the Letter.

A copy of Zimmerman's instructions to von Eckhardt, sent through von Bernstorff, is in possession of the United States government. It is as follows:

"Berlin, January 19, 1917.

"On the first of February we intend to begin submarine warfare unrestricted. In spite of this, it is our intention to endeavor to keep neutral the United States of America.

"If this attempt is not successful, we propose an alliance on the following basis with Mexico: That we shall make war together and together make peace. We shall give general financial support and it is understood that Mexico is to reconquer the lost territory in New Mexico, Texas and Arizona. The details are left to you for settlement."

"Japan Also.

"You are instructed to inform the president of Mexico of the above in the greatest confidence as soon as it is certain that there will be an outbreak of war with the United States and suggest that the president of Mexico, on his own initiative, should communicate with Japan, suggesting adherence at once to this plan; at the same time, offer to mediate between Germany and Japan.

"Please call to the attention of the president of Mexico

that the employment of ruthless submarine warfare now promises to compel England to make peace in a few months.

(signed) "'Zimmerman.'"

This document has been in the hands of the government since President Wilson broke off diplomatic relations with Germany.

Chapter 18

THE CONCIERGERIE

1917

A light comes on and I hear his footsteps before I see him, the soft leather of his shoes on concrete. "Edouard!" I call through the bars as he comes into view; I'm afraid he isn't real. I am in a new cell. It contains three beds, a toilet, a bottle of fresh water.

As soon as he sees me, tears well in his eyes. I've never seen Edouard like this. "My God, what have you done, M'greet?"

"*Nothing.* I swear—nothing!"

"I've been searching for you for weeks. You vanished from Berlin. I heard rumors that you were in Paris and that—"

"I was arrested at the Élysée Palace. I've been in Saint Lazare Prison." It's such a relief to have him here with me, to finally share the nightmare that has swallowed me. "Have you been inside Saint Lazare, Edouard? I had no light, no toilet, no shower. I was left in a cell with nothing but hay and a window with bars but no glass. In this weather, Edouard! I was so cold; the place is frozen in time. I looked out of the window and expected to see the Revolution! I was alone for weeks. It was inhumane."

He shakes his head. "Did they give you a change of clothes, a blanket?"

"They gave me nothing. Not for the longest time." I start to cry, feeling everything anew when I see the empathy in his eyes. "They locked me up like an animal. I wasn't allowed to write letters or to phone anyone. I thought I was losing my mind I was so cold and hungry. When I thought I would surely die, two nuns arrived, and they brought me fresh towels and soap."

"Did they treat you well?"

"One, Sister Léonide, was kind to me." *You must eat, Mata Hari*, she pleaded with me, *or you will sicken.* "They took me to a room with faucet pumps in the ceiling and watched me shower." I feel myself flush. "You don't know how much modesty you have until you are in prison, Edouard. The nuns told me I was being taken to see Captain Bouchardon. That was why I was allowed to clean myself. I couldn't place his name, but I knew I'd heard it before."

"Captain Bouchardon—"

"Le Cigale, do you remember? In the early days. He was a sergeant in the police department. He wanted me arrested for dancing nude." He was a little mustached man I dismissed because more powerful men were protecting me. "Back then he left me alone because I was sleeping with the chief of police. But when I was brought to his office from Saint Lazare, he interrogated me. Now he is a prosecutor. He demanded the names of my German contacts—"

"Do you have German contacts?"

"Are you asking if I'm a spy?" I shrink back from the bars. Who does he think I've become? "*Against France?* Of course not! I told Bouchardon the truth. That I agreed to obtain information to *help* France defeat Germany, that Commandant Ladoux—"

"Commandant Ladoux? Who is he?"

"He's with the French Secret Service. I met him through Jean Hallure, the drunk musician from the Kursaal. Now he's a lieutenant." I'm going too fast for him. Edouard pats his jacket, then his pockets, looking for a pen and paper to write all this down.

"Why have they let you visit me?" I ask.

"They haven't," he says absently, giving up the search. "I bribed a guard to come in here to see you." He gives me a wry look. "Haven't I told you there isn't anyone in Paris I don't know? Now—how many times did this Captain Bouchardon interrogate you?" he asks.

"Sixteen times. Those were the only days I was allowed to shower. I was made to wash myself before they brought me to his office. The prison issued me a *number*, Edouard. 721 44625. I told Bouchardon *exactly* what happened in Madrid. I chronicled every detail. I informed him that I was hired by Commandant Ladoux of the French Secret Service, and that I provided the commandant with important information to aid France."

"How did you get this information, M'greet?"

"I seduced a German in Madrid; his name is Major Arnold Kalle. I spent an evening with him and he revealed a plot to send a German submarine into French territory. I went straight to the French Embassy and reported this information by telegram to Commandant Ladoux! I'm not in bed with the Germans for pleasure, Edouard. I did this for France. But no one will listen to the truth—it's as if the world has gone mad." I take a deep breath. "I need you to represent me."

"I don't know that I can do that, M'greet. I'm not a criminal lawyer."

"That's fine. I'm not a criminal." I grip the bars and he wraps his fingers around mine. But I can see doubt in his eyes. "The cell at Saint Lazare had no furniture at all. It was worse than Scotland Yard. I thought that was impossible. I slept on the hay; it was flea infested and soaked in urine—"

"M'greet, there's something I don't understand. If you are working for the French Secret Service, why have they arrested you? Why are they the ones calling you a German spy?"

"I don't know." Though I've had nothing but time to think it over. "I can't understand it either."

"Are you aware that they're planning a court martial? There must be something you know, something that they want."

"I swear, there's nothing! I've considered everything and none of it makes sense."

"What evidence do they have, then, that you are giving information to Germany?"

"None! They searched all of my belongings. Everything I had with me at the Élysée Palace was confiscated. All they have confronted me with is a tube of oxycyanide of mercury."

"And? Why do they think it is important?"

"Because they are fools—it's my birth control, Edouard!" I say, exasperated. "Bouchardon behaves as if fertility is imaginary. He insists I use it to make 'sympathetic inks.' That's what he said. 'One drop of this,' he claims, 'and you are translating letters.'"

Edouard puts his hand to his temple.

"It doesn't make any sense, I know. The world has gone mad."

"Why did they transfer you here from Saint Lazare? Did they tell you that?"

"No. Sometimes I think I'm in a horrible nightmare. I'm not a double agent, Edouard. You have to believe me. I've only gathered intelligence for France. Do you think this could be about money?" I ask. "Commandant Ladoux never paid me the sum we agreed upon. Also, when they arrested me, they took all the money I saved for Vadime—"

Edouard interrupts me. "What money?"

I tell him about the three hundred thousand marks Alfred Kiepert's family paid me to stay away from him, and the twenty thousand marks I received from Consul Cramer.

Edouard's face pales. "Who is Consul Cramer, M'greet?"

"He's the German consul in Amsterdam. I was given his name by General von Schilling—"

He puts up his hand to silence me. "When were you in Amsterdam? And why did the German consul give you twenty thousand marks?"

I see how it appears through his eyes and feel a stab of fear. "I went to Amsterdam after I left Berlin. I was coming home, to Paris, but the train was stopped by German soldiers. The money from Cramer was compensation for my furs. The soldiers stole them." I don't want to tell him that I promised Cramer I'd keep my eyes and ears open for Germany. I did nothing for Germany. It was Germany that I betrayed.

Edouard shuts his eyes as if he's blocking out terrible images.

"You can clear this up for me, can't you?" I ask, willing myself to stay calm. "Despite how it may appear on the surface, surely no one will believe I'd give secrets to the Germans, not after you explain the truth to them. Even the British understood in the end."

Edouard opens his eyes. "*The British?* How are they involved? M'greet, I need you to start at the beginning. At the very beginning, from the day I left Berlin."

I tell him everything. I even admit that I spied on Non while I was in Amsterdam, awaiting passage home. "She's such a beautiful young woman now, Edouard. Even if I had revealed myself she wouldn't have recognized me; I'm certain of it. Do you think—"

"M'greet, focus on what's important right now."

"Of course. But when I'm released—"

"You may never be released!"

I'm shocked into silence.

"That's how serious this situation is! Right now it's not your daughter's safety in jeopardy. It's yours."

My hands begin to tremble.

"M'greet." He says my name softly. "Why didn't you call me when they arrested you in London?"

I look away. "You were married." I correct myself. "You *are* married."

He reaches through the bars and tilts my chin up toward him. "Do you think anyone else is more important to me than you?"

I meet his eyes and I feel such warmth. The sound of approaching boots echoes in the hall. He turns and a guard gives him a curt nod. Our time is finished. "I'll see you soon," he says.

"When? When will you come back? Please, get me out of here, Edouard!"

"M'greet, I'll do whatever it takes."

That night I dream of the Revolution. I'm riding in my father's bokkenwagen while on the street people throw stones and trash at me. Vile threats pierce my ears: ugly, taunting cries of "seductress" and "traitor." I pull at the reins to make the wagon stop, but it's going too fast. I know that I am heading for the guillotine.

I jerk awake.

My heart is beating too quickly; I can hear the rush of blood in my ears. I pull the blanket tight around my shoulders and weep. What will happen if Edouard can't save me? All Non will ever know about me are the lies she reads in the papers. That her mother was a German spy.

"Mata Hari?" Sister Léonide's face appears between the bars of my cell. "Why are you crying?"

I speak the words that I now fear are true: "I'm going to die." I don't want to leave Edouard. And Non. My God, I have so many hopes for us, for the future still.

She crosses herself and rearranges the rosary beads in her hand. "You should pray."

I am moved to see that there are tears in her eyes.

"This is not the end, Mata Hari. There is always one more road."

An image of my aunt Marie passes through my mind.

"Is it true what they say in the papers?"

In all of our time together, first in the Saint Lazare Prison and now here in the Conciergerie, Sister Léonide has never asked me if I am guilty, whether I have done what the papers and the authorities are accusing me of.

"No, Sister. It isn't." I look through my cell window at the moon. In France and Germany the moon appears for every citizen, every soldier. No one sees a different one. I meet her eyes. "But I thought I could control my future," I admit.

"No one should play at being God," Sister Léonide admonishes me, gently. "It's vanity to try."

She slips away and I am alone with the moon. I blot out its light with my thumb. Everything is an illusion.

I have a surprising visitor the next morning. As soon as the guard announces his arrival I'm immediately embarrassed. What will he think of me in these prison clothes and under such conditions? But his eyes are full of concern, not judgment, and when he clasps my hands in his through the bars, I feel warmth.

"Mata Hari."

"How did you get in here?"

"There's not a mousehole in France I can't sniff out," Bowtie boasts, and I'm not surprised. He sits on the wooden stool provided for him and I seat myself on the edge of my bed. "How are you?"

"I've been better." I cough. It's cold, and I have no jacket, only the threadbare blanket from the bed. I'm too proud to wrap it around my shoulders right now. "How has the war been treating you?"

"No one wants gossip or entertainment. Only news from the Front."

"Is that why you're here? War finally meets gossip now that Mata Hari is in prison for espionage?"

"Is it true?"

"Did I spy for Germany? Of course not."

"I never believed you would." He studies me, and I can't tell if he's doing his job or is under the notion that he might offer me help. "Mata Hari, what happened?"

"What happened? The Secret Service looked at my life and they got it all wrong."

"I can help you," he says. "But you have to meet me halfway. Tell me the truth—you were living in Berlin. You left and went to Amsterdam and Madrid. What were you doing in those countries?"

I study Bowtie through the prison bars. Non will never know the truth about me if I die. To her I'll be a vile seductress, the loose woman who betrayed a country that loved her, that made her famous. Bowtie can change that.

I lean forward. "I was awaiting orders. I was paid to gather intelligence. Not by Germany," I clarify. "England and France depended on my access and my information."

He writes quickly. "Your access and information?"

"Yes." I drop my voice to a whisper. "While I was waiting for orders in Amsterdam I helped distribute a secret newspaper. With an underground mail service. No one suspected me because of who I am. You can publish that; the Germans have already discovered it. I also helped a man across the border. A wounded soldier who needed to rejoin his regiment."

Bowtie sits back. "Where was his regiment?"

"In The Netherlands."

Now Bowtie is frowning. Perhaps he knows that I am lying. "I also joined the Red Cross."

"In France?"

"In Madrid. While I was waiting."

"For orders?"

"Yes."

"Interesting. This is all very interesting." He flips through his notebook, then sits back and watches me for a long time—so long that I am sure he knows that I'm fabricating the stories of another life. Then he says, "Can you tell me about Vadime de Massloff? The Russian you visited near our airbase in Vittel."

I look at Bowtie through the bars. "Are you accusing me of something?"

"Of course not."

"Because not even these monsters think I was spying in Vittel."

"Are you sure?"

"We're going to be married one day soon." In New York. A new world, a new country, a new life. "Vadime is not a casual fling." I will never deceive him.

"Does he know this?"

What an unkind, horrible thing to ask. "I'm finished with this interview!" It's the first time in my life I've sent a reporter away. I turn my back on him until I hear his footsteps fading.

That night I dream of Leeuwarden in September when the maple trees paint the canals red and gold. Frida, our maid, is baking poffertjes *and serving them hot with butter and caster sugar. My youngest brothers— three and two—eat everything on their plates, licking them clean, too young to have manners. Only my older brother behaves himself at the table.*

"Ari, Cornelius, sit still," Frida admonishes, and I glance at Johannes and we giggle, because we are older and know better.

My mother says to my father, "Your daughter causes too much trouble around the house. Frida doesn't know what to do with her."

My father says, "And what kind of trouble is this, my M'greet?"

"I took Mama's pearls and shoes and dressed Ari in them. He was a princess."

My father laughs, rubbing his beard with his knuckles. "Oh no! What else?"

With Papa, I can do anything. *"I told my classmates I was born in a castle."*

"And so you should have been!" Papa cries, with a sweep of his hand. "Presenting the Countess of Caminghastate," he announces to imaginary crowds and then, magically, we are walking hand in hand, past the Tower of Oldehove.

We stop in the bakery near the park where my brothers like to play.

"Ah, it's the baron and little baroness of Leeuwarden," the baker says, and he takes out two pieces of marzipan wrapped in tissue. He hands the sweets to me and turns into the Walrus, gruesome with fleshy jowls and yellow teeth. I turn to my papa for protection from the meaty hands that are reaching for me, but my papa has vanished.

Chapter 19

ANYTHING YOU
HAVEN'T TOLD ME?

*O*fficially, none of the prisoners in the Conciergerie are allowed visitors, but unauthorized exceptions are possible. Edouard has successfully bribed the guards for a second time. I rush to the bars, then hesitate. I haven't bathed since I last saw him. My hair is stringy and unkempt. There's dirt under my nails and on the hem of my dress.

"M'greet." Edouard is dressed entirely in gray. If he is disgusted by my appearance, I can't read it in his face. He seats himself on the stool that Bowtie used and immediately I notice there's something different in the air between us. I wait for him to explain. "I want you to sit down," he says.

I sit on my bed.

"You understand why you were arrested?"

"I do." When he says nothing more, I elaborate. "They claim I'm a double agent."

"Yes. And now there's been a development." He reaches into his suit pocket, retrieves a piece of paper, and pushes it between the bars. It's a typed explanation of my arrest. I read quickly until I come to material that is wholly new and shocking to me. The report says messages were intercepted on their way to Berlin, sent in code, from Madrid, from Major Arnold Kalle.

Kalle's messages describe a spy with the code name of H21. This spy was passing "significant information" about French military operations to Berlin. Credit for breaking the code Kalle used is given to Commandant Ladoux. At the bottom of the report is a handwritten note from Ladoux himself. *"I am of the very strong opinion that Mata Hari is a double agent. Arrest her upon arrival in Paris."*

The paper I'm holding begins to shake as my hands tremble. "Liar!" I shout. My voice echoes in the prison. A few cells down someone shouts, "They all are!" I lower my voice and swear, "Ladoux is a liar, Edouard!"

"All of it, M'greet?" I can see in his eyes that he doesn't believe me.

"Major Kalle is the man I seduced in Madrid." I think of us in his bed, how I believed he was charmed by me, how I was proud of discovering an important secret for France. I am so embarrassed. "Whatever he sent in those messages isn't true. It can't be. I didn't reveal anything to him! I don't know any French military secrets. He has turned everything around. The truth is *he* told *me* Berlin's secrets. Or, I thought he did—I don't know what to believe anymore. I don't understand this at all, Edouard. He's lying."

"If Major Kalle was lying with the intent to discredit you, M'greet, why did he send his telegrams to Berlin in code?" There's fear in Edouard's face. "A person transmits in code to keep a message secret."

I begin to weep. "I don't know."

"Is there anything you haven't told me, M'greet? Absolutely anything that you are withholding? Information you haven't already given to Bouchardon or Ladoux?"

I close my eyes and I am back at Consul Cramer's office. I see him scoffing at my suggestion that he compensate me for stolen property. *"The consulate does not reimburse travelers for lost clothing. This applies in times of peace as well as war."* I hear myself agreeing to his alternative suggestion. I open my eyes as tears burn hot trails down my face. "A small thing. The full reason Consul Cramer gave me those twenty thousand marks."

I am staring at the elephant-headed god Ganesh, the remover of obstacles. I hear Mahadevi telling me, "You have to let him go."

"He was my son. I will never let him go. I want to feel whole again."

"Let go of that desire. You will never be whole again."

I recognize the first words of truth anyone has offered me. She is not vowing that all will be well, or begging me to eat because I still have Non.

"The house is haunted," I tell Ganesh. "My little boy is everywhere."

We both know what I must do. But my little girl . . .

I turn to Mahadevi. "What will happen to her?"

"I was married once. I have a girl, too. She's grown now. If I had stayed with her father, he would have killed me."

The scent of my hair, the touch of my finger running down her tiny nose. What will Non remember of me if I leave her now?

Mahadevi looks straight into my eyes. "He is violent and I have seen how he hurts you. It is only a matter of time. You'll be dead. What good is a dead mother to a girl?"

I wake up shouting Non's name.

When the guards announce his arrival, I turn my back. I don't want to see him.

"Mata Hari."

"I know what you think. It isn't true." In my own ears, my voice sounds raw. I don't understand why they keep letting him in to see me. Who does Bowtie know that he can gain access to the Conciergerie whenever he pleases? He can't possibly afford to bribe the guards the way Edouard does.

"Look," he says. "A peace offering."

I turn and he holds up a newspaper: STAR OF THE EAST IMPRISONED FOR ESPIONAGE: BUT HAS SHE BEEN FRAMED? "I have nothing more to say to you," I tell him and retreat to the back of my cell. "You can leave."

"Mata Hari, please let me help you. I don't believe you're guilty of espionage against France. I think you're being used as a scapegoat."

I study him. I don't know who to trust anymore.

"Let me help you," he says again, and an idea occurs to me.

I approach the bars. "Can you contact someone for me?"

"I can contact anyone. I'll contact the Pope if that's what you want."

If he has access to anyone, then he can communicate with Non.

Something is happening. For the first time in a month I'm allowed to shower. Someone went through my confiscated property; after I am returned to my cell a female guard brings me one of my own skirts along with a green blouse. I haven't seen these items since the morning I was arrested in my hotel room. The clothing feels wonderful and smells so clean I nearly cry with gratitude.

Then unfamiliar guards arrive and I am let out of my cell for a second time. The men—two in front and two behind—escort me down the hall. I am shocked when they usher me outside the prison into a foggy morning and a waiting vehicle.

I don't know where they are taking me and I don't ask.

I wish we could drive for days—for years. To see the world beyond the view from my cell window is now the greatest luxury. I drink in the sights and the sounds. But the trip is over all too soon. The guards accompany me up the steps of an unfamiliar building and escort me down barren halls. I am delivered to a room that has two windows. Behind a desk sits Commandant Ladoux and next to him is Captain Bouchardon, both looking grim and impatient. I freeze when I see them; at that moment Edouard joins me. He puts his hand on the small of my back and pushes me forward.

"There's nothing I want to say to these men," I whisper as I sit next to Edouard. My guards remain at the door. Are they concerned that I will make a mad run for freedom?

"My client has something to tell you," Edouard says. "I believe it will clear up this grave misunderstanding, and we will all come to agree that Mata Hari is being imprisoned unjustly and must be released at once. She is no more guilty of espionage than you or I. She is merely a foolish woman with the regrettable habit of bedding the wrong men. A woman who routinely couples ill-advised liaisons with requests for compensation."

He's calling me a whore. If he believes this will free me, then I will play the role of a foolish whore.

Captain Bouchardon says, "Speak," and everyone looks at me.

"It would be cowardly to defend myself against such actions as I have taken," I begin.

Edouard interrupts me. "The day you met Consul Cramer," he prompts. "Was that the first time you'd ever spoken with him?"

"Yes."

"We've heard this before," Ladoux declares. He starts to stand.

Edouard gestures for him to wait and Ladoux sits down. "When you asked Consul Cramer for compensation for your furs—what was his response?"

"Consul Cramer told me that the consulate never reimburses travelers for lost clothing. That this is true in times of peace as well as war."

Ladoux rubs his temple impatiently.

"He then asked me the market value of my confiscated property and gave me a check. For twenty thousand marks. He said it was a favor, an acknowledgment of who I am. And he said that he would inform his superiors that I agreed to keep my ears and eyes open on behalf of Germany."

There's silence in the room. "I agreed and accepted the check."

"So your payment—" Ladoux begins.

"Was compensation for stolen furs. I never intended to spy for Germany; what he told his superiors was untrue. I agreed to his suggestion because I take when someone has taken from me—"

"My client is telling the truth. She took the money from Consul Cramer because German soldiers seized her furs while she was a passenger on a train bound for Paris."

"When I first made France my home," I add, "I took a train to Paris. I was without money and without clothes—"

"The furs aren't the point!" Bouchardon interrupts. He addresses Edouard. "If she wants us to believe that she regularly travels with twenty thousand marks' worth of furs, so be it. What we find incredibly difficult to believe, Monsieur Clunet, is that a German consul would lie to his superiors about such a sum of money and what its purpose was." Bouchardon is stone-faced. "We are at war. Her story is preposterous."

"What do you believe the truth to be?" Edouard demands.

"Don't concern yourself with what we *believe*, counselor." Bouchardon glances at Ladoux. "Concern yourself with what we *know*. We have proof that the twenty thousand marks in discussion were paid in exchange for espionage, Monsieur Clunet. Not furs. Not liaisons. It was payment from Germany for espionage against France."

"Show me this proof," Edouard demands.

"I'm sorry." Bouchardon stands and Ladoux follows. "It's a matter of national security now. We will see the both of you at trial."

The men leave without sparing me a glance.

The guards escort me out of the room immediately; I don't have time for a single private word with Edouard. I have no idea what to expect from a trial. I just pray that Edouard is able to bribe his way back to my cell and explain it to me.

Chapter 20

TRIAL BY COURT MARTIAL

JULY 24, 1917

*T*his time seven guards are deemed necessary to escort me from my cell in the Conciergerie to the black car waiting outside to convey me to the Palais de Justice. I have had only one visit since my disastrous meeting with Bouchardon and Ladoux—from Bowtie. I haven't heard a word from Edouard.

The drive lasts only a few minutes and before we reach the courthouse I see that the streets are filled with people, many of them chanting my name and holding signs that read *Free Mata Hari* and *Innocent.* Some women in the crowd are weeping. The sight touches me; I didn't realize I had female admirers. If he manages to visit me again, I will thank Bowtie. He promised me that he would rally people in my support.

As soon as we come to a stop, a dozen reporters swarm the car. I regret that I am not wearing something glamorous, an ensemble that represents who I am, an entertainer. Instead I am dressed in a simple blue skirt and blouse given to me by my jailers. One of my guards opens the car door and the ambush is immediate.

"Mata Hari!" a reporter shouts. "Why are you spying for Germany?"

I ignore him and do not let my face betray my emotions. I step out and scan the throng for Bowtie; I don't see him. The guards escort me toward the courthouse and the reporters follow like swarming bees.

"Mata Hari! Why were you arrested?"

I stop and answer this question. "Because I am a woman who enjoys herself very much."

"Keep moving," the nearest guard snaps at me. The crowd is surging and three men appear to clear a path so that I can enter the doors of the Palais de Justice.

Inside it is absolute madness. Reporters are crowding in the halls. I spot Bowtie. "Where is Edouard?" I call to him as I am herded past.

"He's here—don't worry. He's already in the Cour d'Assises," he answers and reaches out for my hand.

"No touching the prisoner!"

I'm taken down the hall to a paneled courtroom. I see seven tall wooden chairs that I imagine are meant for my judges, a long table, and behind that a French flag that covers an entire wall.

Edouard is sitting alone at a smaller table. It strikes me that his hair is almost completely white—was it still peppered dark when he first visited me in prison? He looks as though my arrest has aged him ten years. Next to him is an empty chair.

At a different table sit three men I don't recognize, together with Captain Bouchardon. The table is weighted down with stacks of documents. All four men watch me as I enter. None of them stand.

As soon as he sees me, though, Edouard rises. He guides me to the empty chair and catches me looking up at the image of Justice painted on the ceiling above our heads.

"M'greet," he says quietly, drawing my gaze downward. I can see that he's nervous. He's not a criminal lawyer, yet here we are. The files on Bouchardon's table are so thick. What can possibly be written in them? I imagine they are lists. Lists of every man I've slept with.

Edouard whispers in my ear, "That man." I follow his gaze: He means the tall one dressed entirely in gray. "His name is Andre Mornet."

For a moment we are together in the Rothschilds' jasmine-scented garden and he is saying *Don't speak at length with anyone who appears drunk, in particular the German ambassador . . . von Schoen.*

"One of the best prosecutors in France," he says, and I am snapped back into the awful present.

"I want you to answer him in simple sentences, M'greet, no matter how he phrases his questions. For your own sake, don't embellish. Do not attempt to describe your version of events. I'll do that for you. This is a military tribunal. All of the judges"—he inclines his head toward the seven still-empty chairs—"are members of the military. Do not try to charm them. Under these circumstances they will respond to facts, not stories."

I wish that I were anywhere in this world instead of inside the Palais de Justice. I want to be at the top of the temple of Borobudur with Sofie, watching the sun set over the misty hills of Magelang. I want to be exploring the Javanese beaches with Non, picking my way across the rocks as the warm breeze tangles her hair.

"In a few moments the doors will open and the public will be allowed in," Edouard is informing me. "Then the seven judges will enter. After they are seated, Andre Mornet will call witnesses."

Witnesses? "Who do they plan to call?"

"I was not given that information. I'm sorry. A court martial is unlike a trial in the civilian world—"

"And our witnesses? Who has agreed to testify for me?" I have conflicted feelings immediately. How wonderful it will be to see familiar faces, and yet how horrible to see them under these circumstances.

"I'm sorry, M'greet." Edouard pushes a glass of water into my hands.

"You are sorry? Why are you sorry? Who turned me down?"

He recites the list quietly. Guimet and Givenchy. Baron Rothschild. Felix Rousseau, my "banker." Jeanne is dead. I've made so few real friends in my life.

"Has anyone agreed to speak on my behalf?"

"Yes. I located Henri de Marguerie. He will tell them you are of good character."

A handsome man who spent the night with me after one of my shows. *Salome? Cleopatra?* Maybe *Tristan and Isolde.* I can't summon an image of his face, but I remember his wristwatch—it was the first one I'd ever seen. I think back and eventually it comes to me. Henri de Rothschild's château. I'd just performed *Lady Godiva* and the string quartet was playing something slow. A dark-haired man asked me to dance. He was wearing a Rolex. "It's a wristwatch," he said.

A guard opens the doors and spectators rush to get inside.

"At least I have Vadime," I say, searching the crowd for him. Vadime knows the true me. He will set these men straight.

"Vadime de Massloff declined as well. I'm sorry."

This can't be true. In my mind's eye I see him, wrapping his scarf around my neck, pulling me toward him. *"I love you, Mata Hari. I've loved you since the first time I saw you."* Who will I live with in New York? *All of my hope for the future rests with you,* he said.

Edouard sees my devastation. "I'm told his superior officer forbade him to speak on your behalf. Don't let this undo you, M'greet. Stay strong. This is the performance of your life."

"Are you certain—"

"We believe in you, Mata Hari!"

I am cut off by the noise and excitement of hundreds of people scuffling to find a seat; the commotion is so great that the prosecutor starts shouting, "These civilians must be removed!"

There is absolute mayhem for several minutes and the room

threatens to dissolve into chaos. The judges enter and confer and it's immediately decided that the trial will proceed *huis clos.*

Edouard looks at me. *Behind closed doors.* Without a single reporter watching the trial with a critical eye, anything might happen. I look up at the image of Justice holding her heavy scales and wonder which way they will tip. Is justice truly blind? The Roman goddess is depicted as impartial, meant to uncover the truth, and to do so objectively, without fear or favor, no matter the wealth or weakness of the person who is standing before her. I look at the judges and they stare straight back at me.

Andre Mornet has been detailing the case against me. He has revealed that French agents spent more than fifteen months following me from Berlin to Amsterdam, from Amsterdam to Madrid, and back again to Paris.

I have racked my memory but I cannot recall any moment when I thought I was being followed.

He has detailed my liaisons with men in every city—during many years, not only for the past fifteen months. He knows where we went to eat, where we went to dance, and always where we were intimate. Most of these men I barely remember. He has spent a great deal of time speaking about past lovers who are German: officers, captains, colonels. But the man who interests him most is Russian: Vadime de Massloff. Hearing his name makes me want to weep, and I can barely listen as he describes our relationship and the importance of the airbase in Vittel. None of what he says is true in the way he describes what happened, and why it happened. But now I recognize that it is damning all the same. I can see the terrible picture that the best prosecutor in France is painting, stroke by stroke.

"Can you tell me about Vadime de Massloff?"

"Are you accusing me of something? Because not even these monsters think I was spying in Vittel."

"Are you sure?"

"The English understood that this woman cannot be trusted," Andre Mornet says. He describes how they arrested me, and I am stunned to learn that while they were paying for my stay at the Savoy the British informed Commandant Ladoux of their belief that I was working with the Germans. Now I understand why I heard nothing from Ladoux beyond that terse telegram telling me to return to Madrid. This revelation leads directly to the most damning evidence Mornet has: Arnold Kalle and the coded telegram he sent from Madrid to Berlin, identifying me as asset "H21" and crediting me with passing "significant information" about French military operations to Berlin.

Due to the "sensitive nature" of the information decoded in these missives, the contents are not described to me in any detail. I cannot defend myself against the unknown.

When, at last, Mornet calls me to the stand, my legs are trembling; I hope it isn't obvious. I sit and try to compose myself as he instructs me to answer every question as briefly as possible. "There are to be no histrionics, no drama, no performing, Margaretha Zelle. Mata Hari's audience has left. So, shall we begin?"

I nod and he says, "Is it true that you were invited to observe army maneuvers in Silesia and that this invitation was extended by a German cavalry officer by the name of Alfred Kiepert?"

"Yes, but—"

"Answer only with a yes or no, Miss Zelle."

I glance at Edouard. He nods. "Yes."

As he describes the importance of an invitation I never accepted, I look at the seven men who sit in judgment of me. They are old and humorless. Men who were probably alive and even fighting during the Siege of Paris.

There is a pause, and I realize that Mornet has asked me something. "I didn't accept his invitation," I say.

"That isn't what I asked you, Miss Zelle. I asked you why you took such a great number of German officers as lovers."

When will I be offered the chance to explain that I never saw military maneuvers with Alfred Kiepert? "I love officers. I have loved them all my life. I'd prefer to be the mistress of a poor officer than of a rich banker. And I like to make comparisons between the different nationalities. I have known an equal number of French officers."

Mornet shakes his head; the seven judges look disgusted. "General von Schilling," Mornet says, counting on his fingers. "*Officer* Alfred Kiepert; *Major* Arnold Kalle; Alfred von Schlieffen, chief of staff of the German army; Günther Burstyn—"

"I prefer men in uniform."

"Men in *German* uniform," he says, as if he is speaking an obscenity.

"That isn't accurate," Edouard objects.

But Mornet is not deterred. "This tribunal does not find it credible that the astonishing sums these military men paid—three hundred thousand marks from Officer Alfred Kiepert, twenty thousand marks from Consul Cramer, for example—were money paid for the favors of an aging mistress."

"Object!" Edouard says. "The reason for these payments are in her deposition."

"You must be very expensive," Mornet says to me. His tone is mocking.

"Definitely," I reply.

"Object!" Edouard repeats, sounding outraged.

"What do you think you are worth?"

"All or nothing," I say, defiant.

None of the judges paid Edouard the slightest attention when he shouted his objections, but now Mornet addresses him directly. "We have read her deposition, counselor. What I am saying is that we do not believe her claims. We believe she is lying." He pauses, as if he is considering his next words very carefully. "On December first, Monsieur Clunet, fifty thousand Allied soldiers were killed. Miss Zelle provided the Germans with information that led directly to these deaths."

"That's a lie," I shout and Edouard is immediately on his feet. "Show me the proof! Fifty thousand men? There wasn't a single story in any newspaper in this country—"

"It is confidential information," Andre Mornet replies. "We are at war." He turns to me on the stand. "You betrayed France, Miss Zelle."

The room has become oppressive. "France is my home!" I say. "For most of my life I have lived in Paris. Am I a courtesan? Yes. A traitoress? Never!" I have to rest my head in my hands to compose myself.

Mornet calls his witnesses, and one after another, officers I've never met detail romantic liaisons that never took place. The entire trial is a farce. The last to speak is a short colonel named Goudet. If I searched all of France, I'd never find another man as fat or smug. Mornet introduces him as the head of French counterespionage.

"I have studied the case of the accused with great care," Colonel Goudet says. The room is absolutely silent. I realize I am holding my breath. "Margaretha Zelle"—Goudet clears his throat—"is the most dangerous spy of the twentieth century."

All seven judges begin talking at once.

"Look at this woman," Mornet says, as he finishes his summation. He has detailed my fluency in several languages, my relationships with dozens of military officers, some real and some pure fantasy; he has challenged my intelligence, my morality, and my lack of conscience.

"This is a woman who is accustomed to getting what she wants: men and money. She uses her charm and her fame to convince the world that she is harmless, but do not be fooled. She must not get what she wants this time because she has betrayed France. She has taken money and given information to our enemy that has cost French soldiers their lives. She must not walk free. Make no mistake. Margaretha Zelle is guilty of treason!"

I'm taken directly from the courtroom to a car. I'm not given the chance to converse with Edouard or talk to any of the reporters who wait for me outside of the Palais de Justice.

In my cell I can't sleep. I am too numb.

After my son's death, I stopped talking. I lay in bed and stared at the ceiling. I don't remember what I dreamed about, or what kept me occupied during the day. I stared at the white ceiling for long periods of time, thinking about Norman and where he was, if he would recognize me when I got to heaven, and if he did, whether he'd still be a boy or a man. My servant, Laksari, stayed by my bedside, talking to me about my daughter, urging me to spend time with my little girl. Now, as I stare at the bars of my cell, I wonder if I will see Norman before I see my daughter again.

I am returned to the Palais de Justice the next morning and there are a thousand people crowding the marble steps, yet I am so distressed I can barely hear them calling my name. Inside the courtroom the trial resumes at eight o'clock. It's Edouard's turn to speak in my defense.

He calls the only witness who has agreed to speak on my behalf: Henri de Marguerie. We spent one evening together and haven't seen each other in more than a decade.

"You're military?"

"I was a pilot."

I allow him to continue complimenting me as we cross the dance floor. An orchestra replaces the string quartet and the new musicians strike up a waltz. He tells me about his family in London. I tell him about my time in Bombay. Then the musicians abandon Johann Strauss and begin playing a more scandalizing tune; I learned the accompanying dance my first week in Paris. The handsome aviator raises his eyebrows at me, asking if I'm willing to accept his invitation.

Henri speaks kindly about me but it is apparent that none of the judges are interested in the warm memories of a long-retired aviator who bedded a woman easily at a party, and Mornet makes short work of him.

"Before spending the evening with you did Miss Zelle ask about your military affiliation?"

"I was retired—"

"Yes or no?"

"Yes."

In no time, it's Edouard's turn to deliver a summation and I feel like a passenger on the *Titanic*.

"Margaretha Zelle, better known to the world as Mata Hari, is one of the most photographed women of our time. Her image has appeared on everything from cigarettes to packages of tea. How can any person in this courtroom today believe that she could be a successful spy for the Germans? What man would trust her with secrets—a dancer, an actress, a *courtesan*? My client stands on trial today not because of secrets divulged—for we have heard no compelling evidence that she had access to *any* sensitive information—

but rather, for the number of men she's taken to her bed. Of this, we have heard ample evidence. Can you condemn her for the life she's chosen to lead, one of financial and moral promiscuity? Yes, but you cannot convict her of treason. Is Margaretha Zelle guilty of making poor decisions? Yes. Is she guilty of seduction? Most certainly. But is she guilty of treason against the nation of France? Absolutely not."

After the judges withdraw, we are instructed to wait. I lean over in my chair and Edouard takes me in his arms. "They're going to find me guilty," I predict.

"If that's the case, we will appeal," he says. "Immediately."

I start to weep. "If they deny the appeal?"

"Then we will submit another one," Edouard whispers into my ear. "Pray for a quick end to this war, M'greet. When it's over, this country will regain its sanity and everyone will see that the only thing you're guilty of is being a foolish woman."

It hurts to hear him call me foolish. But it's true. I should have married him. I should have left Berlin with him when he asked me to leave. If I had done that simple thing, none of this—none of it—would have happened. Vadime de Massloff never would have loved me; he was a foolish distraction. The weight of this realization hits me hard and I bury my head in his chest. "I love you, Edouard," I say.

His arms tighten around me. "I love you, too, Margaretha Zelle."

It takes the judges forty minutes to reach a verdict. They file back into the courtroom one by one and refuse to meet my gaze. I decide that I am not going to cry in this room again.

"Margaretha Zelle, also known as M'greet MacLeod, also known as Mata Hari, the judges of this tribunal find you guilty of espionage against the country of France."

"What shall the sentence of the accused be?" the prosecutor asks.

"The sentence of the accused shall be death by firing squad."

Chapter 21

WHAT LEGACY CAN I LEAVE HER?

*I*nside the Conciergerie, I'm moved to a new cell: It's called the Slaughterhouse. Two women join me: one a convicted murderess, the other a young girl also charged with espionage. We rarely speak to one another. Instead, we keep to ourselves and sleep as often as we can, trying to dream away our misery. I can dream while I'm awake now. Today, it is August in The Hague, and the pink azaleas are in bloom. *"Tell me about our lives in Java,"* I say. *"Tell me again."*

"It's going to be magnificent," Evert promises, sprawling on the clean cotton sheets. *"We'll buy a house by water so clear you can see to the bottom."*

"And our children?" I feel perfectly safe with him.

"We're going to have three of them. Two boys and a girl. We'll name the boys Evert and Hans. And the girl shall be—"

"Not M'greet." I say, decisive. For the first time I know my future.

"But M'greet's a lovely name."

"I like the name Antje." Our family will be cradled in tropical nights and sands the color of eternity.

He runs his fingers through my hair. *"Whatever you wish."*

* * *

As I sit on my cot I stare at my hands: The fingers painted with henna in Java, the wrists that Guimet's silver bangles adorned. I look at the arms that held Norman and Non. I study my feet. Someday soon they are going to walk their last. The court hasn't said when I am going to die. Someone will simply come one morning and take me away. Unless I win an appeal.

On the last day in September, Sister Léonide tells me that I have a visitor: Edouard Clunet has arrived. "Are you willing to see him?" she asks.

My cellmates stare at me, stricken. There is only one reason that one of us would be allowed an official visitor. My voice trembles when I ask her to please, show him in.

I can hear his footsteps. I believe I would recognize his gait if he were walking among thousands. Sister Léonide brings him a chair—not the stool that the bribed guards offer illicit visitors—and he sits. We stare at each other through the bars. Then he tells me what I already know.

"They rejected your appeal."

"So this is how the show ends," I say. "The last dance." Edouard buries his head in his hands and cries. I try to be brave for us both. "It's all right."

"I wanted to take care of you," he whispers, gaining control of his emotions.

"I know. And I should have let you."

He takes my hand through the prison bars. "This is an abomination of justice. What has the world come to?" He is devastated.

"Buddha said, 'In life there is suffering because of the impermanent nature of things,'" I offer, holding on tightly. I imagine Edouard going home this evening to his aubergine chair, taking a brandy while his pretty wife reads to him from *Le Figaro*. That was the role I should have played. Not this. We could have created a family. For so many years I believed I offered the world "the dance of destruction as it leads to creation." Now I understand the truth: I confused the order of things. I created pain; I danced to my own destruction.

I feel the pinpricks of hot tears. "I'm going to miss you so much," I tell him.

He rests his head against the bars. "I do not think I can bear this."

It should be crisp and clear this early in October, but beyond my cell window there is only rain. I dream constantly of the sun. Of beaches and water and warm temple stones. I sit on the edge of my metal bed and remember my first weeks in Java, when anything seemed possible. That's what's so wonderful about beginnings. They promise everything: love, happiness, eternity. I wonder what eternity is truly like, and whether Marie Antoinette thought about this more than a hundred years ago when she was sitting here, waiting to be taken to the guillotine from this very prison. Did she hope there would be a last-minute reprieve? Did she agonize over what was to become of her son? I think about my daughter living in Amsterdam and I wonder what she will make of her life. Will she be happy? Can there ever be happiness for a child whose mother abandoned her? I hope so. With Rudolph, I was once foolish enough to believe I could make us both happy. Now I know that people must make their own happiness.

Sister Léonide announces another official visitor. It's Bowtie, holding an envelope in his hands. We watch each other through the bars in silence; there is no more need for artfulness between us. Bowtie's eyes fill with genuine tears.

"No use in crying," I say gently. "It's not going to change anything."

He hands me the envelope. "As promised."

Inside is my daughter's address and a current photo of her. I experience a rush of emotions gazing at her image: She looks so like me and yet I can see that she is kinder and so very innocent. I hope Rudolph doesn't ruin her.

"Thank you," I whisper, running my finger over her hair, her wholesome dress, her face. We will never meet again in this world. Everything she'll ever believe about me will come from papers like *Le Figaro*.

Bowtie sits in the chair Sister Léonide brought him and watches me.

"One last interview?" I say, for old times' sake. I'm surprised when he takes out his pad of paper and a pen. "What do you want to talk about?" he asks.

I think about it for a while. "Poppies," I say. I've been remembering a poem I read in *Punch* magazine a couple years ago. I recite it for him:

In Flanders fields the poppies blow
Between the crosses, row on row,
That mark our place; and in the sky
The larks, still bravely singing, fly
Scarce heard amid the guns below.

We are the Dead. Short days ago
We lived, felt dawn, saw sunset glow,
Loved and were loved, and now we lie
In Flanders fields.

Take up our quarrel with the foe:
To you from failing hands we throw
The torch; be yours to hold it high.
If ye break faith with us who die
We shall not sleep, though poppies grow
In Flanders fields.

For several long minutes he is at a loss for words; together we listen to one of my cellmates sob.

"Are your parents still alive?" he asks quietly, with embarrassment.

"No." I check myself. "I'm not certain. My father may be." I tell Bowtie about him. What he would say to me when I was a child. *White is a nice color, M'greet, but it's not your color. Your color is red. Because red is passion. It's life.*

"Do you regret your career?"

I've thought about this a great deal in the Conciergerie. If I had it all to do over again, would I have taken those lessons with Mahadevi? Do I regret touring France, and Spain, and even Germany? "Not entirely." If I had never danced, I would not know Edouard.

"What I regret most is losing my daughter. I thought there would be time for us to reunite . . . I dreamed that we'd escape this war, that I'd bring her to live with me in New York where we would be safe." I look him in the eye. "I've lived almost forty years," I tell him, "and I've made enormous sums of money. A lifetime of jewels, apartments, furs. But now, in the end, what do I have left that matters? What legacy can I leave her?"

"A lock of your hair," he says quietly. "Your memories."

"Could you tell her how breathtaking Java is?"

"Whatever you wish."

I tell him my best memories of that faraway place. I tell him about jungles and rare flowers and dancing with Mahadevi until the sky turned pink at dawn.

When Sister Léonide tells us that our visit is almost over, Bowtie requests a pair of scissors and she complies without question. I cut off a long lock of hair. I fold it into the envelope and give it to him. A gift for my daughter.

"Mama, Mama, wake up!"

"Oh, Non, liefste, it's too early—"

"No, Mama. Something's wrong!"

I'm jolted awake. Someone is shaking my shoulder. My God, it's Bouchardon. It's happening. It's real.

"Get dressed," he says.

Immediately I feel like I'm going to be sick.

He leaves my cell and his footsteps disappear down the hall. The other women are staring at me, their eyes haunted. One day he will come for them as well.

They watch me dress. A black hat, a black skirt, and a long dark blouse. Sister Léonide arrives and she walks me to the last car I will ever ride in. The drive to Château de Vincennes is a heartbeat. A group of reporters and military officers are already waiting for me. Bowtie is among them. And now I see Edouard.

Many have gathered to witness my death, yet as I walk to the field behind the château all is silent. Then I hear Edouard shouting my name and I run.

I embrace him until my guards force us to part.

They escort me to a wooden stake in the ground. As they tie my hands I feel as if I'm watching myself from a distance. I am offered a blindfold, but I refuse. I can hear Edouard weeping. I want to be strong for him. I want him to be the last person I see on this earth.

Twelve men take a stance across from me. They aim their rifles at my chest. I look one last time at Edouard. I remember him as he was on the day we met, tossing that rose out of his car. I conjure the day in the museum when he posed like the statue of Charles V. I appreciate for the final time how hard he labored to deliver Non home to me. I will miss him.

God, how I will miss him.

EPILOGUE

$\mathcal{C}$ustomers are trying on coats, asking questions about the furs, demanding different cuts. The woman wearing the expensive rings—who's already been here six times this week—is demanding another cup of tea, sinking back into one of the soft leather couches, expecting the staff to fetch her refreshments.

"More biscuits, madam?" Of course.

"More tea?" Yes, and be certain it's hot this time.

It's unlikely that Ring Woman will buy anything from Joossens today; still, the biscuits and tea have to be produced. The shop girl is on her way to refill the woman's cup for a fourth time when she sees him, standing near the winter hats.

"Jeanne MacLeod?" he asks, startling her. He is wearing a green bow tie. It should look ridiculous, but he wears it with style—he looks to be twenty, maybe twenty-five.

She tries to place him. A friend of her father's? A previous customer? He holds out his hand and she shakes it.

"Ancel Dupond. I was a friend of your mother's."

She nearly drops the teacup and saucer she's holding. She inspects the man more closely. There are fine lines around his eyes. Now, as she studies him, she decides he's closer to thirty-five. She realizes the implication of his words. "*Was?* Why do you say *was?*"

"I'm sorry. You don't know?" He takes the teacup from her as it begins to rattle in its saucer. He guides her to a couch. He sets the china on a table and asks, "You're Jeanne Louise MacLeod, am I right?"

"My mother called me Non. That's what I prefer to be called."

"Is there somewhere we can go to talk?"

"Miss," her customer calls, waving bejeweled fingers. "I'm still waiting for hot tea."

"It's right there," Non says. "Feel free to get up and pour it." She turns to her mother's friend. "Why don't we go across the street?" She retrieves her coat from the back room and puts on her hat. When she leaves Joossens with Ancel Dupond, she has no intention of returning.

As they make their way to the coffeehouse, Ancel recognizes Mata Hari in the girl: the same dark beauty and a similar willfulness, too. He wonders how this girl's father has managed to control her.

In the bright light of the coffeehouse Ancel orders coffee for both of them and waits for the girl to ask questions. He has some of his own. What was it like to be raised by a man who didn't want you? Were you aware of how badly your mother yearned for you?

"My mother is dead?" Non asks.

"Yes. I'm very sorry." Ancel reaches into his bag and retrieves an article. It's not one he wrote, but it's a kind and melancholic piece that describes the trial and Mata Hari's execution. He feels uncomfortable watching Non while she reads it, so he stares across the coffeehouse at a pair of women laughing together over their porcelain cups. There can be such joy in the world, he thinks. And so much sorrow. When he looks back, Non's eyes are red. She's so young. Sixteen? Seventeen? Mata Hari told him her age but he can't remember and it would be rude, now, to ask.

"This is so terrible," she whispers, trying not to cry. "Why didn't anyone tell me? I've been working. I was saving money to visit Paris and find her."

"I'm very sorry." All he can offer her are words. He takes out a folder. Inside is everything he's ever written about Mata Hari. His article covering her debut at Guimet's library, her triumph at the Kursaal, the lies he published about her time in Berlin.

He pushes it toward Non.

"What is this?"

He hopes he isn't making a mistake. But this was what Mata Hari had wanted. "Your mother's press," he says. "Whatever your father's told you about her, she loved you deeply."

"How do you know?" There's an edge in her voice. She mistrusts her mother, but at the same time she's looking for reasons to love her.

"Because I was one of the last people to see her."

A woman arrives with their coffee but Non doesn't drink. She stares at the steam rising into the air, visible and then gone forever. "My father never told me she was in prison," she says flatly.

"For a long time, very few people knew." Though surely, Rudolph MacLeod was one of them.

"You knew."

"I'm a reporter for *Le Figaro*. It was my job to know."

"Was she mistreated?"

"No." He tells the lie without hesitation.

"I'm glad to know that."

"She was innocent, in my opinion."

"Then . . . why?" Non's voice begins to rise. "Why did they execute her?"

"Publicity. During war, sacrifices are made." Ancel knows how bitter he sounds. "The story of a *femme fatale* betraying France could only end in death." His guilt is gnawing at him: Without Mata Hari he wouldn't have a large office overlooking the Seine. Without him, the sensation that was Mata Hari might never have existed. Fueled by his articles, France had built her up and then tore her down.

Non doesn't open the folder. "Do you know why she abandoned me?" she asks.

"She was afraid of your father. Afraid that he would kill you if she came for you."

"She tried to take me once," the girl whispers. "She didn't succeed. When we got home, my father beat me so badly I wasn't able to walk for two months."

Ancel doesn't know what to say.

"I live with him. If he knew the two of us were meeting here, he *would* kill me. But don't worry. I won't give him that chance."

If there was any doubt, Ancel is now certain this is Mata Hari's daughter. "She left you this," he says, reaching into his coat pocket and handing her a locket. It's silver, and he had Non's initials engraved on the front. He purchased it the day Mata Hari clipped off a lock of her hair and handed it to him through the prison bars. He wanted to create a nicer presentation than hair wrapped in paper.

Non is weeping now, clasping the locket to her chest. Other customers have started to stare; Ancel wonders what this scene looks like to them. Non opens the locket and sees her mother's hair. "It's unfair," she manages to say.

It is. Ancel can't spin the story any other way. He watches as she fastens the locket around her neck and he thinks of how similar mother and daughter are in their body language. *Were.*

"You quit your job," he observes. "What will your father say?"

"I don't know. I don't care. He won't be able to find me where I'm going."

*   *   *

She stands at the rails of the ship *Outlandia* and closes her eyes, imagining the warmth of Java. No one on this ship knows who she is. She had been afraid that her father was having her followed, but now, with the sea air to clear her head, she can think better.

She is finally free. At last.

She has memorized every article given to her by the journalist from *Le Figaro*. She has weeks, possibly even months, before her money runs out and she has to find employment. Until that happens, she will visit the cities where her mother once lived and meet the women her mother once knew. She plans to fit together the broken pieces of her childhood, putting faces to the names that echo in her mind: Norman, Laksari, Mahadevi. And, of course, the most important name of all: Mata Hari.

After so many years, finally, she is going home.

AUTHOR'S NOTE

On October 15, just before dawn, Captain Bouchardon woke Mata Hari from her sleep and ordered her to dress. She was given several minutes to compose herself, then driven from the Conciergerie to the Château de Vincennes where reporters and military officers were waiting. Among those present was Edouard Clunet. Witnesses said that as they embraced for the last time, Edouard became hysterical.

At 5:45 a.m., Mata Hari was taken behind the château and tied to a wooden stake that had been placed in the ground. Twelve men aimed rifles at her chest. She nodded her head when she was ready and, at 6:00 a.m., the twelve men fired. Only three of the trained riflemen hit their mark, but one of the bullets pierced her heart. Mata Hari died at 6:06. She had refused a blindfold. When the execution was over, no one was allowed to claim her body. In accordance with tradition, an officer emptied his pistol into Mata Hari's ear. Afterward, her body was brought to the University of Paris for medical research and experimentation.

Mata Hari's daughter, Jeanne Louise MacLeod, did sail to Java a few weeks shy of her twenty-first birthday. Shockingly, she died while en route, and her cause of death is uncertain. Her early passing guaranteed that she would never learn the truth about her mother's arrest.

Many more years would pass before the world would learn that Arnold Kalle had sent his "secret" messages from Madrid to Berlin in a code that the British had already cracked. Recognizing Mata Hari for what she was—a very amateur spy working for France—Arnold Kalle neatly orchestrated her downfall. He sent a series of telegrams to Berlin written in this broken code, fully anticipating that the British would share the contents with their French allies, and that France would then indict Mata Hari.

If the French knew that Mata Hari was set up, they weren't interested in seeing the truth revealed. In 1917, there was one thing the Germans and French agreed upon: Mata Hari was most valuable dead. Germany likely resented the hoodwinking of Consul Cramer; seeing Mata Hari killed by the French would have been a victory. France was in dire fear of losing the war and desperate to convince her citizens that the government could swiftly destroy all enemies. Mata Hari's sensational execution answered the same need that the deaths of three hundred other French "spies" accomplished: The wartime propaganda machine was fed.

If Mata Hari did "pray for a quick end to this war" in the hope of saving herself, her prayers were answered too late. The truce that halted fighting went into effect at the eleventh hour of the eleventh day of the eleventh month of 1918. Today, that day is commemorated in the United States as Veterans Day.

Even so many years after Mata Hari's death, fact and fiction are still hard to separate. Much of her success can be attributed to her ability to fabricate—like her father, she was an extraordinary teller of tall tales. The stories she fed to the public were often aggrandized and the result is that the exact truth of her life is nearly impossible to prove. And as time has passed, her legend has only grown. Today, the fantasy of Mata Hari has more substance than the reality of Margaretha Zelle. I believe the girl from Leeuwarden would want it no other way.

MATA HARI'S LAST DANCE

MICHELLE MORAN

In the glow of prewar Paris, Mata Hari seems to have everything: a successful career as an exotic dancer, scores of rich lovers, her own apartment, and the attention of the elite European art clique. But as a world war dawns, Europe begins to change—and so does life for Mata Hari. In the midst of this changing world, Mata Hari must learn to navigate growing tensions between rival superpowers Germany and France, as well as her own personal battle for her estranged daughter, Non. Despite all her efforts, Mata Hari fails to win back her daughter and her old way of life. In the end she finds herself poor, alone, and sentenced to death for a crime she swore she never committed. At once tragic and beautiful, *Mata Hari's Last Dance* chronicles the line between fact and fiction, creation and destruction, and life and death.

FOR DISCUSSION

1. *Mata Hari's Last Dance* opens with a newspaper article detailing Mata Hari's death by French firing squad—an article that claims she was not only guilty but "one of the most dangerous of the Kaiser's agents in France and England" (page 2). Discuss how this article compares to the story that the character Mata Hari tells us. Is there any overlap? In general, why do you think the author chose to use so many newspaper articles throughout the novel? Do the articles give us a different perspective? How so?

2. Mata Hari describes her small, run-down apartment as a place where "the carpets stink of urine and mold" and the landlord is "a man who beats his wife" (page 18). Would you describe Mata Hari as a strong female character? Is she a feminist? Do you attribute her ability to lift herself out of poverty as an indication of her strength?

3. Discuss the relationship between Edouard Clunet and Mata Hari. Would you call their relationship odd? Unrequited? Problematic? Do you think the two are truly in love with each other? Why or why not?

4. The snake handler tells Mata Hari not to be afraid of the snake, but to "Treat her well . . . and she will never harm you" (page 48). Is the snake a symbol of the main character? Both Mata Hari and the snake are exotic, dangerous, and arguably misunderstood. In the end, do you believe Mata Hari is as harmless as the snake? Why or why not?

5. What do you think is Mata Hari's goal? Does she want simply to be famous, or is it something more? Why do you think she seeks out the attention of Bowtie and the media?

6. The famous fashion designer tells Mata, "women like us prefer to forget we had a past. Too painful. We'd rather create" (page 64). Discuss Mata Hari's creation. What kind of creation does she make when she dances? What kind of life does her art create? What kind of image? In the process of creation, does she also do as the epigraph to the novel suggests: "This is the dance I dance tonight. The dance of destruction as it leads to creation" (page vii)?

7. Revisit the scene in which Mata Hari reveals the truth about her husband, daughter, and her deceased son (pages 93–94). Is this the first glance we get into the "real" Mata Hari? Did you believe she was removing the mask of her dancer persona in this scene? Why or why not?

8. Bowtie tells Mata Hari "you're good for my career" (page 121). Discuss the ways in which the characters in the novel use one another. Are any of their relationships sincere, or are they all born from opportunity? Consider Bowtie, Mata Hari, Edouard, Mata Hari's father, and Rudolph MacLeod in your response.

9. What is the symbolism of Mata Hari's characterization of herself as "an orchid among buttercups" (page 129)? Do you think she values herself for her distinct appearance, her distinct way of being in the world, or both?

10. Do you think death acts as a catalyst for change in the novel? How might the deaths of Mata Hari's mother and son cause Mata Hari to transform herself into someone new?

11. Do you forgive Mata Hari for her decision to leave her daughter, Non? Do you think she tried everything in her power to get Non back? Is Mata Hari any different from her own father in the end? Why or why not?

12. How does the tension between the real and the fictional serve as a theme for the novel? You may wish to consider Mata Hari's family, her job, and her accusation as a spy in your response. Do you agree that *Mata Hari's Last Dance* presents the point of view that perhaps the "truth" is a composite of fact and fiction, as exemplified in the fact that Mata Hari is not from India but did live in Java?

13. What is Mata Hari's "last dance"? Do you agree with her that she "danced [her] . . . own destruction" (page 246)? In some ways, does Mata Hari's death also create something new? Consider the role of women during her lifetime in your response. Does Mata Hari leave anything but tragedy as a legacy for her daughter?

A CONVERSATION
WITH MICHELLE MORAN

Mata Hari's Last Dance follows the theme of your other books in that a strong female from history is brought to life. How do you select these women from history for your novels? What inspires you about Mata Hari in particular, and female figures in general?

The women in history who appeal to me the most are often the ones who did something extraordinary, although very little is known about them by the public. In my novel *Rebel Queen*, Sita trained to become one of the queen's personal guards at a time when most women were in purdah and not allowed out of the house. In the case of Mata Hari, I found her rise to fame fascinating. She overcame great personal odds—the death of her child, her husband's abuse—to remake herself and become one of the most recognized dancers in Europe.

Why did you choose to begin the novel with Mata Hari's death? Do you think starting with her execution and working backward helps us get close to the truth?

I think when people hear the name *Mata Hari*, a few things immediately come to mind, one of which is her execution. I thought it would be interesting to start with what people already know and work from there. Mata Hari had an extraordinary life. It was an incredibly complicated one, and the entire truth of what she did (or didn't do) may never be known.

Besides Mata Hari, who is your favorite character in the novel and why?

Her lawyer, Edouard Clunet. He was there throughout her life, even at the very end when she was executed. The fact that he witnessed the entire arc of her career made him an interesting figure.

Do you think Mata Hari was innocent? The story presents us with both possibilities through the newspaper articles. What is your stance? Or do you think the possibility exists that she was both a little guilty and a little innocent?

I think Mata Hari fell prey to all the wonderful press that was written about her—that she was a great seductress and a stunning beauty. My guess is that she thought she could get away with spying because she was such an irresistible woman. Her entire adult life she'd been told this. So yes, I think she did spy, but I think she did it for France and that she did it very poorly. I don't believe for a moment that she was interested in secrets or war. Money was her goal—it had always been her goal since her father had lost everything when she was a child.

In your research, do you think you discovered the "real" Mata Hari? Or does she remain as mysterious to you as ever?

I think the real Mata Hari is in these pages somewhere—in the glimpses of her childhood, in the pain she describes at seeing her father living with another woman after he abandoned her family, in the memories of her husband's cruelty. Her personality was forged in the fires of abandonment and abuse. But always, even at the end, she held on to the dream of reuniting with Non.

Discuss the title. In your opinion, is Mata Hari's last dance her death? Or does her legacy reach beyond her execution?

I think her last dance was certainly her death. It was a performance, only this time it was on a political stage and she wasn't able to orchestrate it.

How did you bring to life prewar Paris and Berlin? Did you travel to these cities to capture their spirit? Share with us your research method.

Whenever I write a book, I travel to the locations where my characters spent much of their time. For Mata Hari, that meant going to Paris, Berlin, and the Netherlands. But Paris proved to be the most important, in particular the Musée Guimet, where Mata Hari made her debut.

What do you think was Mata Hari's true goal in life? In some ways, she seems vain. In other moments, she is a heartbroken mother. What is your take on the real person's desire?

I think she was many things, just as all of us are. She was beautiful and vain and ambitious and wounded. She was a wife and mother and dancer and courtesan. She searched desperately for love and couldn't seem to recognize the real form of it when it came. I think that the biggest mistakes she made in her life (in terms of what she did during the war and the men she allowed to court her) go back to this desperate search for acceptance.

Do you understand Mata Hari's popularity as a form of exoticism? Is this problematic for you? How did you tackle such a large issue in the novel?

This is such a great question. There's no doubt that Mata Hari's success came from her perceived exoticism. This is something she tried very hard to cultivate, going as far as changing her name and place of birth whenever she spoke with the press. We know she fell in love with Hinduism at some point in Java, but whether she practiced it at home is highly doubtful. She probably embraced it much the same way her audiences did—as something new and interesting. However, when you really look at her dances and how they incorporated Hindu gods, what she was doing was shocking. Nothing like that was happening in any temple in India or Java. I'm sure she knew that and I'm sure it didn't concern her. She was an entertainer.

You ask "what is truth and what is propaganda?" in the novel (page 167). Can you answer your own question in light of Mata Hari's arrest and conviction?

That's a difficult question when writing about Mata Hari. She tried so hard to obfuscate her past that in some ways she really succeeded. In terms of her death, though, I have very strong feelings that it served both France and Germany's need at the time. I talk about this in my epilogue. It's a sad thing to realize just how grossly justice was miscarried in her case.

Is there a historical moment of interest to you right now? What are you reading?

Yes! Ancient Egypt. Every few years I feel the need to return to the world of the Pharaohs, now more than ever. Currently I'm reading a book about life under Pharaoh Hatshepsut. She was a fascinating woman who reigned as a king long before Nefertiti and Cleopatra.

ENHANCE YOUR BOOK CLUB

1. Part of the appeal of *Mata Hari's Last Dance* is the fact that Mata Hari is not just a fictional character in a novel but was a real woman tried and convicted of treason during World War I. Host a movie night with your book club and watch the 1931 film *Mata Hari*. After the movie, discuss her life as it was presented in the film and in the novel. What conclusions can you draw about her? Is she a sympathetic figure? In the end, do you believe she was innocent and simply out of touch with the reality of the war?

2. Mata Hari has the great fortune—and perhaps misfortune—to travel widely throughout Europe during the height of her fame. Travel goes hand-in-hand with Mata Hari's desire for transformation, her wish to lose her "real" self in furs and fancy apartments, or undressed and dancing. With your group, look at photographs of Mata Hari's two favorite cities—Paris and Berlin. Imagine what it was like to live in these glamorous places before the war. Over dinner, share with your book club a place you have been that changed your life. Share photos and memories about this special place. Do you feel like Mata Hari—exotic, new—when you travel?

3. Just before her execution, Mata Hari talks to Bowtie one last time. When he asks her what she wants to discuss she says "poppies" (page 247)—a topic inspired by a poem she had recently read and perhaps also from her belief in herself as an "orchid among buttercups." Return to page 247 and reread the poem with your book club. What images does the poem bring to mind? What feeling did you get hearing the poem? Why do you think Mata Hari had this poem on her mind right before her death? Try writing your own poem inspired by "In Flanders Fields." Make the first line of your poem "In _____ the _____ grow." Share your poem with your group.

4. Michelle Moran has written several other historical novels. Chose another era to go back in time with Moran, such as the one depicted in *Rebel Queen* or *Nefertiti*. Compare the strong female characters in all of Moran's novels. Do these characters share common traits? What are they? How do you think this author breaks stereotypes for women across the ages?

ABOUT THE AUTHOR

$\mathcal{M}$ichelle Moran was born in Southern California. After attending Pomona College, she earned a master's degree from Claremont Graduate University. During her six years as a public high school teacher, Moran used her summers to travel around the world, and it was her experiences as a volunteer on archaeological digs that inspired her to write historical fiction. She is the internationally bestselling author of the novels *Rebel Queen*, *Nefertiti*, *The Heretic Queen*, *Cleopatra's Daughter*, *Madame Tussaud*, and *The Second Empress*, which have been translated into more than twenty languages. Visit her online at MichelleMoran.com.

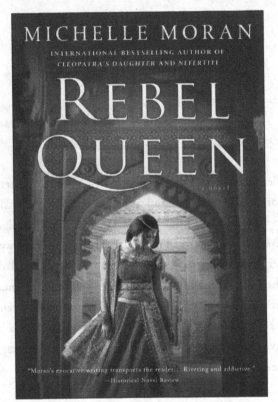